Fenella took the jug before Alasdair could prevent her, and drank a great mouthful of the water. It was bitterly cold, and tasted of peat and rock. She shivered all over, and a sharp tingling started in her hands and feet, and spread over her whole body. She felt her heart begin to thud faster and faster, and a dark cloud was swirling in her head—like a whirlpool—like the waters of the well—and the roar of them grew to thunder—and she was falling—

Alasdair gave a wild shout. "Where is Fenella?"

And she was nowhere. There was the little jug lying on its side on the earth. There was the Bocan doubled up with laughter. The moon shining on the thorn trees. But the girl had gone.

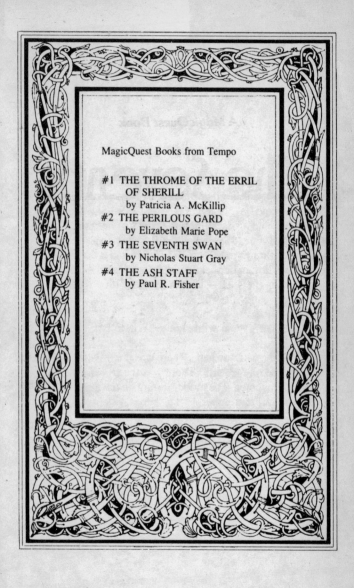

A MagicQuest Book

The Seventh Swan

NICHOLAS STUART GRAY

TEMPO BOOKS, NEW YORK

To
That Island

This Tempo Book contains the complete
text of the original hardcover edition.
It has been completely reset in a typeface
designed for easy reading, and was printed
from new film.

THE SEVENTH SWAN

PRINTING HISTORY
Dobson edition / 1962
Tempo edition / January 1984

ISBN: 0-441-75955-6

Tempo Books are published by The Berkley Publishing Group,
200 Madison Avenue, New York, New York 10016.
Tempo Books are registered in the United States Patent Office.
PRINTED IN THE UNITED STATES OF AMERICA

CONTENTS

Note:

A short Glossary of Gaelic words used in this story will be found at the end of the book. A wonderful version of the "Wild Swans" legend is among the stories of Hans Christian Andersen.

1. WINGS OVER KINROWAN

They were dancing in the great hall of Kinrowan castle. It was a gaily colored scene, full of laughter and quick movement, and the exciting skirl of music. Most of the men were wearing long bright plaids that swept back over their left shoulders. And some were kilted also. So that the greens and reds and blues of the tartans made a fine background for the paler colors of the women's full round skirts and stiff bodices, their jewels and embroideries. The eyes of the dancers were shining in the light of torches and candles, and of the huge fires burning in the stone hearths at either end of the hall.

Without being too obvious about it, nearly everyone was covertly watching two who danced with them down the long lines and dividings of the reel. A young man and a young woman, partnering each other. No, she was only a girl—not yet eighteen. Very small and slender, she had soft brown hair and blue eyes. There were pearls sewn on her cap, and a little white ruff at her throat. Her dress was white, and so were the slippers that skipped so lightly under her swirling skirt. She was neat in all her movements, and very clever at making nothing of the fact that her partner used only one hand for their dancing. His other hand—and indeed his whole arm—was concealed beneath an unusually heavy plaid that was draped, against all sense and custom, over his right shoulder. It was hard to see how he could use a sword with his sword-arm so enfolded. But then Alasdair never had used a sword, nor ever would. His hair was dark and curly, and he was outrageously handsome, though there was a look of great unsureness about him.

By one of the fireplaces, a man was standing. He was tall and finely made, and though he, also, was very good-looking, his was an assured and authoritative face with humor at the edges of mouth. At the moment he had a speculative expression. Then he glanced down at the small hand that was suddenly laid on his green velvet sleeve, and he smiled. The dark lady smiled in return.

"Ranald," said his wife, softly, "you're watching them. Don't let him see or he'll grow self-conscious."

A note of anxiety crept into her voice.

"Oh, do you think he's enjoying it—just a little? Perhaps, for once, his mind is on the piping and dancing. With maybe a thought or two to spare for that pretty girl!"

"Who knows what your brother is thinking?" said the Chief.

Seeing the shadow that flickered over her face, he added quickly, "He seems not as unhappy as usual. He talks to the Lady Fenella when they move near enough for speech."

"It is she," said Agnes, rather amused, "who does all the talking. A gay bright child. Alasdair has hardly said a word."

"He may be listening," said Ranald, hopefully.

And then, while his relatives spoke thus of him, and watched with kindly concern, the young man stopped dancing—so suddenly that he caused utter confusion among the other dancers.

While they got themselves into a fine tangle trying to avoid collision, he stood quite still with half-shut eyes. His head was lifted and tilted sideways as though he was listening intently to something far away. His partner came to his side, as swift as an arrow, thinking he might be ill, but her hands dropped before they touched him. There was a look of grief and despair on his face that made her halt and gasp.

The pipes faltered and died away in discord. Startled silence fell on the castle hall. And, in that silence, Alasdair turned and ran from the place like a deer.

A murmur rose from the motionless dancers. And the young girl, left alone in hurt surprise, covered her face with her hands to hide a glimmer of tears. And that was the end of merriment.

Alasdair was gasping to himself as he ran, almost sobbing, and hardly looking where he was going. He stumbled on the uneven flagstones of the passages, and on the stairway, where he met a man and a woman who stood aside to let him go past, and then turned to stare after him in concern. He did not even see them. Nor anyone else that he encountered. He was going by instinct alone, it seemed, to his own quarters where he might be sure of protection and concealment. He longed for both.

Kinrowan was a small enough sort of castle, and immensely strong. This strength was not just for show either. The Highlands of Scotland were not at any time noted for their peaceful qualities. In 1520, there was no actual official war in progress with that popular adversary England—nor was Kinrowan's clan embroiled in a specific feud with another clan—yet it could be only a matter of time before someone started something. James V was on the throne, and doing his best to bring some order into his unruly kingdom, but people had tried that before. The keep of Kinrowan castle was massive and square, with a small bailey court, high-walled, between it and the gate towers. All the windows, apart from arrow-slits, were on the court side. There were big, round towers set at the two outer corners of the keep, each with a two-floored turret to it. And in one of these towers, Alasdair had quarters for himself, his half dozen retainers, and their captain.

At the end of a narrow corridor was a sharp turning, the foot of a spiral stair to the upper floor of the tower, and a heavy closed door. Here, also, were two men wearing belted plaids of Alasdair's own tartan. Being, as he was himself, from the Lowlands, they would not normally have dressed so, but it was a gesture of courtesy to their Highland hosts. One man, the older, was sprawled on the lowest tread of the stairs. He was a burly fellow, with dark hair and beard. The other, as lithe as a leopard, sat on his heels near the door, and now he snatched up a pair of dice from the ground, dropped them into his leather sporran, and got to his feet in one move as he saw Alasdair.

"What is it?" exclaimed the older man, rising also.

Alasdair barely glanced aside at them. He just shook his head dumbly, and the young man jumped forward, threw open the door, and let the fugitive hurry into the room beyond. He put out a hand to steady his master, as the boy went past him. But the door slammed, and he looked at the other man and shook his head.

Inside the room, Alasdair leaned his back against the heavy door, as though holding it shut against pursuit. In the soft light of candles and log-fire, his face was pale and haggard, though its extreme good looks were not greatly impaired by these drawbacks. He shut his eyes, and fought for breath.

It was a plainly furnished room, decorated rather grimly with the mounted heads and horns of deer, and by trophies of arms on which the firelight glinted, making bright streaks on swords and dirks, and the studs on leather targes. A narrow, arched opening in the far wall led into the turret, and this was full of the moonlight that spilled through its thin windows. In the main room, too, the arrow-slits showed bright.

A man was sitting sideways on the table near the fire, with a goblet held between his hands. The glow of the fire lit his tawny hair and close-cut beard. He was plainly dressed compared with the dancers in the hall below, and in a manner befitting the soldier that he was; yet there was a sort of arrogance in his chased-silver buttons, the glove-soft deerskin jacket and thigh-boots, and the fine great plaid-brooch that he wore. The plaid itself and his tight-fitting trews were of Alasdair's tartan. He might have been any age between the late thirties or early forties, but he was one of those people whose attraction depends almost entirely on their mood. At the moment, he looked dour and hard. He never lifted his eyes from the wine that he was swishing round and round in the cup for all the rush and scurry of Alasdair's entrance.

That young man was rubbing his left hand over his face in a distracted movement, and catching his breath into a long and shaken sigh. The other remained quite unmoved, as though he had noticed none of it. In fact, he had missed nothing.

After a moment or two, and realizing he would get no reaction, Alasdair said with a sort of gloomy defiance, "I've run away again!"

There was silence in the room. He received no answering word or look.

"Can't you say something?" cried the boy. "I tell you, I've run away!"

"I noticed," said the other, calmly, in a very soft and cutting voice.

There was a slight sound from beyond the door, and Alasdair started, and sprang across the room to a door in the right wall. But the soldier moved faster than he, and blocked his path. Alasdair caught him by the shoulder and looked in panic into his bleak gray eyes.

"Ewen, let me pass!" stammered the boy. "Don't let them come and find me here!"

But the other just looked back at him without sympathy. Short of actual violence, it was impossible for Alasdair to get past him. He knew he was no match for the soldier. Though he was so much the younger, and indeed the taller of the two, the other man was heavily built and strong, and would take a deal of shifting. He was saying, in a light voice, that held the lilt of the Highlands somewhere behind its deliberate coldness, "No one will come. You've just worked yourself up—as usual."

He surveyed the effect of this remark, and then looked across at the main door, and called sharply, "Lachunn!"

The door opened, and a bearded head looked in, with some caution. It seemed to be expecting trouble.

"Shut the door," said Ewen, and then snapped, "Not *yet*, fool! When I've done speaking. Let no one in at all. Stay on guard."

And, after a moment, he said, carefully, "Shut—the door—*now!*"

"Yes, captain," said the head.

It shook itself thoughtfully, and withdrew. The latch clicked. And the soldier turned a sardonic eye on the young man beside him.

"There," said he, unkindly. "No one can come and bite you. You may relax."

He got a resentful glare, and Alasdair moved away, saying it was all very well for him to be sarcastic and unpleasant—

"You'd sing a different tune if it was you that people sneered at—if they stared at you!" said the boy, crossly. "All whispering and nudging one another!" Then he came back to Ewen, and said in an urgent rush of words, "I know what they whispered—'poor thing, how strange he looks!' And then the pitying smiles—and through all that din—the whispers and the laughing and the music—I heard the swans go over—"

He had wound his left hand into the thick folds of green-and-blue tartan across Ewen's breast, and was shaking him with the stress of his outburst. The soldier's mouth curled a little, but it was not a pleasant smile.

"I dare say not one soul noticed you," said he, "until you managed to draw attention to yourself, and make everyone miserable by your behavior."

The boy released him abruptly, and backed away.

"I might have known I'd get small kindness from you," he said.

"You might, indeed."

"There are times," the boy told him, "when I wonder if you're human!"

Ewen shot him an odd look. And Alasdair gave a small choked cry. He cringed away from the words he feared would follow. But the other merely said, in a casual sort of way, "I thought you were for braving it out this time?"

"I promised nothing. I only said I would try."

Then he rallied with what was, under the circumstances, a gallant effort, and said accusingly, "You expected me to fail, didn't you! You just sat here patiently, and waited for me to come slinking back to your feet! Knowing I would run away—"

"Fearing," said the other, dryly.

He took a long swallow of wine from the cup he still held. And over the rim his guarded eyes met those of the boy in a look of mild derision. The boy recoiled from it.

"Don't," he said. "Don't look at me as though I'd fled from a battle!"

"Haven't you?"

Alasdair went to a big chair by the table, and dropped into it. He seemed suddenly exhausted. He hunched his shoulders and said, rather incoherently, "Is there shame in deserting a lost cause—if the cause be one's own—?"

He got no reply, and he lifted a look full of pain at the other.

"You have a glittering reputation as a soldier," he said, "but have you never been forced to surrender?"

For a moment, Ewen stood still. Then he crossed to the fire, and stirred at the logs with his booted foot. It seemed he did not intend to reply. But at last he said, in a distant voice, "I'd be sorry to see you do it."

Alasdair opened his mouth to tell him this was no sort of answer to his question, but there came a disturbance from outside the door. A man's voice raised in command, and then a growling sort of uproar. Alasdair sprang to his feet, his hand to his throat, and said chokingly, "No! Not yet! Not yet—please!"

The soldier cast him an expressionless glance, and strode to the door, where he set his hand down hard on the latch to keep it from lifting. He shouted, "Lachunn! No one is to come in!"

They could hear this information being excitedly relayed to somebody else, and through the welter of argument and explanation that followed, a clear deep voice said, slowly, "Get out—of my—way."

Ewen looked startled.

"Mo Dhia!" said he, "The Chief!"

And he threw the door wide.

The guards were still crouched defensively before it, and their dirks were bare in their hands, though they seemed very unsure what to do with them next. In fact, they looked completely confused. Ewen resolved their difficulty by saying in a most cutting tone, "You Lowland sheep-heads!"

They fell back, one against either wall, and eyed him nervously. Lachunn licked his bearded lips and said, "Captain, you told us—clearly—and with your own mouth—"

Ranald took this opportunity to stroll past them into the tower room.

"There! He's in!" said Lachunn, plaintively.

"It's his castle," said Ewen.

"But you said—"

Ewen shut the door on his men. He turned and found the Chief standing in the middle of the room, with a most forbidding gaze directed at him.

"You should have shouted your name," said the soldier.

Ranald looked him up and down, and seemed not to care over-much for what he saw. He did not rise to the intentionally irritating remark, but after the one uncomplimentary glance, turned his shoulder on Ewen, and spoke sternly to Alasdair.

"I allow you to keep your bodyguard about you in my house," he said, "but I would prefer them kept in some control. I will not have drawn steel and guarded doors. Do you hear?"

Alasdair mumbled something, and the Chief swept on, "Your own behavior is something to wonder at! You should be locked up until you learn manners."

He took a pace toward the young man. And found his way blocked. He stared at the obstacle in a way that most offenders found quelling. Ewen merely stared back.

"Be good enough to allow me speech with my brother-in-law," said Ranald, evenly.

And then added, with a sort of wry humor, "Oh, be at ease, man! If I ever truly wished to use him harshly, I'd first set my men on you."

The weather-tanned face of the soldier, with its dour lines, changed suddenly and surprisingly. His eyes glinted as wild and bright as moonlight, and he gave the Chief a fleeting and most wicked smile.

"Have you men enough?" said he.

"More than enough," Ranald told him darkly, "but the time is not come, yet."

For a count of three, Ewen stood quite still; then he gave ground and let the other pass.

Alasdair watched his tall relative approach with some misgiving. When he came near, the boy said, "I know you're angry with me, but truly I—"

"The girl went weeping from the hall," said Ranald, "doubtless in search of her father—who is now at his third supper in the buttery, good man! Before he comes raging to me, demanding satisfaction for the insult offered to his daughter, I would suggest *you* go to *him*—and apologize."

Alasdair gave a quick and involuntary shake of his handsome head. The Chief sat down in the big chair by the fire, and stretched one hand to the glow. He sighed, and then said, "My good boy, an explanation is really the least you can offer."

"Must I?" said Alasdair, crossly. "Tell the whole miserable tale once again, to a stranger—"

"He is not exactly a stranger," Ranald told him in a patient voice, "he has been here before. And your tale is not a secret. Oh, come, you know you've behaved abominably! You were dancing with young Fenella—our guest—and you dropped her hand as though it burnt you, and fled from the hall. She must think you took a loathing for her."

Alasdair looked quite startled.

"Oh, no! You must explain, Ranald—indeed, I scarcely noticed her."

"A most consoling explanation!" said the Chief.

Then he went on, more seriously, "I have risked a good many clan-feuds for your sake, mo chridhe. And I'm a peaceable man. If you really must fly out at people—flee from them—offend them in so thoughtless a fashion, and so often—you must learn to deal with the consequences yourself. I cannot protect you much longer."

The latch of the door gave an anxious rattle, and a subdued shout came through the solid oak panels.

"Is her ladyship to enter?" it wanted to know.

Kinrowan struck the arm of his chair with a clenched fist, and got to his feet.

"Ewen! Call your dogs to heel!" he said, fiercely.

But the soldier had already opened the door, and the Lady Agnes swept in.

"We had to ask you," said Lachunn defensively.

His captain shut the door on him once more.

Her dark-crimson skirts glowed richly in the firelight, as Agnes went across the room to her brother. She said nothing but looked so straightly at him that he lifted his hand as though to defend himself.

"I didn't mean to upset anyone," he said, rather hoarsely, "I forgot I was dancing. But, Agnes—people were whispering. And I heard the swans go over—"

"It's the last time that I try to find a bride for you," said the lady.

"I've never asked you—"

She raised her voice a little, and overrode his protest.

"Fenella is most gentle," said she. "Why couldn't you make friends with her? Talk to her? She would understand—"

"Must I ask pity from every girl you choose to invite to your house?" Alasdair was stung to indignation.

"Better than insulting them," put in Ranald.

"I didn't intend—"

And now the Chief's deep voice bore down his argument.

"Better anything than running away. So that now the girl's father will demand an apology from me—or maybe declare a feud!"

Behind them, the door opened quietly. No challenge had

been raised by the guard outside, which seemed to have lost confidence in its ability to guard anything at all. Ewen moved quickly as though to hold the door himself, but seeing who entered, he shrugged his shoulders and let Fenella by. He then stood in the open doorway and favored his men with a whispered diatribe on their shortcomings.

Fenella curtseyed to the other three in the room.

"Am I intruding unforgivably?" said she.

Agnes sank into the big chair, and held out her hand, and the girl went across the floor like a ripple of water to take it.

"Forgive us," said the lady of Kinrowan, "we are behaving very badly. Our guests must be most bewildered."

"No, madam," said the girl, "they seem calm enough, almost as though they are accustomed to such—incidents."

Ranald shot her a quick look, and then said in a deep growl, "Ewen! Either come in, or go out! But, for God's sake, stop bullying those men, and shut the door!"

The soldier stepped back into the room, and slammed the door with a bang that made everyone jump. The Chief looked speculatively again at the young girl in the white dress, standing so quietly with folded hands by the fire. He gave a small, apprehensive cough, and said, "Did you find your father, my dear?"

"I didn't look for him, sir," said Fenella.

Ranald's brow cleared a little.

"Are you very cross with us all?" said Agnes.

"Not now," Fenella told her. "Only puzzled. No one has ever actually fled from me, before—not once. Naturally I would like to know why your brother did so. Do I dance clumsily? Talk too much? Does he find me ugly and repellant—?"

During all this, Alasdair had been standing with averted head in the background. Now Ranald moved to his side, and put a compelling hand on his shoulder, and pushed him forward a little. He responded to this spur with a nervous glance, and a stumbling move toward the girl. He gulped, and found a rush of words.

"No, no—nothing like that," said he, "you dance well enough—and I suppose you're quite pretty—and truly I never noticed what you were talking about—"

His voice died away at the startled look she gave him. There was a sudden glint in her blue eyes. The men regarded her with some trepidation, but Agnes realized she was trying not to laugh. Alasdair in desperation forced himself to further explanation.

"I heard the wild swans flying over Kinrowan—"

The girl's eyes took on an even brighter gleam, and her voice shook slightly.

"I'm sure bird life is most absorbing," said she.

Agnes found her sight blurred with a sudden rush of tears. And Ranald put up a hand to hide the smile that twitched the corner of his mouth. But Ewen said something under his breath that sounded like the hiss of a snake. He stared at Fenella in a most unfriendly way, and his soft voice had a very chilling edge to it as he said, "It's nothing to laugh about!"

Fenella turned a startled gaze on him, and was about to reply placatingly, when Alasdair gave a wild exclamation and threw back his head. He whirled around so quickly that the heavy folds of his plaid swung out about his right side, and he went in a run to the turret. He pushed open one of the narrow horn windows, and stared out eagerly into the dark of the night.

"He's done it again!" said Fenella, blankly.

"Oh, child," said Agnes, "it was the swans again."

The girl turned her gentle eyes on the lady of the castle, and said without malice, but quite clearly, "Is he insane?"

Silence fell in the tower room. The wind blew in at the window, and stirred some hanging tapestries, and made smoke come eddying from the fire. By the door, the soldier had stiffened, and was looking very grimly at the girl. And Agnes caught her husband's eye, and bit her lip.

In the end, however, it was she who spoke. She said, "Surely you must know Alasdair's—you have heard his story?"

"Someone must have told you," said Ranald.

Fenella looked from one to the other of them, and then she shook her head.

"I know nothing at all about him," said she, "nor ever heard his name until I came here today. Madam," she appealed to Agnes, in a voice that was suddenly very young and self-conscious, "if I have said or done anything tactless—as it seems to me that I have—please forgive me and let me withdraw. I truly didn't mean to be inquisitive."

Agnes gently reached out and touched her tightly clasped hands.

"I think you should be told everything," she said.

And Fenella's smooth brow crumpled a little as she looked at the young man by the window, still staring out at flying clouds and moonlit sky.

"Oh, no," said the girl. "He can't wish to be discussed so— behind his back—as though he was in another world—"

"And so he is," said Ranald, heavily. "Nor would he notice now, if you set a pin in him!"

Fenella looked a little frightened. And Ewen came quickly to face them all. He eyed the girl as though he hated her.

"It's not for you to judge Alasdair," he told her, cuttingly, "until you have some dim notion what you're judging!"

Ranald put a restraining hand on his arm, but the soldier jerked himself free. Fenella looked deep into his unfriendly eyes for a moment, and then said, "You are perfectly right, sir."

She turned back to Agnes, and added very softly, "Tell me, then."

2. *THE WILD SWANS*

Agnes sat perfectly still for a few minutes, then she gave a long sigh and lifted a hand to shield her face from the too revealing light of the fire. But Fenella had seen the focus change in her eyes. The Chief's wife was looking right through the stone walls of Kinrowan, beyond the moors and the mountains, to some place far away and very long ago. When she spoke, it was so quietly that it seemed she spoke mostly to herself, and not to the girl.

"It's a strange, sad tale," she said, "and you will not like the telling, for I think cruelty is not in you. When I was born, my mother feared I couldn't live. She was in great distress, poor soul, for I was her first daughter, much longed for, and I had come too soon. She was ill, and weak. She begged and prayed my father to send their seven young sons to the wishing well on the fringe of the forest—for water to christen me— just in case—"

Fenella dropped to her knees beside Agnes, with a whisper and rustle of silk as her skirt spread around her, and she took the cold hands into a sympathetic clasp.

"This is making you cry," said the girl. "Don't—please don't tell me any more. Truly, you need not."

She tugged a small handkerchief from the bosom of her gown, and put it into Agnes's hand. That beautiful lady gave a shaken little laugh, and a sob, and pressed it to her eyes. And Ranald came to the back of the carved chair, and touched his wife's shoulder very gently.

"Let it go, my darling," he said. "There is no need—"

"I think there is great need for me to tell," said Agnes.

She began to do so. And Fenella seemed to see the cruel tale unfold. Beyond the moors and the mountains, far away and very long ago. While the quiet voice of Agnes spoke in the quiet room, Fenella could picture the seven young boys leaving their home, in haste and excitement, and running as fast as they could go to the fringe of the forest. Robert, the eldest, who was sixteen. Hugh and Maurice. Ellyot, who was ten. Keith and Kenneth and Alasdair. Little Alasdair must have been a sore drag on them, thought Fenella, at only three years old. Poor baby. She saw him—stumbling and being pulled along, and asking questions—not understanding at all why there was such need of haste. Perhaps weeping, and wanting to go home—wailing for his mother. Fenella gave a big sniff, and Agnes was too lost in her memories even to return the handkerchief.

Ranald said, in his deep, grave voice, "I don't know your views on magic, Mistress Fenella. But it's a thing that can happen. It can happen! Even in the prosaic Lowlands, where you might think the easy living, the rich fields and fat cattle, would dull men's minds to the depths of mystery. It happens."

And Fenella saw it happen—almost as clearly as if the next words of Agnes carried her back twenty years to that Lowland forest. She saw it happen.

An old rune, of terrible power. Lying somewhere on the ground—or lurking in the dark tree shadows—gleeking out from the crannies of the well-coping—or waiting, half-submerged, in the water. Who could tell where the boys had run upon it? They never knew themselves where the thing was waiting for them. At one moment they were hurrying along, calling to one another, intent upon their task. And then they were in the air, great wings threshing wildly as they flew in bewildered circles. Slowly coming to realize that the seven brothers, who had come to the forest as boys, were now wheeling over it—as seven wild swans.

And one of them still soft and fluffy, thought Fenella. No more than a cygnet. Stumbling about the sky, as he had stumbled on the ground.

She said aloud, "Their poor mother. And their father—"

Ranald shook his handsome head very slightly.

"A great mercy was given to their mother," he said. "She died before a shepherd came to the castle to tell what he had seen."

Agnes sat silently for a while. Fenella wondered if she meant to say no more. Although the girl longed to hear the rest, she would ask no questions. She glanced about the room at the three men, trying to guess their thoughts.

Alasdair was still at the window, his hand on the stone edge, his head bent. No one could guess his thoughts, for he was far away and lost completely in his own mind. He had no ears, no eyes, for any other person.

It was not easy to know what Ewen was thinking, either. He was leaning his shoulder against the wall where it opened out into the turret. His arms were folded, and his eyes were veiled. He seemed quite relaxed and aloof. But Fenella had a strong suspicion that it was the aloofness, the relaxation, of a cat guarding a mouse hole. That he was perfectly ready, in mind and body, to move very quickly indeed in almost any direction.

Ranald was intent upon his wife, and at last she gave a long sigh, and a glint of a smile at Fenella.

"I did not die, after all," said she, "as you will have guessed. The tale was kept from me, a kindly guarded secret, and I thought myself an only child until I was sixteen. Then there was a night when my old nurse was ailing and fevered—and I was sitting up with her—and she talked. Oh, I ran to my father, in disbelief and horror! And he was a man who could not tell a direct lie. After that, sleep deserted me. Night and day I thought of those lost seven. Until it came to me that I alone could seek them, and find them, and bring them home."

"She set off secretly, to wander the world," said Ranald, in a somewhat disapproving way, "and herself little more than a child."

And while Agnes went on with her strange tale, Fenella

could picture very clearly in her mind that young girl setting off to find her brothers.

In the night, with everyone asleep and the ways of the castle so well known to her, there went Agnes. In a dress of plain wool, an old plaid wrapped about her, stout shoes to her feet and a staff in her hand. With a knapsack slung on her shoulder, containing some bread and cheese, a few coins, and a battered old raggedy doll that she loved—there indeed went Agnes.

The search was long and increasingly discouraging. From place to place she went; into England, and over the seas beyond; and she saw many swans—but they were only swans. And in her aimless wanderings, she came back at last to Scotland, to the Highlands, to a place of mountains and high moors, and bright rushing waters. And she passed one day a little shieling and an ancient woman who was brushing its doorstep, and she stopped—more from habit than hope.

"I'm in search of my brothers, ma'am—"

"Indeed, my dear, I hope you find them soon. For you look so tired and hungry. Have you far to seek?"

"The whole world. And they, perhaps, not in it!"

"Are they living, then?"

"Who knows? It is more than seventeen years since they were turned to swans, and flew away."

And the old woman cried out, and then caught Agnes by her hands—and rough little hands they were, now, for the girl had worked hard to buy her food wherever she went—and she said in a breathless and wondering voice, "You tell me a strange thing, my daughter! And I have stranger to tell you! Last evening, when I was coming home with my little dog, by the side of the loch—away down there" —and she pointed through the trees—"I saw seven swans swimming. And my Sheila went splashing and barking after them. And the biggest turned his long neck, and spoke to her in the voice of a man. He said 'Go away, you silly dog!' And you should have seen Sheila go!"

She stopped. The girl's eyes were shining like stars, and she touched the old woman's cheeks with her lips, and went speeding off down the little glen toward the water that glittered at the far end of it. All her weariness and despair forgotten in an instant.

But there were no swans.

And Agnes sat by the shore and cried herself to sleep. In the night she woke to the sound of voices. The swans had come back to the loch.

"I feared to startle them into flight," said Agnes, "so I began to sing, very softly and slowly. I sang the cradle song I'd learned from my nurse—the song my mother sang to her sons before I came to destroy them all—"

"It was not your fault, m'eudail," this was Ranald, in protest.

"No, but it was my doing," murmured Agnes.

After a flurry of wings, and a half-move to rise from the water, the swans had settled back, and stayed very still for a while; all gazing at Agnes with their bright, black eyes, with heads turning and craning, and their white feathers reflected in the loch. And Agnes stopped singing, and held out her hands, with the tears running unheeded down her face.

"My brothers—" she said.

The largest and boldest of the swans, he who was closest to shore, said wonderingly, "Is it—Agnes?"

And the smallest, he who was farthest away and still prepared for instant flight, said, "She doesn't look much like our sister."

"Well, she wouldn't," said Robert, "not as we remember her, for she was no bigger than a rabbit, then, and very ugly indeed. If you are Agnes," said he, to the girl, "give us news of home."

While she did so, the seven swans drew nearer and nearer, sending long arrows of ripples over the loch as they moved—until they came up on the pebbly shore, over to her side—until they settled around her, with their strong wings folded, and their feathers brushing her hands, her knees, her feet. And, after a while, Robert put forward his black-tipped beak and touched her cheek. And Alasdair laid his long neck across her lap, and snuggled his head down. And the girl tried to hug them all, and she laughed and she wept. And she told them of home. Of their mother's death, and her own searching. And they wept, too.

"A merry meeting," said Ranald, dryly.

But he was holding his wife's hand very tight.

And then the swans told their sister the terms of their bondage.

"Our life as swans will be eternal," said Robert.

"But we may never go home—not even to fly over its roof," said Hugh.

"And never again shall we be men," said Maurice. "Unless—"

"Unless—unless—" said Ellyot, excitedly, "—unless our own sister should find us—"

"And weave for each of us a shirt," said Keith, slowly. "A shirt made from stinging nettles, spun and woven into cloth—"

"Nettles gathered in the dead of night, from the edges of graveyards," said Kenneth. "Ugh! An eery task!"

"And never—never—never must she say one word to anyone—not a single word—nor write a single word—" cried Alasdair, "until the shirts are made, and the spell ended."

"Well," said Agnes, "that all seems quite simple."

Fenella came back to the tower room with a gasp, and a sigh of relief.

"How lovely!" she breathed. "You were all together at last. And knowing how to set them free!"

"It wasn't quite like that," the Lady Agnes told her, gravely, "though indeed it was lovely—they were alive, and could be freed! But they didn't stay with me. They said it was not allowed. I had to work alone until the shirts were ready. So I found an old, half-ruined shieling, away up on the hill some distance from the crofts, and there I made my home. I herded sheep for one of the crofters, and so earned my bread. And the walls of the ancient burial ground were almost overgrown with nettles. Oh, my grief!" said she, ruefully, "my hands are prickling still, just to remember them!"

There was a tentative tapping on the door. And Ewen moved, as fast as Fenella had thought he would, and threw it open. Lachunn recoiled from him slightly and then said in a very defensive voice, "Yes, well, I know you wish for no interruption, captain—but it's this fellow wanting the Chief! He said he would shout and bellow, if we refused to knock on the door. I thought you'd rather have the knocking than the shouting—"

His voice trailed away, and he said, rather hopelessly, "A wee knock is less alarming—"

Ewen directed the full force of his cold glare on the man who stood in the background. He got an equally disapproving glare in return. For this was one of Ranald's own clansmen, who was perfectly prepared to take on Ewen and his guards, and fight his way through to his Chief if it became necessary.

But it was not, as it turned out. For Kinrowan came up behind Ewen, and said, "Stand aside, please."

Not very graciously, he was obeyed. And then he said to his man, "Speak, then."

Fenella heard none of the colloquy that followed between them. She sat back quietly on her heels, watching the face of Agnes. For a look of great tenderness had settled there, and a remembering smile.

"When I was weaving, one day, in the doorway," said the dark lady, very softly indeed, "in the sunshine of the spring, a man came riding by. He was the Chief in these parts, and he saw smoke from the roof, and came to see who was there. I couldn't speak to him, because of the spell, but he saw that I was a stranger, and harmless, keeping sheep for one of his farmers. He did not order me away."

Ranald had closed the door at the other side of the room, and returned to the fire in time to hear these last sentences. He gave a sudden, surprisingly boyish grin, and said to Fenella, "It didn't need words to show me how beautiful she was! Order her away? In a fortnight she was my wife."

Fenella gave him a look of mild wonder and admiration. He had seemed so very imperturbable a person, but it came to her that he was a good deal more impulsive than he appeared. And yet the integrity of Agnes shone from her dark eyes. It was not, after all, so wild a decision on the part of the Chief. He was speaking, now, to his wife.

"That was Alan at the door. Wanting to know what to do with our guests. Apparently they grow restless. Unsure whether to go or stay—to take their leave at once, without a word, or pretend there is nothing amiss."

"What did you suggest they should do?" said Agnes.

"Dance again, and be merry. Saying we will rejoin them soon."

The note in his voice shifted, and became grave. "Go back to them, now, Agnes. If you really want this tale told to the end, I will do it. For it grows ugly. Better that you shouldn't have to endure the memory again."

"It isn't very nice," she agreed, "but I'd rather stay."

"As you wish."

Ranald looked down at Fenella on the white, thick sheepskin

rug, her hands in her lap, and he said, "Even when she was
my wife, she must still gather the nettles and weave the cloth.
She could not speak, to tell us why, nor could she write it for
us to read. We thought her dumb, and everyone pitied her
disability—for a while. Then—people saw how she went out
in the night, and gathered the weeds in the churchyard, tying
them in bundles and taking them to the castle. They saw her
spin the thread, and weave the cloth, and cut those strange
small shirts with the too-wide sleeves—"

"For the wings," put in Agnes.

"*I* knew there was no wrong in what she did," said Ranald,
harshly. "I did not understand—but I knew there was nothing
evil in her."

The tone of his voice, and the spark in his eyes, again
brought it home to Fenella that his apparent impassivity was
the result of strong self-control, and not entirely natural to him.
She thought he would be most alarming if that control really
slipped. And, at this very moment, there was a dangerous look
to him as he spoke through stiffened lips.

"A whisper began to run and spread among my people—
that she was—a witch! It grew to a wild and frenzied clamor of
fear. For there was a bad harvest, and a cattle raid in force by
Fergus and his men from beyond the hills. And they blamed—!
They came to me and dared to demand that she be—burned!"

Fenella gave a startled cry, and clutched at Agnes's crimson
skirt.

"You! Burnt!"

Her wide-eyed stare of horror swung back to Ranald's grim
face.

"How could they!" she cried.

He wore such a look of anger that the girl caught her breath
sharply.

"Even now," said the Chief, "I dare not think too long on
what they did! I had to go on a hunt, for we were very short
of food. And then—while I was away from home—they did
the unthinkable thing! My own people. They came to the castle—" he bit his lip hard, and stopped speaking.

"Some tried to hold them back," said Agnes, soothingly.

"Not many! And the others—took my lady out into the
courtyard—and tied her to a stake!"

Agnes put her hand on one of his, for he was standing very

close. She looked down at the pale face of the girl at her feet.

"They were afraid," she said. "It wasn't cruelty or hatred that moved them to do it—only fear. Remember, I was a stranger to them, or very nearly and my actions were—curious. I have never blamed them."

"I have," said Ranald, "and do!"

The Highlander spoke in him, who finds it hard to forgive or forget. And Agnes quickly took up the tale. She tried not to paint too clear a picture of the events that followed—but they were still too vivid to be pleasant. Fenella saw it all.

As though she was standing herself in that courtyard, she saw Agnes bound upright to a wooden stake. The faggots and brushwood piled high about her feet. The people of the clan, men and women, huddled together in fear and dreadful determination. Then a glimmer of fire, and the lovely face of their victim through a haze of smoke. And her hands still sewing busily at a small shirt.

"The last one was nearly finished," said Agnes. "More than a year's work lay behind."

She had caught up the little pile of shirts, with her needle and thread still left in a seam, as she was seized in the castle. Faithful to the end, she was trying to complete her task. So, in the rising flames, she stitched with fingers that shook.

And over the loch came seven swans flying fast.

Whatever the spell that bound them, it had at least allowed them one mercy—to come before the shirts were quite ready. They circled around the courtyard, necks extended, and wings throbbing, making the clanging sound of their war cry. And the people cowered away from them. Before the flames could touch the body of their sister, they dived to her through the smoke, and she threw the shirts into the air, one after the other. Robert came boldly in, so close that he scorched his breast, and dived into the first shirt as he flew. Then came Hugh—and Maurice—then Ellyot—Keith—Kenneth—last of all, hissing with fright and rage, Alasdair. And then—

"Then my brothers were at my side," said Agnes, breathlessly, for the telling had made her shudder, "stamping through the fire, and cutting the cords that fastened me. Lifting me free. They were very angry!" she gave a hoarse little laugh. "They snatched the plaids from the nearest men, to clothe themselves! And they took their swords as well."

"I wish they'd used them," said Ranald, through his teeth.

"When your people recovered a little from their shock—when *our* people pulled their scattered wits together," said Agnes, "there was quite a show of swords and dirks among them. But at last I could speak, and I stepped between them and my brothers before any blood was spilled, and told them the truth. There was no further talk of fighting, or of burning."

Ranald said, "She even persuaded me to forgive the clan, when I returned—at least, to pardon them!"

Agnes rose, rather exhaustedly, and gave him a gentle smile.

"It's over and done with," she said, "two years ago."

"And a happy ending at the last," said Fenella. "The spell broken, and all come right."

She stopped abruptly, and put her hand over her mouth.

Both Agnes and Ranald had turned their heads to look at the young man by the window. And Agnes said, very quietly, "The last shirt was not finished. It had no right sleeve. Alasdair has still the wing of a swan."

There was a pause. Then Ranald said, "So—he thinks himself a creature not quite human—"

"Nor can he fly," said Agnes.

She covered her face with her hands, and went very quickly to the door. Ewen opened it for her, and the lady of Kinrowan fled from the room.

The Chief was watching Fenella thoughtfully. For a few moments she sat quite still, twisting her hands together. Then she drew a long breath, lifting her small face and wide eyes.

"Is that *all* that distresses him so?" said she.

Ranald's brow cleared a little, and his set mouth relaxed. He considered her question for a while, and then said carefully, "He thinks he is a target for scorn, and aversion. That people will blame him for being neither a man nor a swan."

"But—he is himself!"

"If you could persuade him of that," said Ranald, dryly, "you will succeed where everyone else has most signally failed."

He glanced again at Alasdair's averted head, and drew his brows together.

"There was a great deal of—shame—among my clan, for what they had done. They have all tried to atone by their behavior to him. They would, I think, die to help him! All of them! For Agnes's sake. But he will not listen or heed. When his brothers went home, he stayed here. But he withdraws more and more from everyone, and I fear for his reason—"

He fell silent. And the girl got to her feet. She smoothed her skirts, and pushed a lock of softly curling hair under the cap she wore. She gave the Chief a grave and thoughtful look.

"May I—would you allow me to stay here for a little while?"

A corner of Ranald's mouth twitched.

"And welcome, my heart," said he.

He turned away, and then swung around to say casually, "Do you want Ewen removed?"

From where he was standing, the man he named turned his head abruptly so that Fenella caught the sudden lively flash of his eyes. She said hastily, "No, no! I have to do some careful thinking, and I think more easily when there isn't noise and tumult."

"I see what you mean," said Ranald.

He glanced from Ewen to Fenella, and bowed to the girl with great courtesy, and strode from the room. She wondered why he seemed to be smiling.

Then she jumped as Ewen shut the door with yet another slam. For a moment she half expected Kinrowan to return and demand an apology, but that wise man evidently decided to ignore the matter.

Ewen turned and favored the girl with one of his less endearing expressions.

"You wished to hear a tale," said he, "I trust you enjoyed it!"

With that, he marched over to where the turret curved out from the room, and stood with his back turned, between Fenella and Alasdair, as though he had placed himself on guard.

3. *THE MAN WITHOUT A NAME*

Fenella gave a nervous little cough. She was the dear and only daughter of a chieftain, and in all her life had only lifted a finger to be loved. She could well have been shockingly spoilt, but for the fact that her father and her clan had not allowed her to rule them too openly, for her own sake. Besides, she was sweet-tempered by nature, gentle and generous. She had other qualities too, which had not yet been put fully to the test; a daring spirit, and a very determined will.

She lowered her head a little, and surveyed Ewen calculatingly from under her lashes. She wanted his help, and was considering the best means of getting under his very formidable guard. At the moment, back turned and head held stiffly, he looked quite unapproachable.

She tapped her fingers on her skirts, and then went and prodded the logs on the hearth with her toe, to the peril of her slipper, and jumped back to avoid the sparks that ensued. She wandered across the room to examine a trophy of arms on the wall, and touched one of the swords and brought away a fingerload of dust. She looked again at the soldier, and sighed. No brilliant plan for coping with him had matured. She thought that she had better, perhaps, just be simple. She said, "Captain Ewen, is he listening to us?"

"No."

"Well, may I talk to you?"

"Who can stop you?"

Fenella gave another small cough. But then she never had supposed he would be easy to handle. She went on doggedly, "Is—is he your own Chief?"

The man turned a little toward her. But not in any friendly spirit. A rather curious expression settled across his face, of mocking irony. But whether it was aimed at her, or at himself, the girl had no way of telling.

"I have no chief," he said, lightly, "I belong to no clan, and I have no name—except the first, and the rank I have made for myself! I wear Alasdair's respected tartan as a mercenary in his service. My sword is sold to the highest bidder."

Ah, thought Fenella, wisely, it is himself he mocks.

But she was not to be sidetracked. She narrowed her eyes and said with great innocence, "Kinrowan has more money than Alasdair. Why doesn't he buy you?"

She now received the doubtful pleasure of his full attention. He swung right around, and there was no sort of lightness about him. He looked most forbidding.

"I sell my sword where I choose!" he snapped.

Stung into a spurt of temper, he was suddenly vulnerable. Fenella was quick to follow up her advantage.

"I have no money at all," said she, wide-eyed, "so I ask you only to *lend* me your sword."

Before he could say anything, she hurried on, "I am going, I think, into a sort of battle, and would be very glad of your company."

He gave her a startled look, as though he was seeing her for the first time. She seated herself in the chair by the table, and gazed gravely back at him.

"But—what like battle?" he sounded baffled.

Fenella was off on another tack.

"Sir," said she, "in the course of your chosen career as a hired man—"

She was on easy ground. He was not used to being teased. But she ignored his expression, and hurried on, "You must have traveled far! Seen so much, and done so many things—not all of them pleasant—"

"What are you after?" he said, shortly.

"What is your experience of sorcery?" she countered.

His jaw dropped slightly. He seemed thrown off balance. Then he came to the other side of the table, and faced her across the stained and unpolished surface.

"Are you mad?" he said.

She put her head back against the high chair. She gazed at him as though he was a very junior officer and she his commander. And he perfectly understood, and glowered at her. It was rather an ugly look.

"Madam," he said, sneeringly, "forgive my bluntness. I withdraw the word 'mad'—and substitute 'daft'!"

Fenella had the uneasy feeling that she had gone too far. She put both hands on the table, palms upward, and spoke with all the appeal she could muster, "Forgive me for teasing you. And let us not speak of madness—or even daftness! It *is* sorcery that we must face, so let us discuss it calmly. Oh, why do you distrust me so! I'm sorry if I've annoyed you, sir. But—you are trying to protect Alasdair from me—what do you fear I shall do to him?"

"Hurt him," said the other, bleakly.

He brushed aside her protest.

"I've seen it happen," he said, and a flush of anger ran over his tanned face. "Whatever Kinrowan may think of people's loving kindness, I've seen them—affronted by Alasdair's indifference to them—fleering at his feathered wing—!"

He stopped abruptly, and shut his mouth into a harsh line. A straight lock of hair had fallen over his eyes, and he now stood lowering at Fenella from under it.

"He has met some odd people," said she.

"Oh, leave him alone," said the soldier, roughly. "Leave him in such small peace as he can find!"

"I will not," said the girl. "I will do everything in my power to help him. And if you won't assist—you must just stand by and watch. For I mean to study sorcery!"

Ewen stared at her. Then he turned on his heel and strode to the door.

"I shall warn your father," said he.

"Tell-tale!" snapped Fenella.

He stopped in his tracks, stiff-backed. And the girl jumped from her chair, and ran to get between him and the door. She put both hands on his plaid.

"I didn't mean it!" she cried. "And nor did you! Of course you won't tell anyone! I'm sorry. Oh, Ewen, don't be so unfriendly. I mean no harm—to you or him! I like you both."

"Good God," said he, "you don't even know us!"

But Fenella knew she had out-maneuvered him. She moved back toward the fire. He would not run away, now.

"Is there a house-brounie in this castle?" she asked.

"Of course not! What a childish question."

"Lots of places do have them," she told him. "They live about the house, and bring it luck. And if you ever need special help, you can summon them by calling them three times, and sticking a knife into the table. Lend me your sword," she said.

She held out her hand, and he retreated a pace.

"You're not sticking that in the table!" said he.

Fenella went quickly to him, and took hold of the basket-hilt of the heavy sword he wore. And he brushed her away, but quite gently. There was a faint edge of laughter in his voice when he spoke, "Get your fingers off it!"

She had only seen him smile in gibing fashion until now, but when he chose, his smile could lift all the hard lines of his mouth and eyes, making him a much younger and very much more attractive person. His eyes had gone almost blue, instead of their usual bleak gray. Ewen had lowered his guard at last.

He put a hand to his belt and slid a long black-hafted dirk from its sheath, and held it out across his palm.

"This would surely be more suitable," he said.

"Well, I didn't see you had it."

"And what's more," he went on, "there's no call to ruin the furniture. Tapping it on the table should suffice."

"Perhaps," allowed Fenella. "You tap, and I'll call for help."

Ewen cast a wry glance toward the door and said she had better go easy with shouting for help.

"If Ranald hears, he'll think I'm murdering you. And he'd enjoy a clash."

"If there's a brounie here," said Fenella, "he will come if I merely whisper."

"Whisper, then!"

Fenella went to the table, and leaned on its edge with her hands. She did begin by whispering:

> "Help for this house in need, brounie!
> Help for grief! Help for despair!"

And then forgot caution, and lifted her voice to an urgent cry:

> "Show yourself without fear, brounie;
> Help! Help! Help—if you're there!"

Ewen noted that neither of his men outside the door took the slightest notice of this appeal for aid, and promised himself a word with them. He said, "A poet, too."

"Ssh—it's an old rhyme. Tap with the dirk—three times!"

Quite solemnly he obeyed.

The last sharp sound was still in their ears when a door was opened. And it was not the main door, but the small one, half-hidden in shabby tapestries in the side wall. A draft swirled in from a dark and unheated room beyond, that was rarely used at all. And a man came in and stood looking at them in a startled way, as though they were part of a strange dream.

There was something odd about the newcomer, though at first it was hard to define. After a while no one would think of it again. He was thin and tall, with white hair that fell softly around a deeply lined face. Bright intelligence and humor sparkled in his light-brown eyes, and in the sweet curve of his mouth. As he moved forward, it was with an awkward and lagging gait. His arms were carried with curious stiffness, and now it was only too obvious that he had a great hump on his back.

"What are you shrieking for?" he said, in a gentle and most melodious old voice. "And why is that madman brandishing a knife?"

"Oh—Hudart!" gasped the girl. "Just for the moment I thought you were—!"

She took a long breath.

"We were just doing a spell, Ewen and I."

"*She* is doing a spell," said Ewen, firmly.

"Then you're both wander-witted!" said the old hunchback. "Put the dirk away, man, or you'll cut yourself."

He came over to the fire, with his gawky movements, and shook his head at them reprovingly. But he had the kindest eyes in the world, and it was hard for him to look as strict as he intended.

"Spells!" he said. "Are you children to play with fire!"

"I wanted the brounie." Fenella was unrepentant.

She looked at him sideways, and added softly, "How long have you been bard to Kinrowan, sir?"

"Since the Chief's grandfather was Chief, and—" the old man broke off, and then said, "Why do you want to know?"

"Maybe you can tell me if there's a spirit that guards this house."

"Maybe," said Hudart.

"Maybe you can tell, or maybe there is?"

"Maybe both," said the bard.

He turned to warm his bony long hands at the fire.

"I wish I hadna come in here," said he, plaintively. "I don't like such silly talk. I was on my way down to the great hall, to sing my new ballad for the Chief's guests. And I stepped aside into that empty room, just to run over the words again. My memory—"

Fenella said sadly, half to herself, "The Lady Agnes went to the doors of death to lift a spell. I hoped to follow her path a little—if I have the courage."

"You shouldn't even be thinking of such fearful things!" said the old man, nervously.

He looked at the soldier, standing square and stolid and watchful, and flicked his fingers at him in some agitation.

"Do something, child!" he said. "Distract her!"

"Do what?" said Ewen.

"Dance! Sing! Oh, can't you see her thoughts are dangerous! Listen to my new ballad—"

Before anyone could say anything, Hudart began to sing. He had a beautiful voice, as clear as a bell still, and he sang very quickly.

> "Twas black mirk nicht,
>   An' still as stane;

Ah, Ballindalloch!
The bluid wis reid,
The toun wis ta'an—
Wae tae Annandale!"

Ewen laughed, and Hudart frowned at him, and said severely, "This is a very serious song, my darling!"

Fenella gave the old man a pleading look.

"Surely you know something of magic at your age—" she began.

"Listen to the next verse!" said Hudart, and started to sing again.

"Tho' focht ye weel,
An' deeved them
  sair—
Ah, Ballindalloch!
Fu' mony leel
Return nae mair—
Wae tae Annandale—"

And then added, casually, "I used to know a bit of magic once."

And then he clapped a hand over his mouth, seemingly appalled by his own words.

"Hudart!" cried Fenella, with great excitement.

"Oh no! No, no, no!" said the bard. "I don't mean the sort you mean! Not at all, just conjuring! Little tricks and jokes between my songs, to puzzle people and make them laugh. Look—"

He turned from the disappointed girl, and went over to Ewen with his lagging gait, and put his hand behind the great plaid where it crossed the soldier's breast.

"Oran, copan, talla, tor!"

And from under the heavy folds of tartan, the hunchback produced a little bunch of stiff bright flowers. He laughed hopefully, but no one else joined him, and he stopped and looked sad.

"Not puzzled? Not amused?" he said.

"You do it to everyone," said Ewen, "and I've seen the trick before. A child could do it! The flowers are paper and they fold flat, and you had them in your hand all the time."

"You're not a very kind young man," said Hudart.

And he turned to the girl.

"I'm very old," he said, "and my wits fail a little. I never was very clever at this sort of thing. Though I can still sing quite nicely." he ended on a more hopeful note.

"Are you sure you can give me no advice about magic?" said Fenella.

"Mo chaileag, I *have* advised you! Have naught to do with it!"

She ran toward the turret, and turned, one slender hand thrown out toward the young man who stood still by the window with his face to the night.

"Does it not grieve you to see him like this?"

"I grieve," said the old man, somberly.

"Then help me. For I think you know more than you pretend—"

"No, no! I do not, then!"

"Look at him!"

The bard struck one clenched fist into the palm of his other hand. He cast a frenzied look at Ewen, who merely lifted his eyebrow unhelpfully. And Hudart clutched his head so that the long white hair stood on end.

"It isn't safe! I wish I'd gone straight to the great hall! This is real madness! And I'm not allowed—I've retired—given up all my small tricks, my bit weather-charms and the like! They will be angry—They'll punish me for sure—"

"I'll protect you from anything you fear," offered Ewen.

But he was wearing his most sardonic and unkind expression, and the old man snorted contemptuously at him.

"Oh, you will, will you, my hero! Take your hand from your sword and think again! You're talking of matters outside your element, let me tell you, and steel would be no help— not the way you think to use it. All that dirk nonsense," he muttered, turning away, "though the girl had a useful bit of a charm—"

He started humming to himself in an absent way, and he shut his eyes, and tapped his fingers on his forehead. Ewen's mouth curled, and Fenella frowned him to a less mocking look. After a few minutes, the old bard lifted both arms above his head, and shouted wildly into the shadows of the raftered ceiling:

> "Oran, copan, talla, tor!
> Just a word, if nothing more!"

Then he wrapped his arms around his head, as though he expected the skies to fall on him.

Nothing happened.

In the silence the fire was hissing and sputtering to itself—and talking.

No—the voice was not coming from the fireplace.

Fenella turned and stared at the mounted head of a deer on the wall behind her. Its glass eyes held no life, not a hair stirred on jowl or neck, and the antlers jutted wide but quite immobile. Yet its jaws were moving slightly, and from them came a small, clear, icy voice:

> "First word spoken holds the clue:
> Let us hear no more from you."

The jaws clicked once or twice, and were still. Hudart was standing quite rigid, with his arms bent over his head, and his eyes shut. And Fenella was open-mouthed with surprise. And the soldier laughed.

"Well, well!" said he.

Hudart drew a long and shuddering breath, and covered his face with his hands. After a moment, he said in a muffled voice, "There! They're angry, just as I said They would be! And They told us nothing at all."

Then he lowered his hands, and stared at Ewen. He said, breathlessly, "But They did—They did! 'First word spoken holds the clue'—and you, my son, spoke the word."

"*I* did?"

"You said, 'Well, well,' and in mockery—but that was it."

The old man turned to Fenella.

"I suppose They mean there is a clue in—or beside—a well."

"There's a well in the castle bailey—" she began, in high excitement.

"I will meddle no further in this matter," said Hudart, firmly. "It's all quite daft and useless! But I would say They mean the well in the thorn-wood, away over the hills, by the Standing Stones—"

"You mad little man," said Ewen, "don't encourage her!"

He got a glare from the bard.

"I'm *warning* her!" snapped Hudart. And stamped across the room until he came eye to eye with the soldier and said, *"You* stop her, if you can! You're a bold man, my heart, but I think you've met your match!"

And he went out quickly. There was an excited and startled uproar from the guards outside. They had not known he was in the room.

Fenella said slowly and thoughtfully, "Is he the brounie?"

Ewen suddenly seemed impatient with the whole episode. He gave her a quelling look and said, "He's the castle bard. Don't be silly! Are you so easily gulled by a few childish tricks? I've seen men before who could throw their voices and make dumb objects speak. He's naught but a hired jester!"

"Selling himself, I think, where he chooses," said Fenella.

The mercenary eyed her impassively for a moment, then he went to the table and tilted the big flagon over his wine cup. He spilt some of the blood-red wine over his hand, but ignored the fact, and he sat himself down in the big chair and looked again at Fenella. Their positions were reversed, and he in command. The girl bit her lip, for he was as unapproachable as ever, and she felt alone and rather frightened. She made a forlorn little gesture toward Alasdair.

"If you have any love or pity for him—"

"I've no special feelings for anyone," the soldier said.

And he looked it. Fenella tried another line of approach.

"Ewen," she said, pleadingly, "I'm only a girl. I've never gone into any sort of danger before—"

"Do you expect chivalry from a mercenary?"

He laughed. Fenella wondered why she had ever thought him likeable. She gave up her attempts at coercion. She was very cross with him. She stamped her foot hard, and said waspishly, "Let us start afresh! I shall go to the well in the thorn-wood alone. And at midnight, for good measure!"

He lifted his wine cup toward her.

"Slainte mhath!" said he, mockingly.

He took a few hearty gulps of the wine, looking at her wickedly over the rim. And she gave him a small inclination of her head, and went with dignity from the room.

Left alone, the soldier grinned to himself. He looked across at the deer head on the wall, and his brow creased a little. He sat gazing at it for some time, drinking his wine slowly. Then he put down the goblet, and went across to the trophy to look more closely at it. He tapped it on the jaw. And it bit him.

"Dhia!" he exclaimed, springing back.

Yet it was only a stuffed head, and the light in the eyes was just a reflection of candlelight. Ewen examined the thing suspiciously, and then gave up and went back to the fire, catching up his goblet as he passed the table, and swallowing the rest of his wine at a gulp.

And Alasdair stirred at last. He threw back the plaid from his right shoulder. Then very slowly he stretched a huge, white wing across the dark window. The primary feathers were nearly two feet long, with a sheen like ivory, and the farthest tip was a couple of yards from his shoulder at its fullest stretch. It was a strange thing to see, that spread of wing, but the boy did not look at it. He dropped his beautiful head against the soft underfeathers in a movement of weariness and despair, and stood still.

4. *WRITTEN IN THE WATER*

There are many things easier to describe than perform. Fenella had talked lightly enough of going to the well alone at midnight, but, when it came to the point, it was no simple undertaking. Far from it.

She had gone back to the great hall of Kinrowan, where she had danced and smiled and chattered, most resolutely, with the other guests. Under the approving eyes of her father and her aunt, and of the Chief and his lady. No one had asked her any questions. Only Aunt Mary watched her with faint misgiving. She had taken the place of Fenella's mother when that gentle lady had died, so much too young, and had brought up her brother's child. So she knew very well the look of bright-eyed candor. It meant Fenella was about to do something of which her relatives would disapprove. But Mary was a placid person, so she made no comment. Which was lucky. For Fenella, though unaccustomed to guile, had no intention of giving away her plans to anyone.

By ten o'clock, most of the guests had gone. But those who lived too far away were staying at the castle, so there was still some dancing, and extra late supper, and Hudart had sung many

songs. He was singing when Fenella went quietly to her aunt
and Lady Agnes, and asked her permission to retire. She said
she had a bit of a headache. And this was very nearly true, for
she had been thinking and thinking—about sorcery, and Alasdair with the swan's wing, and the icy voice from the head of
the deer, and Ewen's mocking glance—until her mind had
become slightly blurred.

"Let me just slip away," she said, "I'll disturb no one. I
think I need some sleep."

She caught Agnes's eye, and that lady gave her a little nod.
She knew, as Fenella's aunt could not, what sort of thoughts
might be haunting the girl. And Fenella went, as she requested,
and almost unnoticed, from the room, having refused all offers
of hot milk and soothing herbal brews.

Once in her own bedchamber, she refused all these again
from her worried waiting-maid. She allowed the woman to help
her off with the fine white ballgown and all its petticoats, and
to unpin the pearl cap from her hair. When these were being
carefully put away in a big oak chest, she sat down on the bed
with a thump.

"I'll need you no more tonight, Morag," said she.

She overbore the ensuing protestations, and went on, "Go
and dance with all the others. Enjoy it, and don't worry for
me. I'll be asleep in moments. And I don't wish to be disturbed
again—not for any reason whatever!—until the sun is up, and
it is morning. Good night, now."

She was so convincing that the young woman went off quite
happily and left her to her rest.

But it was a burst of activity that followed the closing of
the door. Fenella hurried to put on a heavy, dark woolen riding-
dress, and soft knee-length boots. She tied her hair back with
a fine veil and knotted the ends under her chin again for greater
security. She put a plaid over her head and shoulders and pinned
it at the breast with a silver brooch. Then she made for the
door.

She glanced back as she got there, and made a tutting noise,
seeing the candles all burning and throwing bright light over
the empty bed. So she got a long cloak from a cupboard, and
rolled it into a sort of bolster which she set under the covers,
with a sheet drawn closely about its top end. It was not a good
likeness of herself lying there, but probably good enough to

deceive Aunt Mary or Lady Agnes if they came to see how she did. And did not look too closely, thought the girl.

Picking up one candle, she blew out all the rest, and left the room to the dim glow of the peats in the hearth. She went out into the corridor, quite forgetting to look first if it was empty. By chance it was so.

Empty also was the narrow little staircase at its far end. This led down to some storerooms, and kitchens, and living quarters for the house servants. But most people used the main stair instead, for it was broad and light; and this one was of rough stones, slippery and with no windows. No one saw Fenella go down.

She came from the stairwell into a long stone passage with doors at either side, and she went flitting along like a small dark ghost, her candle throwing a dancing shadow on the walls. Once she thought she heard a soft footfall around a corner just ahead of her, but when she came to it there was nobody in sight. She stopped and listened. Nothing but silence, and from another part of the house, the distant sound of music. She went on until she came to a door, with a cold wind blowing under it. And again she stopped, rather suddenly, staring at the short chain that should have held the door safe-fastened. It was unhooked, and swinging slightly.

Well, someone has just gone out, thought the girl. A servant, or a groom. If I wait for a moment or two he'll be away and out of sight.

She waited. Wondering why so small a thing as a swinging bit of chain should make her heart jump so. Then she put the candle on a nearby shelf, and drew a long breath, and lifted the latch with great caution, and opened the door. As she had hoped, it led to the open air. She blew out the candle, and left the shelter of the keep. A rising full moon was throwing bright moonlight over the bailey-court, and making fine black silhouettes of the gate towers at the far side. Fenella took a few steps forward.

A hand came down hard on her shoulder from behind, and a hand went over her mouth. A soft whisper told her that if she screamed she would be instantly throttled. She choked instead, and the hand on her mouth slid away.

"A fine game!" said she, glaring at its owner. "To jump out and startle me to death!"

"Ssh! You aren't dead."

And before she could do more than gasp with indignation—

"Call the guard then, you little fool!" hissed Ewen. "Or come with me and hold your tongue!"

He moved off into the shadow of a buttress without another glance at her, and she gritted her teeth and went after him.

Several times he put out a hand and halted her behind him, while he looked on all sides before crossing a patch of moonlight. He was going around the court close to the walls, keeping very cleverly to the shadows whenever possible. Once the girl, not seeing him stop, walked into him and got some remark from the side of his mouth which, luckily, she did not catch. While they stood there, two men came by—so close that Fenella could have reached out and touched a breastplate. If the men had glanced into the darkness beside a buttress—but they did not. They went past, laughing and gibing with one another. And the other pair came without let or hindrance to a little, barred sally-port in a corner of the side wall of the bailey.

"I'd never have got here alone," whispered Fenella.

"No. You would have marched to the main gate, and been turned back by the guard. Silly chit!" said the soldier.

And a man stepped out of a dark niche in the thickness of the wall, and put a sword to his throat. Fenella managed to choke back her scream.

It was hard to see exactly what happened next. The sally-port was deep in the castle wall, and the shadows were black there. Fenella saw only a swirl of Ewen's plaid, and a scuffle, and heard the clash of a fallen sword, and then a choking noise. A man had been hurled to the ground, and the other was kneeling on him, both hands on his neck. The choking died away. Fenella put her clenched fists against her mouth. Then a breathless whisper said, "The rope—back there on the wall—"

She lifted down the coil of rope that was hanging from a nail, and handed it over. A few minutes later, Ewen got to his feet. He pulled the unconscious and tightly bound man into the darkest corner, and straightened his own plaid and pushed his hair from his eyes.

"Is he hurt?" said Fenella, anxiously.

"Just a wee thing strangled," she was told, "but he'll live to stick out his neck again."

"Ranald won't like it," said the girl. "One of his own men, and doing his duty in halting us!"

"Ranald wouldna like any part of this," said Ewen.

He unbarred the little door, and pushed it open. The moonlight fell full across his face and Fenella saw the dancing light in his eyes, and realized with some surprise that he was thoroughly enjoying himself.

"Stand still now," he said, softly. "When that cloud covers the moon—run like a deer for the shelter of yon bushes."

Within a second or two, the scene was darkened and they set off. But it was rough going, and the ground sloped steeply downwards so that Fenella found it hard to keep her footing. She stumbled and tripped, and caught her foot in her skirt and sat down heavily. Then she was hauled up and propelled most ungently into a clump of hazel. She gave a squeak of pain as the branches whipped across her face.

"Hold your noise!" hissed Ewen.

She lost her balance and sat down again. This time she was offered no assistance in rising. He merely said, in a disgusted whisper, "It's like leading a herd of bullocks!"

Fenella opened her mouth to say firmly that, bullocks or no bullocks, *she* was the leader in this expedition. But she said nothing. It was no time for an argument. And besides, Ewen was already away, slipping silently through the bushes.

After a while, they came out on an open hillside dotted with rocks. A good way below them lay a small loch, bright under the moon like a sheet of silver, and beyond that were more lines of hills. Kinrowan castle was hidden now behind the hazelwood. And Ewen relaxed a little, though he was still wary as he led the way to where a stony gully cut straight down the hillside. He clambered into this until only his head showed, and then looked back at Fenella hesitating on the brink.

"Now be careful!" said he. "Don't go tripping and squealing, and turning your ankle! If they hear us back at Kinrowan, they'll think we're a cattle raid, and turn out the clan."

"It's not so easy to move at all in this great skirt," said Fenella.

"Then kilt it up. What a thing to be wearing, anyway, on a ploy like this!"

Fenella thought of several retorts, but she bit them back and scrambled down into the gully. She could see the soldier going down ahead of her, very sure-footed, and wondered if he would do so well in a heavy skirt. The thought made her giggle, and he snapped over his shoulder at her to hold her racket. And she slipped on a wet stone and sat sideways in the quick-flowing, shallow burn that was also using the gully to get down to the loch.

Luckily, she was not hurt beyond a small bruise here and there, and she rose at once, but she was very wet. Ewen made no comment, unless a snort counted, and Fenella went more carefully until she found herself at last on a pebbly beach by the loch-side.

Ewen pointed across the still water.

"The well is over beyond that hill there," said he.

"If you expect me to swim—!"

"Well, I don't," he said, "for I'm sure you'd drown us both. I have a boat."

So he had. Carefully hidden in a great clump of reeds and tied to a rock. Fenella looked approvingly at him as he stooped to unfasten the knot.

"I do think you're—"

"Just get in," said he, "and stop clacking."

She bit back the "clever" that had been on her tongue, and substituted "rude"—but it was under her breath. Then she wrung some of the water from her soaking skirt, and stepped with dignity into the coracle. It tipped wildly, and Ewen grabbed it by its side and Fenella by her arm, and set them straight again.

"Like elephants!" he said.

With even greater dignity, Fenella seated herself in the bottom of the boat—in a couple of inches of water. She could not get much wetter but she found she could get colder. However, she made no complaint. And Ewen embarked with ease, and took up a rough paddle, and pushed off from the shore.

But my weight held the boat steady for him, thought the girl, resentfully, and there's the skirt—

And she was unused to dealing with boats, an honest afterthought added. Though she had traveled in them, fished from them, there had always been so many willing hands to hold her steady, to guard and cherish her.

It was not a wide loch and very soon the boat grounded on another little beach of pebbles, and thin gray bent. Ewen stepped into water that came to the knees of his long boots, and he scooped Fenella up in both arms and swung her ashore. He had given no indication of his intention, and took the girl by surprise so that she was quite off-balance. She clutched him frantically to keep from falling, and he detached her, saying irritably, "Can't you keep your footing for three seconds at a time!"

He tethered the boat and set off up the hill.

Fenella, following, found herself wishing fervently that he would fall flat on his face.

He did not. And nor did she. The hill proved a gently sloping one and easy to climb. The heather and bracken, their beautiful bright September colors grayed by the moonlight, caught wickedly at Fenella's hampering skirt, but she managed to keep upright. She was not so far behind the soldier when they came to the summit, and she glanced at him, triumphant and panting, but he had no compliment to offer. He just nodded toward a couple of miles of moorland that lay ahead.

"Just over here," he said, as though he spoke of a narrow lane. "Are you sure you're for going on?"

"Are you raving mad?" she countered, coldly. "If you think I've come this far—"

He did not wait for her to complete the sentence, but set off across the moor. And Fenella smiled a little behind his broad back. She was beginning to know him.

It took them over an hour to cross the upland. Fenella was getting tired, and in spite of herself her feet began to drag, and she had a stitch in her side. The air was cold, and every breath she took was like swallowing small knives, she thought. The soldier spared her a glance from time to time, and, although he said nothing, yet he went more slowly, and occasionally lent her a steadying hand.

And then, at last, they were looking down at another, and far larger, stretch of water, with a range of high mountains like a black wall beyond. The moonlight was brilliant, and they could see how the bare bones of the hill jutted out below them. The ground fell in a series of shelfs and ledges, little rock precipices, and slopes of scree. And all down these levels grew thorn bushes, leaning sideways from the prevailing wind, with their branches interlocked and their ancient roots half-exposed. Under them, the shadows were black.

Down near the loch the ground flattened out a bit into a fairly smooth curve ending in a ten-foot drop to the water. And there, black and somber against the glitter, stood a tall ruined tower with empty windows and a broken and roofless top.

"The Black Keep," said Ewen. "They say it's haunted. And there's your thorn-wood."

"And there are the Standing Stones!" said Fenella, with a gasp.

From the ruined keep to the rise of the ground ran a double line of great monoliths. Some were upright, and some lay on their sides, and some were too broken to show much more than as a hump among the bracken. They had once been hewn four-square, but wind and weather had softened their outlines until they seemed almost part of the hill itself, and not set there by human hands.

"They go up toward the well," said the soldier, following Fenella's gaze.

"Must we go near them?"

"They won't hurt you."

"They look as though they'd like to."

"Rubbish."

Fenella bit her lip. She battled valiantly with a strong desire to slap him. Ewen, too quick-eyed, noticed this and grinned. Then he said, "What about the cairn?" and he pointed.

A huge black hump stood just below the hanging wood, and some little way from the menhirs. Ten feet high, and as wide, it looked as sinister as the Standing Stones. For the first time Fenella felt a chill of fear run through her blood, and she shivered.

"No one comes here," Ewen was going on, unsoothingly. "They go miles out of their way to avoid the place."

"One can see why," whispered the girl.

She shivered again. Ewen seemed unimpressed by the eeriness of the scene but then, she thought, he would never let anyone know what he really felt. Fenella suddenly realized that she herself was cold and exhausted and very wet.

"Are you afraid of these things?" said the soldier.

"Yes."

He laughed softly and in a very aggravating manner.

"Well!" said he. "Here's the brave warrior who would take up arms against sorcery! Cowering at the sight of a few old bits of stone, and a man-made mole house! My torture!" he scoffed. "I'm glad you were not one of my troop in a real battle. If you were a mercenary, you'd find little employment!"

Fenella looked into the wicked dancing of his eyes. She drew a deep breath and said, "And if you were married to a man, he would have you ducked for a scold!"

This thought seemed to have its effect. Ewen said no more, but turned and began to scramble down the rocky hillside. Fenella suspected that he was laughing. And his remarks had steadied her, given back her courage and her resolution, and she followed him carefully.

When they came to them, the trees were stumpy and twisted, with angular, long-thorned branches and twigs. They also had some very nasty and treacherous spikes that grew from their trunks, and made it almost impossible to grab at them to ease the descent. For it was not easy going. A deer would have had no difficulty. Rabbits would like it. And Ewen seemed quite unworried, slithering quietly down mossy patches, or jumping from rock to rock. But Fenella—face and hands scratched, slipping, falling, dragging her skirt from the clutches of the thorns, rescuing her veil from the same, disentangling locks of hair, and almost weeping with weariness and vexation—Fenella was beyond being afraid of cairn or keep or standing stone when she finally fell into Ewen's outstretched hands in a small clearing. He patted her bracingly on the shoulder, and said, "You'll make a trooper yet," and added, "Cavalry!"

But she gave him a grateful smile all the same. And looked across the clearing that was bright in the moonlight, and saw the well waiting for them.

Right up against a precipitous wall of rock, down which a burn came tumbling in a series of cascades to fall into a deep basin a dozen feet below the level of the clearing, was a circle of battered stones. It was not easy to see it through the overgrowth of moss and fern, bramble and briar. Just here and there the gray of the stones showed hard and still against the wind-moved weeds. It was about six feet from side to side, and roughly two feet high, though once it must have been higher than this, before the years had silted the peaty soil against the sides.

Fenella suddenly stiffened. She whispered to Ewen, "We are being watched!"

He stood quite still also for a moment.

"Who would be here to do the watching?" said he, at last, and went to the middle of the clearing.

The girl ran after him, and caught his sleeve. And the wind dropped, so that there was a great stillness about them.

"The wood's listening," said Fenella, with a bit of a quaver in her voice. "It's probably full of witches and things."

"Your head's full of maggots," she was told.

And then she remembered that she had, after all, come in search of magic. So she let go of Ewen and walked very firmly across the soft ground to the side of the well.

There was a sound of gurgling and sucking from deep inside, and the rush and splash of the burn tumbling down the rocks into it. Fenella hesitated, and then she stooped to peer over the low coping into the darkness within. And Ewen thrust her aside with absolutely no courtesy.

"Get back!" said he. "You'll fall in!"

"Do you think I'm off my head?" she demanded, indignantly.

"I think you're not precisely on it."

And he put one foot on the coping and looked into the well.

"What's down there?" said Fenella, recovering her temper.

"Water."

"Oh, is that all!"

"There's a notice saying 'Private—keep out.'"

He turned and gave her a brief grin.

"Och, it's just a well," said he, "full of dirty, scummy water."

And then he threw back his head like a startled stag, and shoved her violently toward the shadows of the nearest thorn trees. His sword flashed as he drew it.

Fenella clutched at a branch and it pricked her fingers. But she scarcely noted this, and stayed quite frozen with fright. As still as a rabbit that hears the barking of dogs. For now she, too, could hear the approach of danger. Light footsteps, soft on the soft ground, coming down through the shelving levels of the wood.

It may be a witch! thought the girl.

And she choked back a nervous giggle, wondering how Ewen would cope with a witch. Would he, perhaps, be polite for once?

But it was Alasdair who came into the clearing, and stopped with the sword at his breast. As the point was instantly lowered, he said breathlessly and rather crossly, "You *are* here, then!" and he glanced around. "Where's the girl? Hudart told me to come and find you both. Woke me up, he did, and said you were going into danger with that daft child—"

From the corner of his eye, he saw Fenella step from her hiding place, and he added hastily, "His words, not mine!"

And Ewen said, "Well chosen, whoever's! For daft she is. But there has been no sort of danger as yet."

Fenella gave a start of surprise. From somewhere over by the well, out of the empty air, she heard a thin high voice, full of malice, saying like an echo, "As yet—as yet—"

Neither of the men seemed to have heard anything. When Fenella told them, they both gave a quick look around the place; and Alasdair put a hand to his throat, but Ewen said not to talk rubbish.

He then marched across to the well, and looked in. He picked up a chunk of stone from the coping and tossed it down, so that a dull splash came up from below. Fenella thought it was not a thing she would have cared to do. And then she found Alasdair standing close beside her, and he spoke softly as though he had read her thoughts, "He is too sure of himself!"

Then he looked at the girl. A long look, as though seeing her quite newly. He said, very hesitantly, "It was—brave of you to come here, Mistress Fenella. And kind. Hudart said you had a wish to help me by doing so, and I—scarce know what to say. It's more than I deserve. I'm sorry I was so rude to you last night. It—it was the swans—"

"I understand about the swans now," said the girl, very gently.

He gave her a half-smile that touched her heart, it was so sad. He was no longer dressed in his fine clothes, but in a dull yellow cloth trimmed with amber velvet. He had thigh-long riding boots, but there was no cap on his rumpled black curls, and the heavy plaid still fell concealingly over his right arm. He looked gravely at the girl, as he went on, "Then you must understand there is nothing to be done about me. You shouldn't have listened to Hudart's tales, whatever they were. And I am quite at a loss to know why Ewen encouraged you—"

"I wouldn't say that he did, exactly—" began Fenella.

But he caught her arm in a grip that hurt.

"Look! Oh, look!" he said.

He was staring up at the sky, and she did the same.

"Can you see them?" he went on, excitedly. "Driving toward the mountains, with the moonlight on their wings! The wild swans—!"

And he brushed past her, and went toward the place, farthest from the steep of the hill, where the thorn-wood thinned, and one could look out over the lower levels and the loch. Ewen went after him quickly, and caught hold of his shoulder.

"Oh, poor soul!" whispered Fenella.

"Where do you think you're going *now!*" demanded the soldier, in exasperated tones.

The girl moved away from them to a low shelf of rock among the ferns, and she sat down rather wearily, for it had been a strenuous sort of night, and she was not used to such late hours. She brushed her hand idly over some roots of ling, with their tough texture, and then over the softer leaves of violet and clover. She could hear Ewen saying sternly, "The least you can do is to see the young lady home!"

She laughed a little to herself at his sudden excess of chivalry, and she pulled a few sprigs of weed from their shallow soil.

Too late in the year for the flowers, she thought, violets or clovers—

And she shivered suddenly, feeling cold and sleepy. This had all been a silly, useless ploy after all. There was no magic here. No magic in the—

She glanced across at the well. And screamed at the top of her voice.

Ewen got to her first, and she jumped up and clung to him in terror.

"What *is* it?" he said.

He disentangled her hands, and she turned and clutched Alasdair instead, as he hove up on her other side. She said, in a gasping whisper, "What's that, sitting on the side of the well?"

"Nothing!" snapped Ewen.

And Alasdair said, soothingly, "Truly, there's nothing there."

"A patch of mist," said the soldier.

Fenella gulped and tried to pull herself together. She took

another long look at the well, and then she stooped and picked up the little handful of weeds from where she'd dropped them.

"There must be a four-leaved clover—" she faltered.

The two men were looking at her in rather a baffled way, and she held out the leaves to Alasdair, who took them uneasily.

"See what you can see," she told him. "My old nurse always said—"

She saw his face change.

"Now can you see that horrible thing?" she asked.

He nodded, wide-eyed, and gave the spray of weeds to Ewen. The soldier dropped them instantly, without a glance.

"What's the matter with you two?" he said. "That fellow just came down the path without us noticing."

And he strode across to the well. He said in a thoroughly discourteous tone, "Who are you? What are you creeping for, and prying? Frightening the wits from a young maid!"

The person who sat there just looked up into his face and grinned. And the look made Fenella shudder.

Even apart from his expression, he was not an attractive individual. He was small and fat, with little tiny pale beads of eyes shining maliciously under lowering brows. He had hair that was all streaked with black and silver, and stuck stiffly from his head and face in unrelated tufts. He had a huge, loose-lipped mouth, and a pallid skin that was covered with deep furrows in the flabby flesh, and with warts here and there. His clothes were unbelievably ragged and shapeless, and so dirty that it was hard to see exactly what he wore or what color it had once been. He was clutching a grimy, cracked jug in his big hands.

Ewen stared down at him.

"What are you doing here?" he demanded.

"Oh, do be careful—" cautioned Fenella, but not aloud.

The person on the well groped for a moment among the mosses where he sat, and picked up some small object and put it in his mouth. He chewed lingeringly, and then put his hideous head on one side and looked up again at the soldier. He said in a high, gloating voice, "Who are you to question me, Ewen Macrinan of Otterdun?"

Ewen's whole body straightened with a jerk, as though he had been struck. He stared at the fat lump of rags on the edge of the well. And Alasdair spoke in a voice that was suddenly much too loud in the silence of the wood.

"He named you!"

"Wrongly," said the soldier.

But there was something odd about his voice. The ragged stranger laughed. A shocking, cruel sound. And Ewen turned and went stiff-backed out of the clearing toward the open hillside below. This time it was Alasdair who went quickly after him, and caught hold of his arm, and brought him to a halt.

"Ewen—"

But the other stood quite still and rigid, with his eyes on the far mountains, and not seeing them.

And Fenella had gone over to the well.

"Are you—are you magic, sir?" she said.

"I am the Bocan," said the stranger, and he sniggered. "And I heard you—my pretty lady—say I was a horrible thing."

"I was startled," she told him. "One moment there was nothing by the well, and then there was you! I'm sorry I sounded so rude. Please forgive me. Are you—human?"

The Bocan peered at her under his shaggy eyebrows.

"Just go away," he said. "Leave me get on with my supper. I don't like your looks, your conduct, or your conversation!"

Alasdair, having failed to get a single word or glance from the soldier, had come back into the clearing. Now he hurried over to the girl, and said urgently, "Come away, Fenella, and waste no words on this rude fellow."

"Hush!" said she, and then, "It was so strange—we saw him only when we touched the four-leaved clover. It *must* have been four-leaved! My nurse said if one held such a leaf at midnight, one might see strange things—"

"He's strange enough!" commented Alasdair.

"Oh, hush!" said Fenella, again.

She faced the Bocan firmly, though her hands were tightly clenched to stop them shaking. There was something blood-chilling about that heap of dirty, ragged clothes and tufts of hair, and evil little eyes—

"Sir," said the girl, "if you know anything of magic, I need your help. There's a spell that must be broken—"

"Don't!" cut in Alasdair. "I'll not have you telling—"

"Hold quiet!" said the Bocan, contemptuously. "Let the lady have her say. Do you think your—handicap—is so secret?"

Alasdair took a step back from him, and Fenella cast the boy a sympathetic glance, and then hurried on with her appeal to the Bocan.

"I beg you to advise me. I will do anything, however hard or difficult, or dangerous—"

"Ha!" The Bocan laughed gibingly. "What do you know of difficulty! Have you ever faced danger or hardship? How hard can hardness be?"

Alasdair broke in again angrily, "Leave mocking her, scare-crow!"

And took Fenella by the hand, and tried to draw her away, saying under his breath, as she hung back, "He knows nothing of magic! Or anything else! He's naught but an old tinker-man—a beggar—"

"He routed your soldier," said Fenella, "and drove him to a lie!"

But she said the last bit to herself. The Bocan had again found something in a crack in the stones, and was eating it with relish. He licked his thick lips, and peered up at Fenella, and said, "Would you dare look into the well?"

"Look in the—? Why not?"

"After I have said what must be said! When the words are spoken, there will be more than water in the well."

"Of course I'll look."

The Bocan gave one of his high-pitched giggles. He snorted, "Easy to say, my dear! Easy to say!"

"He's just trying to frighten you," said Alasdair.

"And succeeding," whispered Fenella.

The Bocan tittered, and pointed a big fat finger at Alasdair.

"Will you look too, mo churaidh? And the soldier, who dares not face me because I know some names for him—will he look into the well?"

"What will be there, that's so dreadful to see?" said Fenella.

"I'll tell you willingly, my child. When the words are spoken, the water will swirl and bubble. And if anyone is bold enough to look, he shall see whatever he most dreads to see. His own fear—his own shame—his own nightmare. Alive in the well—moving, and speaking, and being!"

There was a little pause. Fenella heard Alasdair gulp, and
his hand tightened convulsively on hers. Then he said, clearly,
"I don't believe it! How could that be?"

The Bocan opened his beady eyes until the whole yellow
pupil showed in mock astonishment.

"You don't believe in magic? You with the swan's wing!"

He grinned evilly as the young man recoiled. Alasdair turned
away, and took a couple of paces toward the shelter of the
trees, and then stopped, although he did not turn around again,
as he heard Fenella say compellingly, "Leave the others alone!
It's I who am asking for help. It's I who will look in your
well."

"Then give me your brooch," said the Bocan.

She quickly unpinned it from her plaid, and handed it to
him. And he scrambled around on the coping until he was
facing the circle of the well, still kneeling on the edge. He
gave the girl a fleering smile, and held the brooch out at arm's
length, above the water far below. And he spoke in a sing-
song gabble:

> "Hawthorn well,
> Hear the spell,
> Gift taken,
> Power waken—
> And show clear
> Their fear."

He opened his hand, and turned it, and the brooch fell.

The sucking and gurgling of the water changed its note and
began to splash and bubble, as though someone was striking
and stirring it with a paddle. And the Bocan bounced up and
down on the coping with horrible glee.

"There!" he cried. "It's starting to spin! In a whirlpool—
deep down, and black as terror! And look—the gleam in the
deepest dark of all!"

And indeed, out of the well a pale glow was shining.

"Now look, my lady, if you dare!"

Fenella took a step forward. But she felt as though her limbs
had turned to lead, and the temptation seized her to turn tail
and run and run, and never stop until she was safe in her own
home far away over the mountains—and she found Alasdair
between herself and the well.

"I'll look first," he said, rather grimly, "and if it's some jest—"

He warded Fenella away with his outstretched hand, and leaned over to look into the depths.

"Oh, don't!" she said, instinctively.

And stopped herself. Alasdair was not a child to be protected and guarded from everything. He was forcing himself to do this, and must not be prevented. But she watched his face with some anxiety. The light from the well showed his wide, dark eyes, and straight nose, and the fine lines of his mouth. It also showed with cruel clarity the look of horror that dawned, and the way he threw out his hand between himself and whatever he saw down there. He said, in a harsh and horrified voice, "Faces—and shouting mouths—laughing and calling me 'Monster!' Ewen!" he cried, and then, more pitifully still, "Robert—!"

But the soldier had not heard, and the elder brother was far away. Fenella ran to Alasdair, and before she could reach him he recoiled and threw both arms above his head, so that his plaid fell back and the great white feathers were spread between himself and the well.

"They throw stones," he cried, "to break my wing!"

Fenella reached up and took his left wrist and pulled it down, and held his hand very tightly between both of hers.

"No, no," she told him, "there are no stones—no shouting. It's just a nightmare that you saw. It wasn't true at all."

He turned on her a wild look of terror and despair.

"Oh, I saw—I saw—!"

But the huge wing folded, and the feathers lowered into their smooth order again. And Fenella gently covered it with the heavy plaid. Alasdair pulled his hand away from hers, and rubbed it over his eyes and mouth. He said, "What's the use of trying to comfort me with lies! I saw a true picture. Whatever they pretend, men look on me with revulsion and with fear—!"

His low voice cracked, and he ended in a whisper, "They know I am not—quite—human."

Fenella was trying to find the right words to calm him. Now she said, "Alasdair, he told you—the Bocan said—! Oh, you saw only your own fears in the well, not the truth. Let me look now, and I'll tell you what I—"

But he stretched his arm out to prevent her passing him, and shook his head violently.

"No! No, you must not! It's horrible—"

And he shouted across the clearing, "Ewen! Ewen, stop her! Keep her from the well!"

This time his voice cut through whatever thoughts had been holding the soldier so still and silent, and he came. And the Bocan laughed derisively, and pointed at him.

"You!" he gibed. "Will you dare to look? I wouldn't advise it! For you, of all men alive, should spare yourself that looking!"

It seemed that Ewen had himself well under control again, for he stared at the Bocan with eyes like stone. He said, evenly, "It's easy to frighten children."

The Bocan put his ugly head on one side.

"And you too old for magic, bhalach?" said he. "Then put down the sprig of rowan that you took in the wood to shield you from its power."

Fenella, in some wonder, watched the soldier take a small spray of rowan-leaves and berries from under his plaid. He dropped them on the ground, and his cold eyes never left the grinning face of the Bocan. Only the muscles of his mouth tightened until they might have been carved from flint. Then he looked down into the well.

There was a long silence. Ewen's face did not alter in any way. He just stood and looked. Until the Bocan said in a hoarse whisper, "Are you hearing a song, Macrinan?"

And Ewen lifted his head. His eyes were quite blank, and he walked slowly across the clearing toward the steep hill ledges, as if he would crash into the rocks unheeding. And Alasdair again ran and put out a hand to halt him.

"What has he done to you?"

The older man did not even glance at him. And, after a moment or two, the boy dropped his hand and stepped back.

"What could *I* do?" said the Bocan, softly. "All that was done, he did to himself. No one forced him to look at it."

And Alasdair suddenly realized that the girl had gone to the well-side, and now was gazing wide-eyed into its depths.

"Ah!" said the Bocan. "What can the lady see there? What secret does she hide in her heart? Terror—or guilt—or despair—"

"None of them!" snapped Alasdair, coming back to glare at him. "What should she have to fear?"

"Fear?"

The creature cackled with laughter, until all his rags heaved and bounced on the well's edge.

"Fear has many shapes," said he. "The worst of all is to see too clear a view of one's own self!"

"I fear failure," said Fenella.

And she went across to Alasdair, and looked at him with grief and great concern. She said, "I saw you, down there in the moving water. With the swan's wing grown huge, over-shadowing your whole life. And I could not help you!"

The light in the well was fading away, but its last glow showed him the soft, troubled blue eyes, and the trembling of her lips.

"Alasdair," she said, compellingly, "it was not truth that I saw, but my fear. Nothing but that. Surely"—and she hesitated and went on in a little rush—"surely, even if there is no way to lift the spell from you—you might learn to live with it? To endure? To be happy?"

Then she spun around and faced the grin of the Bocan and the glint of his evil eyes.

"I have looked. What must I do, now?"

"Drink some water," he told her.

He tipped the jug in his hand so that some slimy creatures fell into the well with soft plops. And he took a coil of wet cord from somewhere in the rags about his middle, and he tied one end to the handle of the jug and lowered it carefully down into the well. Then he hauled it up again, dripping, and half-full of water. He offered it to Fenella, and cackled at her expression.

"It will not poison you," said he.

"Don't drink that!" said Alasdair, sharply. "That foul water!"

"It's lovely," said the Bocan.

"All those slugs—!"

"Delicious," said the Bocan.

And Fenella took the jug before Alasdair could prevent her, and drank a great mouthful of the water. It was bitterly cold, and tasted of peat and rock. She shivered all over, and a sharp tingling started in her hands and feet, and spread over her whole body. She felt her heart begin to thud faster and faster, and a dark cloud was swirling in her head—like a whirlpool—like the waters of the well—and the roar of them grew to thunder— and she was falling—

Alasdair gave a wild shout. "Where is Fenella?"

And she was nowhere. There was the little jug lying on its side on the earth. There was the Bocan doubled up with laughter. The moon shining on the thorn trees. But the girl had gone.

Then there was the Bocan shrieking in a shrill and piercing way. The creature was on his knees, clutching and scrabbling at Ewen's hands that had closed on him like steel, one on his neck and one twisting his arm behind him brutally.

"Don't! You're hurting—you'll break my arm."

"Where is she?"

"I'll tell! I'll tell everything—if you won't torture me!"

Ewen gave a sharp cry. He released the Bocan. So abruptly that the creature fell over, and then scrabbled frantically back on to the edge of the well where he sat rubbing his arm and muttering to himself. Then he peered up at the soldier and said viciously, "I'll tell you, all right! She isn't here. Go and look for her at Kinrowan!"

And then added, very softly, in a sort of savage, hissing glee, "Know her, if you find her—for her poor sake!"

Alasdair strode over to him, and he cowered away as the young man looked at him in open loathing.

"I hope we do find her—for *your* sake! Or be sure I'll find *you*—and make you talk—!"

"Be easy," said the Bocan. "You haven't done with me— nor I with you, cygnet!"

And he grabbed up his jug, as Alasdair took a threatening pace forward.

"Lost my fine supper!" squealed the Bocan. "And every slug for miles scared away!"

He jumped into the well, as Alasdair struck at him.

There was a great splash; a sound of wallowing and sputtering; then only the lapping of water. Alasdair stood staring down into it in great astonishment. He said, "Where did he go? Right under the water?"

He moved back a little, and then said in some horror, "If she fell in there! If she's been down there—drowning—while we did nothing to—"

He looked frantically at Ewen, who said in a numb sort of way, "She's back at the castle—he told us—"

"Lying, maybe—to delay us while she drowned!"

"No," said the soldier, "I think he meant her more harm than drowning."

"At the castle? Then we must hurry. To put a stop to whatever—"

The young man paused, and then said perplexedly, *"Know* her? Why should we not know her?"

He got no reply. And he turned to Ewen. And was a little shocked by the man's set face and haggard look. It had always seemed to him that Ewen was a person with no feelings at all. He was feeling something now.

"Forget whatever you saw in the well," said Alasdair, moved by a most unusual rush of sympathy. "It—it wasn't true—"

As Fenella had tried to comfort him, so he echoed her words to comfort his soldier. But Ewen gave a short, mirthless laugh, and said, "I knew fine what I would see."

"Fool, then, to look!" Alasdair told him.

And he got a funny glance from the other, and a twisted grin. Ewen said, "I was goaded to it, as you were. One can't be constantly out-braved by a chit of a girl!"

Alasdair saw how his hands were clenched until the knuckles showed the white of the bone. And Ewen dropped his gibing tone, and said through his teeth in a voice of shaken fury, "I wish I'd strangled that foul brute!" and added, lower still, "Does he think me so childish I can still be made to cry?"

"Can you not?" said Alasdair.

Ewen gave him a hard stare. Then he laughed again, and said in his usual soft cold way, "I am not you, leanabh!"

And he spun on his heel and marched across to the side of the clearing, and started to go up the steep, rocky hill through the thorn trees, at considerable speed.

Alasdair took a last look at the battered stone circle of the well. He called aloud, "Why does the Bocan think we won't know her?"

There was no reply. He heard a soft rattle of stone on the hill above. And he saw the moon shining over the black outline of the ruined keep below on the shore, and the sinister bulk of the Standing Stones. He thought there was a rustling in the trees on the far side of the clearing.

Alasdair turned and ran after the soldier as fast as he could go.

"Wait for me," he called, in rather a quavering tone.

But even through his sudden fear, he was thinking about Fenella, and wondering what Ranald would say if the girl had not returned to Kinrowan.

5. *THE LOST ONE*

Ranald had quite a lot to say. And the saying exhausted his hearers as much as it did himself.

The little room where Hudart lived, at the side of the castle courtyard among others that belonged to Kinrowan's entourage, was lit by a lantern hanging from a nail on the wall. The small, steady light showed the tall figure of the Chief standing with his back to the fireplace. It shadowed the deepened lines around his mouth, and the watchful eyes; picked bright glints from his red hair; and revealed that he had changed from the fine clothes he had worn earlier, and was now clad only in a shirt and a long plaid belted in folds about his waist, with the ends thrown over his shoulders, and rough leather shoes on his feet. But he was looking no less a Chief. Hudart watched him with respect and admiration from his wooden chair by the side of the hearth.

Alasdair had hunched himself on a stool in a very listless attitude, and somehow managed to look as if he was cold, in spite of the blazing fire. And Ewen was leaning into a narrow window embrasure, staring beyond the horn-window at nothing. The Chief's measured voice swept over them both, and flayed from them the last rags of any self-esteem they still possessed. It seemed that Fenella had not returned to the castle.

The shock of this information had deprived Alasdair of any ability—or even any wish—to defend himself against Ranald's anger. Indeed, it almost took the sting from his words, for after a while Alasdair hardly heard them. He leaned his back against the wall behind the stool, fighting a mad desire to burst into tears. He hoped none of the other men had noticed this, and glanced sideways at Ewen. But there was no indication that his quick-eyed henchman had seen anything amiss, for once. Alasdair tried to fix his attention on the man's torn sleeve, ripped up from cuff to elbow, and the gaping throat of his jacket where some of the silver buttons had been dragged off. The return to the castle had not been all that simple.

As they had made their way back, the rain had started on the hills, a thin, fine drizzle that made them both thoroughly damp in a short time. And Ewen had been much concerned to find his boat was still on the far shore of the loch where he had left it.

"How did *she* get across?" he kept repeating. "Maybe she wouldna trust herself with the oars—but it's four miles around the side!"

And he had set a fast pace after that. They had come up the water-gully in the castle hill as though it had been a ladder. And then they stood in the hazel-spinnery and looked at Kinrowan, so black and still and with no sign of life on its tall bleak walls and battlements. Though that, as Ewen remarked, did not mean it was unguarded. Alasdair had wanted to go straight to the gatehouse, and bang for admittance.

"Thus rousing the whole hive!" snapped Ewen.

"I went out that way, and no one was especially roused!"

The soldier said acidly that getting out was a very different matter from trying to get in.

"Even to you, Alasdair, the gates of Kinrowan will not open in the night without question."

"Well, we have some questions, too! They'll know at the gate if Fenella came back. We must ask everyone—"

"Dhia! And let them all know she was out running the hills!"

"There was no harm—"

"Of course there was not!" Ewen was at his surliest. "But

it is not the usual habit of a young gentlewoman. Would you have her criticized?"

"I am no expert on the habits of gentlewomen," said Alasdair, stiffly, "so I must take your word."

Ewen came off his high horse a little, and shot the boy a funny look. But Alasdair was quite serious.

"We'll find a waiting-maid," said Ewen, grinning, "and send her to see if the Lady Fenella is safe in her bedchamber. We can say you have fallen in love, and cannot sleep till you know she is resting quietly!"

And he had brought them with the utmost caution to the sally-port from which he had taken Fenella out of the castle. The door was still unbarred, as he found when he pushed it open so carefully that it hardly creaked. Then he slid through into the black shadow beyond. Alasdair followed. There was a scuffle of feet, and a torch flared into vivid life. The door was slammed, and he was hurled back against the wall, with the breath knocked out of him. In startled dismay he stared at the circle of fighting men about them, tensed for action. And Ewen was standing between them and Alasdair, and his sword was in his hand. For a moment no one moved. Then Alasdair lurched forward, and grabbed his soldier's arm.

"No! They're Ranald's men!" he gasped.

Instantly, three of them drew themselves on Ewen, hampered as he was, and Alasdair was again pushed back to the wall. There was a fierce but very brief scrimmage. None of the other men moved, though they were ready to, in emergency, and they relaxed visibly when the first three stood back. One man laughed. He was holding Ewen's own sword pointed at its owner's heart. And Ewen looked at him dourly.

"You got free, did you? And fetched some of your friends to give you courage to lie in wait for me!"

The man drew back the broad and gleaming blade. And one of the said friends grabbed his arm, in turn, saying urgently, "Not now! The Chief wants him!"

And then, politely, to Alasdair, "If you'd be good enough to come with us—"

"Is Ranald still awake?" said Alasdair, with a sinking heart. They said he was indeed. And waiting.

And they led the pair of them across the bailey court to

Hudart's room at the side of the keep. To the lantern light, the glow of the fire, and the frown of the Chief.

He rose from a chair by the hearth as Alasdair and Ewen entered the room with their eager escort clustering in the doorway. He looked hard at them all, and demanded to know if there had been any sort of brawl at the gate.

"They handled us tenderly," said Ewen, fiddling in an obvious way with his torn sleeve. "They broke no bones, and kindly spared our lives."

Ranald turned a cold eye on his men.

"I never told you to disarm him!" said he.

"Kinrowan, he drew on us," some of them told him, quite reasonably.

"What would you expect?" put in Ewen. "The place might have been attacked, and taken by enemies, during my absence."

There was quite a satisfying reaction to this gibe from the men around him, and he added, even more annoyingly, "Please note that I didn't hurt you when I knew who you were."

"And please note," said Ranald, dryly, "that no one has hurt you much. Now hold your tongue."

He made a sign to the man with the sword, who brought it to Ewen and handed it over, with a condescending and lordly gesture. There was a glint in the soldier's eye, but he took it in silence. Also his dirk when it was given to him. Ranald congratulated his men on their efficiency, and sent them away rather hurriedly. Then he leaned his arm along the mantel shelf, waited just long enough to fill the little room with tension, and said icily, "Where is the girl?"

The ensuing explanations sounded very thin, under his searching gaze, even to those who were making them. When they fell silent, the Chief drew a long breath and proceeded to favor them with his views on their characters, their conduct, and their intellect. This took him a goodish while.

Old Hudart, sitting silent in his low chair at the corner of the hearth, began by regarding the culprits severely. Then his gaze became rather sympathetic. And finally he grew restless. He got up, unobtrusively, and went to a cupboard where he busied himself in filling a shallow bowl with milk. He tiptoed to the door. And Ranald said, without the slightest change of tone, "Where are you going, Hudart?"

The old man started, slopped some of the milk over his

shoes, and looked at his Chief with the anxious eyes of a chidden dog.

"Just putting out a drop of milk for the hedgehog—"

"Your pet can wait!"

Hudart stepped quickly back from the door. And Ranald said to Alasdair, "What you tell me is like the raving of an unsound mind. Boiling water in a well! Faces shouting from it! Four-leaved clovers! It's naught but a gallimaufry of muddled folklore and hysterical imagining—"

"And it isn't exactly a pet," said Hudart.

The Chief was taken aback.

"What?" he said.

"It's a sort of a stray," the old man went on, eagerly. "It just came to my door a while since, and crying. It's crying now. Can't you hear it? Hungry, I don't doubt."

Ranald, it seemed, was not in a compassionate mood. He told Hudart to shut the door at once. While he obeyed, the Chief eyed his bard coldly and said, "I blame you for starting this nonsense in the girl's mind. Telling her a load of rubbish about the well—"

"I never dreamed she would go there alone!"

"She didn't go alone," said Ranald, balefully.

Alasdair sighed and Ewen braced his shoulders, as the Chief's eyes came back to them.

"It just boils down to this," said Ranald, "that you took her out on the hills and lost her."

They had been over this point several times already, but Alasdair did not feel capable of saying so. He said hopelessly, "The Bocan said she'd be back here."

"And is she?"

"No."

"Then you've lost her, haven't you! A young girl—a guest in my house. Left alone on the hills at night, with wolves and cattle thieves, and the good God knows what else!"

"So you keep saying, Kinrowan," and Ewen stepped in where Alasdair had feared to go. "You've made your point. Now be done with this court-martial. The whole blame lies on me, and I've said so. I could have stopped her. Brought you word of her intention—"

If he meant to draw Ranald's fire from Alasdair, he was entirely successful. The Chief glared at him.

"I am well aware where the main blame lies!" said he.

And Ewen gave him one of his flippant looks, and said, "Chief, I've often heard you say that a guest in your house must be denied nothing. Who am I to contest your wish? The young lady asked me—"

Alasdair was forced to admire the control of his brother-in-law, who cut in quietly, "And if a guest of mine expressed a desire to set fire to the place—?"

"Surely you would expect me to assist?" said Ewen, in a voice as soft as the purr of a cat, and he smiled very sweetly.

Conversation lapsed.

Alasdair wished, not for the first time, that he had some sort of control over his henchmen. Hudart gave a little dry cough. And at last Ranald stirred. He straightened himself until his red head almost brushed the rafters. Alasdair jumped to his feet, and said hurriedly, "Ranald—you have every right to be angry, but—"

"I am more than angry," the Chief told him, in an even voice. "How shall I tell the girl's father that two grown men of my household stood by and watched, while she jumped into a well?"

"We—don't know that she did."

"You don't know *what* she did! You've lost her. And what do I tell her father?"

Ewen chose this moment to put in his oar again. He said, "Tell him this castle can stand siege for a year."

Ranald blinked.

"Will that soothe him?"

"It'll hold him," said Ewen.

And Ranald put his hand to his mouth and bit hard on the knuckle. Alasdair flinched. But the outburst of fury that he expected from his relative did not materialize. Ranald merely said, "Suppose I don't want to be besieged for a year?"

"Oh, we'll get back!" said Alasdair. "If it takes a *hundred* years!"

Old Hudart gave a startled exclamation.

"Don't say so!" he cried. "It may come to that, with sorcery about!"

"And I am not prepared to wait so long," announced the Chief.

He took a long-striding walk through the room and back.

"What possessed you two fools? You didn't even look for the girl!"

Alasdair said defensively that indeed he had wished to go down into the well in search of her.

"What stopped you?" snapped Ranald.

"I did," snapped Ewen.

"You're both deranged!"

Kinrowan moved across the room again, and came to a halt in front of the soldier, who met his gaze with no outward sign of alarm, if indeed he felt any.

"I wish I knew how to handle you," said Ranald.

"If it calms you at all to keep moaning at me—" said the other, and smiled again.

Alasdair shut his eyes. But Ranald merely said, in a voice like that of a lion who has just been offered some sugar, "I would like to horsewhip the pair of you."

He took a deep breath, and added, "But I fear the Lady Agnes would protest."

"So would I," said Ewen.

Ranald marched rather quickly back to the fireplace. He stood with his head averted, and both hands gripping the shelf, and told them how he had been wakened, close after two o'clock, by Agnes saying she had been in a fearful dream. She had seen a flight of huge black wings over the towers of Kinrowan, menacing the castle and all who lived there. She said she had heard the voice of Fenella, crying for help from far away. Nothing would satisfy her but to go at once herself to Fenella's room. And there she had found a dummy lying in the bed. The Chief's wife had sent him to Hudart, knowing the old man had strange cognizance of the castle's activities. What he heard had startled Ranald very much. And a plan of campaign had been organized between himself, his wife, and Hudart, and—

"I came back here," said Ranald, changing his tone, "in time to greet you two, and hear your discreditable account of your exploits! Now I shall go again to Agnes, and let her know the latest—developments!"

"And we," said Alasdair, eagerly, "will go back to the well, and look—"

"You," said Ranald, "will stay here. And not stir one step until I give you leave."

"You *can't* make us—!"

"I command your obedience, Alasdair. As your relative, your elder, and your host! And if you have the slightest authority over Ewen, I lay it on you to make him obey my orders."

He strode over to the door and threw it open wide, so that a shaft of moonlight struck into the room, and turned his hair as black as night. He gave one comprehensive scowl at the three men behind him.

"Hudart," he said, in a meaning sort of way, "I rely on you."

Then Kinrowan was gone, and the door shut.

Alasdair drew a shaken breath and sat down on the stool again. He said, "I knew he would be angry, but I've never known him—"

Ewen laughed, and Alasdair, looking at him in surprise, saw how his eyes were gleaming.

"The Chief was not as angry as he seemed," said Ewen, "I tested him. If his rage had been real he would have struck me."

"And no blame to him," said Alasdair, "you were being very aggravating."

The other shook his head.

"He was thinking coolly all the time. Watching us like a hawk while he scolded. He was playing a game," said he.

Hudart prodded the fire so that the logs fell aside and filled the heart with sparks. The old man snatched up a little basket, made of plaited rushes, that was standing near, and made sure it was untouched. And the sparks died away. Then Hudart put the basket down and went over to Ewen and put a thin hand on his sleeve.

"You are mistaken about Kinrowan," said the bard, "he meant every word he spoke."

"Maybe," said the soldier, "but how did he want them taken?"

The old man shook him slightly.

"Don't be so tiresome, boy!" he snapped. "Why did you let the lady from your sight? I warned you about playing with fire!"

"You didn't think to warn me of the Bocan."

Hudart bit his lip, and lowered his hand.

"I forgot him," he admitted, dismally.

The soldier showed his white teeth in a momentary grin that yet held little mirth in it. He said in a brisk voice, "And now I am going back there, to wring his neck!"

The old bard grabbed his again, with both hands and tightly.

"Not now, you won't!" he cried. "Not until the Chief says—"

Ewen moved across to the door, towing the fragile weight of the old gentleman with him. And he looked over the white head at Alasdair.

"Are you coming?" he said, lightly.

"Oh, Ewen! Ronald told us—he ordered—"

"Don't go from here!" begged Hudart, frantically. "No, no! I shall be blamed—!"

"Even Kinrowan couldna think you'd hold us by force," said Ewen.

"But—oh, look there, my heart! The men posted on the battlements!"

The bard threw out one arm and pointed through the door which Ewen had dragged open. The bailey-wall, and the gate-house showed black against the sky, and men were keeping watch over the courtyard, silhouettes on the ramparts.

"With guns!" cried the old man, and he looked up into Ewen's face and said harshly, "Do you so crave death?"

Ewen stopped in the doorway. The bard, still watching him, said more gently, "And will you leave Alasdair without a sword?"

For a moment the other stood quite still. His eyes were on the gate towers and the armed men up there.

"There is also Fenella," whispered Hudart.

Ewen turned back into the small stone-walled room. He marched across to the fireplace, and stood staring down at the smoking logs.

Hudart gave a sigh of relief, and took the bowl of milk from the table, and set it down outside the door. Then he snapped his fingers close to the ground.

"It's strange to see a hedgehog," he said, "and such a young one. It must have come in under the castle gate."

He looked narrowly at the others. But Ewen was still watching the fire, and Alasdair was watching Ewen. The old man gave a little cry, and said excitedly, "Oh, look! The hedgie is sharing its milk with a little cat! Where did you spring from, pussie? Pretty girl! Wait, I'll refill the bowl!"

He looked again toward the others. But they were lost in their own thoughts. The old man sighed. He put down the jug, and said, "Are you hungry? It's been long since supper. There's some good broth in that pot by the side of the hearth there."

Alasdair shook his head wordlessly, and Ewen never stirred. The bard sighed. He gave each of them a gentle look, from the brown eyes that were so much younger than the rest of his face.

"You're taking it hard, my darlings," said he, "and that's as it should be. It's a terrible thing that has happened. She was a fine sort of lady."

Alasdair slumped down in a chair by the table, and leaned his head on his hand very despondently. And the old man went over to him and touched his shoulder.

"A very fine sort of lady," Hudart repeated, slowly. "Did you think so?"

Alasdair's reply was so low and muffled that it was hard to hear. But Hudart heard it.

"I thought so," the boy said.

After a moment, the bard spoke again, very gently still but probingly, "What did she think of you?"

"She pitied me."

"Is that all?"

He had probed too deeply. Alasdair scowled at him.

"What else!" snapped the young man. "And wherever she is now—she must despise me, too!"

And he jumped and said loudly, with a sort of hurt fury, "I stood by like a silly child, while she was mocked and taunted by that Bocan! I let her look into his nasty well! And whatever happened to her, then, I let it happen! Oh, my grief!" he cried. "Even if I find her again, I can't defend her from danger— lacking a sword-arm!"

Ewen said, without moving, "I've offered to teach you the use of your left."

"And a fine time to remind me of that!" shouted Alasdair.

The door was suddenly thrown wide open, and the Lady Agnes stood on the threshold. Her hands were clasped at her waist, and her face was calm and grave. But Alasdair fell back before the look in her eyes. And Ewen turned, and stiffened. Agnes cast a brief glance over the pair of them, and spoke in a brisk, cool voice. "All right, you two," said she, "I want the Lady Fenella back here and safe in her bed, before sunrise."

Alasdair threw out his hand in appeal.

"Agnes, we also wish—"

She took a step or two into the room, and went on slowly and deliberately, "I don't care how you do it. I don't care if you never return yourselves. But she will come back to Kinrowan."

Behind her, the tall figure of Ranald moved into the moonlit oblong of the doorway, and he waited there listening and watching.

Alasdair made no further interruption. He stood with bent head, while his sister finished what she had come to say.

"I will accept no excuses, and no failure," said she. "Forget your wing, for once, and use your wits!"

She looked across at the soldier, and there was a warning in her eyes.

"Ewen, think twice before you leap."

She turned her back on them and went to the door, and Ranald drew aside to let her pass. But she paused for a moment, and then she faced her brother again, and his swordsman. She said, "Bring that child safely home, or be forever shamed. I lay her life in your hands, and on your heads."

And she went out. Ranald watched her go, and then he also bent a relentless eye on the two younger men.

"And I have a word to add to my lady's commands," said he.

He waited until they both looked at him, and then said in a very stern and forceful way, "Do not go near the Spaewife, by the river-ford. On peril of my deep displeasure."

He spun on his heel, and went out into the night.

Nobody spoke for a short while. Ewen was staring after the Chief, with an odd expression on his face. Hudart, for some reason, was busily dusting the table with a torn cloth. And Alasdair, head lowered, bit his lip in perplexity.

"The Spaewife?" he said, at last. "Why did he mention her?"

"Don't bother your head about that," said Hudart. "Some say she has the Sight—but I don't know about it."

He looked rather slyly at Alasdair, and that young man said, "It hadn't occurred to me to go to her. But surely—the Second Sight could be useful to us, now! She might be able to advise—"

"Ah no—no!" cried the old man. "You mustn't go against the Chief's orders!"

Alasdair went over to the narrow window, and stood looking out. But he was seeing nothing—even if the thin horn that covered it had allowed much of a view—the boy was thinking. And Hudart watched him expectantly.

"My sister told me to use my wits," said Alasdair, suddenly. "Did she mean me to disobey Ranald? Did he mean it, too? Was it a hint he was giving me—to go to the Spaewife?"

"Now why would he do a thing like that?" said Hudart. "He would not think you had the spirit to disobey him."

Alasdair gave him a very cross look. And his handsome face set a little, as though he was gathering strength of will for some decision.

"The Chief is no trickster," said Hudart, solemnly.

"Is he not?" said Ewen.

Hudart turned quickly, with an apprehensive start. The soldier still had his dancing battle-light in his eyes, and he was smiling grimly. The old man gulped in alarm and dismay, and went to Alasdair. He said urgently to him, "Don't heed that fellow of yours. He's a madman. Now, I'll tell you just what to do. The Spaewife can't help you—her advice might lead you into a bit of danger. You must—you must go—"

He hesitated, and then hurried on in his sweet old voice, "Go to Black Fergus. I happen to know he will be in the Glen of the Pines—over on Mackenzie's land—with a few of his men. Go to him, and ask his help. He's a very nice kind man, and he'll do you no harm at all."

Alasdair moved impatiently. He was in no mood for anything nice or safe. He had keyed himself to meet danger, and the old man saw it written on his face, but babbled on, "I'll tell you a password that will make you doubly secure. A password that will make Fergus your friend—ask him if he likes ox-tail soup."

The bard swung around and snatched at Ewen's sleeve, as that one moved past him toward the open door.

"Where are you going?"

"This much I'll tell you," said the soldier, with a wicked lilt to his voice, "I'm no' going where Kinrowan thinks I will!"

He disengaged his sleeve with depressing ease. He said, "Slan leat, Hudart."

"Beannachd leat," answered the bard, mechanically.

He watched the other stride away into the moonlight. And

then Alasdair was out of the room like an arrow, speeding to catch up with his henchman. The old bard shook his head and twisted his thin hands together. His face was furrowed with anxiety.

"He's too wily for his own good, that man!" he said, aloud. "He'll ruin everything!"

And he stood peering across the courtyard toward the stables, until something stirred in the shadow of a nearby buttress, and the Lady Agnes came and stood beside him. She, too, was looking in the direction taken by the others.

"The gates are open for them," said she, quietly, "but where will they go? Why have they gone for horses?"

"Come into the warm, my lady."

She went with Hudart to the fireside, and sat herself down in the low wooden chair, and stretched out her hands to the warm embers.

"It was cruel to drive them so," said she. "They were wet and hungry and miserable! And we've sent them out into the cold. Did they fall into the trap, Hudart?"

"Maybe so." The old man was kneeling to put a square of peat among the darkening logs. "Alasdair would certainly have done it, left to himself. But—"

Behind them, Ranald came in, stooping his head under the door lintel. Agnes gave him an abstracted smile as he came over to join the others.

"Did it work?" he wanted to know.

"We can only hope," said the bard.

Agnes sighed, and said, "If they had stayed here much longer they must have found Fenella."

"Aye," said Hudart, "and by knowing her, they would have released her from the dreadful thing that has fallen on her."

As though he was making an accusation, Agnes said, "I know we have taken a terrible risk. But—it was her own idea. And for Alasdair's sake. Hudart, what effect has this had on him?"

The old man suddenly smiled at the beautiful, anxious lady in his battered chair, and the splendid-looking man who now sat at her feet, and he said, "For minutes at a time, he gave no thought at all to himself or his wing."

The lord and lady of Kinrowan exchanged a long look. And Ranald took both her hands in his, and said reassuringly, "As we hoped, my darling. It's two years since you—brought him home. And in all that time he has never spared a thought for any *but* himself. I have not been too happy about this plot of yours and Fenella's—but I begin to think it may succeed."

"Oh, surely—surely," said his wife, under her breath. "If he worries about her—if he thinks he has been strong and brave—and saved her—"

She bent over the side of the hearth, and took up the rush basket, and set it on her lap between her gentle hands. There was a sort of nest inside it, of soft torn rags, and from among these came a gleam of olive-green, and two bright eyes blinking up at her. Agnes gave a shaken little laugh.

"They never noticed you," said she.

Hudart snorted.

"Not they!" he said. "Never even glanced at her!"

He waved a hand toward the door.

"I told them there was a young hedgehog outside," he cried, half amused and half irritated, "and a she-cat sharing its milk! They were not interested. Didn't even go to look if it was true! They've no sense at all, those two. I gave them a chance to think!"

"They didn't realize the implication of that bit about knowing her if they found her," said Ranald.

"How did you know her so quickly, Hudart?" said the lady.

The old man told her how the tiny voice had called from the courtyard. And how, when he had opened his door, the creature had come with its straddling walk into the room.

"If a little toad tells you then that its name is Fenella, and that it is thirsty, what would you think?" said Hudart, simply.

It had told him more than that. It had told him about the expedition to the well, and what had happened there. And then Fenella had described how she found herself back in the court-yard of the castle, and in what strange shape. She had been very upset.

"But I have met this sort of metamorphosis before," said Hudart to Agnes. "Very disturbing, but really quite simple to deal with. And so I told her. It needs for one specific person to recognize her—in this case, that person being Alasdair— and she is herself again."

He had gone to his Chief with the whole tale, and Ranald and his lady had come to talk it over with Fenella. And the girl had pleaded with them not to make it too easy for Alasdair.

"We could send him to the Spaewife," Agnes had said, suddenly, "and let her tell him some spell or other to say over Fenella. Warning him that it is dangerous, and not to be attempted lightly. Ranald, send a messenger to old Marjorie and tell her what she must say."

And a young clansman had been dispatched to the cottage by the river-ford to tell the story to the Spaewife. No one knew quite what the messenger thought of his errand, but then no one had bothered to ask him. In fact, he thought the festivities of the previous day had been too much for his Chief, but carried out his mission with great zeal nevertheless.

"Are you sure this is altogether wise?" Hudart had said then, to the others.

"I'm not," said Ranald.

But Agnes would have none of this cautiousness.

"If Fenella is brave enough to take the chance—and what is there to go wrong?" she said. "When Alasdair sees the Spaewife—"

"How do we get him there?" said Ranald. "He will surely suspect us of knowing more than we pretend if we just tell him to go to Marjorie for advice. She has never dabbled in such frightful—"

"That will be easy," said Fenella from her basket. "Tell him *not* to go. If you, sir, will taunt him a little, and make him cross—it will be better still if he thinks he has done the whole thing himself."

"Yes," said Agnes, excitedly, "you're right. And Marjorie must tell him a rhyme—invent a rhyme, Hudart!—and she must say it is very dangerous to him who speaks it. Something awful may happen to him—"

"Two heads?" offered Kinrowan, amused.

"Two *wings!*" said Agnes. "Oh, poor Alasdair! But he must be made to think. To face disaster for someone else's sake. Two wings," said Alasdair's loving sister, firmly.

And Hudart suddenly startled everyone by saying loudly:

> "Tober, torra, clach and dun!
> Here's a rhyme without a tune.
> Set the young Fenella free,
> Though disaster fall on me!"

Another puzzled messenger was sent racing down the hill to the Spaewife with this masterpiece learnt by heart.

Now the Chief's wife was talking soothingly to the small toad in the rush basket, who just sat and blinked slowly at her with its beautiful golden eyes.

"He'll be back soon, now, with the rhyme," said Agnes, "and he'll be brave enough to say it. You'll be your pretty self again."

"Suppose he fears to say the spell?" said the tiny voice of the toad. "What then?"

Ranald looked at his wife, and she bit her lip.

"He will be beyond anyone's help," she said, sadly, "but you shall not suffer. After all, he need only look at you, knowing who you are, and the spell will break. Have no fear for yourself."

"I—I am trying not to," said the toad. "And suppose he doesn't come back at all?"

A brief silence fell. And then Ranald said firmly, "My men will be sent to bring him."

And Hudart, rather distracted, said the words that they had all been trying not to think.

"And—if he doesn't fall into your trap? If he goes nowhere near the Spaewife at all, but out over the hills where he canna be found?"

"Of *course* he can be found!" This was Ranald, again. "We'll track him down like a deer! It just may take a bit longer to get him back here. But I hope it may not come to that. That Alasdair will prove himself a man and not a silly, selfish child."

He brought his brows down in a sudden frown.

"If only that stubborn devil wasn't with him!" said he. "He's a dark horse, that one. And yet I swear I've browbeaten him tonight until he will be glad of any chance to go against my orders."

He looked rather hopefully at Hudart, and the old man gave him a doubtful glance in return, and then said in the voice of one who tries to reassure himself, "He was ready enough to leave the castle when you bade him stay, Kinrowan. My heart was in my mouth! His suspicions were roused already, and must have been confirmed when he was not shot by the men on the walls."

"If he'd gone out then," said the Chief, "he would have been shot."

His wife murmured a mild protest, and he smiled at her, and got to his feet, and stretched his arms widely.

"Go and sleep, mo chridhe," he said, "there's no more to do here, until they return. I'll come and tell you when that happens. Go you, love. It's late hours you're letting Alasdair's nephew, or niece, be keeping!"

Agnes gave him an enraptured smile. And Hudart stooped to kiss her hand. Then she rose, and Ranald folded her plaid carefully around her against the chill of the night wind, and took her out into the empty courtyard.

Hudart scurried ahead of them, and went to open another door into the main part of the keep, and the lady of Kinrowan went in. Then the old bard turned with his Chief and strolled slowly toward the gatehouse.

Ranald said, "What will Ewen do?"

Hudart said nothing for a moment, and then he sighed and quoted an old proverb, "'Who knows what sword is in the sheath till it be drawn?'"

"The girl told us more than she guessed about that one," said Ranald, thoughtfully.

"Has it altered your views on him?"

"No. I have always thought," said the Chief, "that that lot got just what they were asking for, all round!"

They went on in silence to the gates, where they were challenged by a sentry. He was horrified to discover that he had shouted at his Chief, but Ranald soothed him by complimenting his vigilance. Then Kinrowan went back toward Hudart's room with the bard. And as they went, the old man said unexpectedly, "If only he doesn't go looking for Black Fergus."

Ranald stopped dead in his tracks.

"Looking for *whom?*"

Hudart explained. And had the rare satisfaction—only it gave him no pleasure—of seeing Ranald struck speechless.

"I was only adding a little to your own plot," pleaded the bard, "it was just a touch of embroidery. I made Fergus sound so dull and safe that young Alasdair must think more favorably of the Spaewife—if he's left to his own judgment."

Ranald recovered speech and movement.

"Dhia!" said he, explosively.

He strode swiftly back toward the gates. Hudart trotted after him, trying to keep up, and having difficulty because of his own awkward loping gait.

"What are you going to do, Kinrowan?"

"Call out some men. If Fergus is after my cattle tonight, I'll have a welcome for him!"

Old Hudart broke into a run, and managed to get ahead of him. And he stood in his path, so that Ranald was forced to halt. He looked down into the distraught face of his bard.

"Something else, is there?" he demanded.

Clasping his thin old hands as though he was praying, Hudart gazed back at him in great agitation. He said, "I beg you—! Don't go near Fergus tonight! If our two should go to him— and then you arrive—he'll cut their throats! Oh, Kinrowan, I told Alasdair to ask if he liked ox-tail!"

Ranald stared at him in startled disbelief.

"Did you, indeed?" said he. "And he stole thirty of my best stirks last time he came foraying into my land. And my men stole back forty of his—and a girl of his clan. She came willingly to join her love, but it has added venom to our feud. There was plenty blood spilled in my father's time between our people."

He gave an exasperated sigh.

"I'll leave Fergus alone," he said. "You must tell me— since you know so much—where he will be. But I'll go after Alasdair and bring him back. He must not run any risk of falling into Fergus's hands. What possessed you, Hudart? He'd flay the hides off them!"

He turned again for the bailey-towers, but before he could move forward, he heard a challenge ring out at the gate, and an answer. Then the sound of rattling chains, as the small door that was set into the main one was opened.

It was a good thing the Lady Agnes had retired to her bed before the return of the two messengers, who flung themselves before their Chief, panting and defeated—to tell him the Spae-wife was not in her cottage. Nor was she at any house in the village—or in any of the farms. They had, they said, looked everywhere. And no one could tell them where she had gone, or when she was likely to return. They had done their best, they said hopefully. To Kinrowan's next question, they shook their heads, and told him they had seen nothing of Alasdair or his soldier.

Hudart left Ranald calling out a tracking party. The old man went slowly back to his little room, a prey to acute anxiety.

By the hearth he found the little rush basket overturned—and empty.

"Oh, no!"

He looked everywhere, but there was no toad. And the door had been open.

"Where is she gone?" cried the old man, clutching his hair. "She canna go off on her own! She'll never find Alasdair tonight. And if she is away from the protection of my hearth, with its bit magic round it—"

He gave a sort of groan.

"If the dawn rises on her before Alasdair has seen her, and recognized her—she will have the head of a toad forever!"

He gave a weary little whimper, and went very haltingly to unhook a cloak from behind the door. It had been a trying night for a very old man. And the night was not yet ended.

6. *FIRE IN THE GLEN*

Alasdair was sulking. Although he was perfectly used to Ewen riding roughshod over him, he was, for the first time, seriously considering retaliation. The mercenary was exceeding his license—or maybe Alasdair was feeling less compliant than usual.

The first argument had taken place when Ewen assumed they would be taking horses from Kinrowan castle. He continued to saddle a couple while Alasdair contested the matter.

"It's only half a mile to the river-ford!"

"Aye," said Ewen, "if we go to the river-ford."

"Well, that's where the Spaewife lives! And where Ranald meant us to go."

"Maybe. Maybe not. And anyway," said Ewen, cunningly, "if we do go, who knows where the lady might send us? Fenella may be miles away. And I," said he, firmly, "have walked far enough this night."

They took two rough-coated, long-maned garrons and rode out.

Where the lane began to wind its way down between the crofts to the river, Ewen suddenly turned his mount aside into the heather, without a word of warning. Alasdair shouted to know where he thought he was going, and got only an unintelligible answer, tossed casually over a departing shoulder. Alasdair was so cross that when he caught up with Ewen he leaned over and grabbed his reins. Ewen's horse shied—or was heeled—sideways, and Alasdair lost his balance and fell off.

"This is no time for larking," said Ewen, severely.

He caught the riderless horse, and dismounted to hold its stirrup politely for Alasdair. At the same time, however, giving the young man the benefit of one of his less pleasant looks. Alasdair choked back the comment he was about to offer, and rode quite meekly after him.

Ewen led the way across the moor, and up the rise of a hill to a high glen and then plunged steeply into a narrow and winding cleft. He then took to some very devious routes. Deer paths—rabbit tracks—along rocky ledges and ravines, over fast-flowing burns, and slow shallow ones. Alasdair lost all sense of direction. But, after what seemed a very long and tiring ride, they came to the outlying trees of a wide-flung pine forest. Here the mercenary slid off his horse, and looped its reins over a branch.

Alasdair, frowning resentfully, pushed his mount forward till its shoulder jostled Ewen a pace or two backwards.

"You are behaving outrageously!" said Alasdair. There was an uncustomary ring of authority in his tone.

"Be good enough to note that I am not your trooper," he went on. "You tend to forget that you are in my service—"

"Command me," said the mercenary.

Caught completely unprepared, Alasdair merely gaped at him. And Ewen put one hand on the horse's neck, and looked up at his master with an air of innocent uncertainty which went ill with the sardonic set of his mouth. He said, "Have I mistaken your wishes, sir? Did you not understand Kinrowan's meaning?"

"Well—I thought I did. He meant us to disobey him, and go to the Spaewife—"

Alasdair's voice trailed away, as the other shook a pitying head.

"Not?" said Alasdair.

"Not," said Ewen.

He assumed the slow and careful voice of one explaining to a backward child.

"He forbade us to go the Spaewife, knowing our first impulse would be to disobey—"

"*I* got that far!" snapped Alasdair.

Ewen gave him a sidelong look.

"And no further? Well, well!" said he, in simple wonder. "Yet whatever Ranald may think of your wit, he cannot think me so easy to gull. He knew I would go a step further, and do *just exactly what he told us!*"

"Go to Black Fergus?" Alasdair was puzzling it out.

The other patted the horse, as though it had just said something clever.

"Of course."

He took the reins from Alasdair and led the garron to where his own was nibbling at the sparse herbage, and began to loop them around a branch. Alasdair swung his leg over the saddle, and then paused, sitting sideways and looking dubiously down at his retainer.

"Ranald is not so complicated—" he began.

"Hudart and your sister were prompting. And I think they knew more than they pretended about the Lady Fenella."

"Just one moment!" said Alasdair, and jerked the reins back from Ewen. "Where *is* Fergus? Do you know?"

"Hudart said he would be in the Glen of Pines. It's just up this pass a small way—"

"And is there some reason why we must go on foot like servants? At least let us meet him more soldierly!"

Alasdair was sitting astride his horse again, and frowning fiercely. Ewen seemed taken by surprise. He said, rather nonplussed, "A good soldier is not reckless—and—we don't know what manner of person Fergus may be, nor what company he keeps. We should approach him with caution—not go linking down like a charge of cavalry—"

Alasdair had backed his horse away a bit. Now he looked triumphantly at the other man and grinned. He said, "You can't have it both ways, can you! Fergus is not a danger to us, if you understood Ranald rightly. If you're afraid—walk!"

He spun his pony, so that Ewen's grab met only empty air, and went clattering away down the pass.

Ewen said something very rude about him under his breath,

wrenched free the reins of his own garron and rode after, still muttering to himself.

There was no sort of path under the trees. Just wet and boggy ground strewn with stones and boulders. It was dark, too, for the moonlight could find no way through the interlocked branches of the pines. All this made for chancy going. But Alasdair was so pleased with his treatment of Ewen that he rode with reckless speed, wanting to maintain his lead. And he was still some way ahead when the ground began to dip steeply, and he came out through the trees, and looked down into a deep, small valley.

Clumps of pine were scattered on the floor of it, and on the hill that led down there. He could see a gleam of water, and the dark shapes of cattle standing around it. In one place there was a red glow of fire, and a column of smoke rising into the moonlight.

Ewen arrived beside him, and said in a compelling whisper, "Alasdair, for the love of God—!"

The young man flashed him one reckless glance, and sent his pony slithering downhill, scattering stones to right and left. And Alasdair was shouting at the top of his voice, "Fergus! Black Fergus! Who likes ox-tail soup!"

Ewen cursed, and prepared to follow. And he fell forward in his saddle as a man leaped on to his back from an overhanging branch. Another ran in from the side, and caught his right arm in a viselike grip. A third, grabbing the pony's bridle, forced it back on its haunches. Ewen had no time even to shout. More dark figures closed in on him. And Alasdair went down to Fergus entirely on his own.

Still filled with wild exhilaration, he came to the foot of the hill and went at a gallop toward the light of the fire. He saw men springing up and running to meet him, but he went on, still shouting excitedly, "Fergus! Fergus! Ox-tail!"

One large and burly man stood still to face his charge. And Alasdair glimpsed his black beard and arrogantly cocked bonnet with the two eagles' feathers jutting, the belted plaid of dark tartan, and the bright dirk glinting in his hand. Then the pony stumbled. Alasdair pitched neatly between its ears, and landed on his head at Fergus's feet, and lay still.

"Dhia!" said Fergus.

There was an excited outburst of exclamation and comment

from those of his men who had come running up, with weapons in evidence, but their chieftain shouted at them and they fell silent. Then Fergus looked up the steep slope of the hill where the pines grew, and he lifted his arm in a sweeping gesture. There was a shrill whistle from the hilltop. A pause. And then another. No more.

"Just the pair of them," said Fergus.

He seemed rather baffled. He rubbed his hand over his strong beard so that it rasped, and drew his brows down until they met across his eyes.

"It's what our picket-guards told us. But what for would two—?"

And he went to stare down at Alasdair, in a sort of irritated disbelief.

Fergus was very conscious of the fact that he was still a good day's ride from his own lands, though he had crossed the border out of Kinrowan's. He was in a neutral area belonging to an elderly and peace-loving landlord, who would not interfere with a clan battle, on either side. Ranald could still arrive with his warriors before Fergus reached safety. And Fergus was even more conscious of the presence of a good many cattle that rightfully belonged to Ranald. His foray had been entirely successful—until now. Yet what could two men do to endanger it—even if they were hostile, which was not yet known.

The basket-hilt of Fergus's sword gleamed in the flicker of the campfire, bright against the dark tartan that swung in heavy folds around his knees. He had a round leather targe slung between his wide shoulders. He was a man of about thirty, and although no one would describe him as handsome, there was an imperious energy about him that was very compelling. Men would follow him wherever he chose to lead them—providing they were his own men, of course.

He looked at Alasdair, and snapped his fingers, and one of his clansmen knelt to turn the young man over, and run his hands around his belt. And then he held out those same hands to show them empty.

"He has no weapons?" said Fergus.

"None."

"It gets odder," said the chieftain, heavily.

It seemed that Alasdair had struck his forehead against a stone when he made his abrupt descent into the glen. There

was a graze just above his left eye that was showing a smear
of blood and swelling rapidly. The boy's eyes were shut, and
his face was very white even by the yellow glow of the fire.
His black curls were disheveled over his brow, and he lay
limp and quiet. But Fergus was not charmed by youth or beauty
or adversity. He was extremely suspicious of the whole business. He turned, still frowning fiercely, to face the men who
were bringing Ewen to him.

The soldier was the worse for wear. His plaid was gone,
and the brooch that had pinned it was decorating the bonnet of
one of his escort. The sleeve that had been torn before was
now half off, and there were no buttons at all on the deerskin
coat—only some long rips that would take a deal of mending.
Ewen's hair was streaked wetly across his eyes, and there was
a considerable amount of mud on his face and person. His
hands were tied behind him, and two men were clutching his
shoulders, but he seemed to be dragging his captors toward
Fergus rather than being dragged himself. As soon as he saw
the dark and burly young man who stood there in obvious
authority, Ewen shouted at him breathlessly, "Have you hurt
the boy?"

"He fell off his horse," said Fergus, staring, "but his neck
seems intact, and he didna bash out his brain—if he has one!"

And then he said, violently, "Just what are you playing at?
Who are you? Kinrowan's men—though not in his colors—?
Does he know of my raid!"

Ewen slumped a little in the grip of his guards. His worst
fears for Alasdair allayed, he began to consider other things.
He wondered uneasily if he had been over-confident about
Ranald's intentions. And now it came to him dimly that he had
heard the name of Fergus spoken in the castle with enmity. He
saw the cattle by the water, and, in the light of Fergus's last
words, he knew why they were there. He gave a sudden sigh.

"Does it matter who we are?" he said, tiredly. "We came
here in peace to find you."

"Then what was all that about ox-tails?" demanded Fergus.

Ewen gave him an odd look. He had just thought of the
same thing. He hesitated and then said, "A—riddle."

Fergus did not care for this suggestion. He strode over to
Ewen, and laid one large hand on his bared throat. In his other
hand the dirk gleamed, unpleasantly near.

"Who are you?" said Fergus again, between his teeth. "Your blood on your head if you lie!"

The man who still knelt by Alasdair gave a sudden shout, and everyone glanced across to see what had startled him so. In searching the unconscious boy, he had pulled aside his plaid. And there, shining in the firelight, a great fan of white feathers was spread over the wet ground. The man had jumped up, and backed away in terror. Others did the same. Ewen felt their shock through the hands of the men who held him. Only Black Fergus stood quite still. Under his curly beard his lip lifted from his teeth like that of an angry hound. His blue eyes moved from the wing to Alasdair's face, and then back to stare savagely at Ewen.

"I know who you are!" said he.

He closed his hand again on the soldier, who lifted his head as though to make it easier for him. But there was a dancing in Ewen's eyes, and he said, "Good. Then you'll also know that the boy is quite harmless. I am only his mercenary, under his orders. So you can stop fearing us, and let me free to tend him."

Just for a second it seemed he had been over-confident again. It was perfectly clear what Fergus's clan thought would happen, and also that they would not lift a finger to prevent it. Ewen choked a little, and Fergus suddenly took his hand from his throat and glowered at him.

"There's more to this business than appears!" said the cattle reiver, "and I'll have it out of you before I—"

He turned away, and jammed his dirk back into its sheath. He called to his men with impatient roughness, "Take the lad into that bit cave up the hill over there!"

For once, none of his men hastened to obey him. They looked at him in great dismay. One or two took a few hesitant steps toward Alasdair, and that was all.

The brow of the chieftain darkened still more. He was a simple man, and not particularly brutal, but he was accustomed to instant obedience. And Ewen, driven as always by a sort of daft streak that made him turn serious matters into ridicule— usually at the worst possible time—said in a pitying voice, "Shame on you, Fergus, to bring such poor little children poaching!"

Fergus turned a lowering eye on him and said rather reasonably, "Are you so short of trouble that you keep wanting more?"

"I want my master looked to!" snapped Ewen. "If your—men—are afraid, let me carry him. He may be more hurt than you think, and the dew's falling."

The chieftain's baleful eye traveled to his men. They quailed a bit under it, and one said rather weakly, "It's the witchcraft, MacIaian Dubh—"

"Never mind what it is! Pick him up, you, Finlay!" snapped Black Fergus. "I want him in the cave, and the cave mouth guarded. Coll! And David—Angus—carry him there! Hell take you, do you hear!"

Four men moved reluctantly to obey. They heard. One sheathed the sword he carried bare in his hand. Another slung his long gun behind his shoulder. And Fergus watched in frowning silence as they knelt to lift the still senseless Alasdair. They were hampered by their extreme reluctance to touch the feathers.

"Wrap his plaid around them!" shouted Ewen, angrily. "And gently, you fumble-handed ninnies!"

The men, rather gratefully, followed his suggestion. But it earned him no pleasant look from the chieftain. Alasdair was lifted and carried around by the side of the pool to where a stream came rushing down a rocky gully from the brae-top. And they then proceeded to scramble up toward a dark opening in the rock, about fifty feet above.

"You," said Fergus, curtly, to Ewen, "get up there after him!"

His guards began to pull the soldier away, and Fergus bellowed at them, "Leave him walk by himself! He can't escape."

The men fell back, and Ewen gave the chieftain one of his mocking looks, and said, "I was beginning to think you overtimid."

"I'll tell you what, my buckie," said Fergus, with spirit, "if you want a dunt on the head to equal your master's, there isn't an awful lot that stops me giving you one!"

He brooded darkly for a moment, and then said, "I'll be having some further discussion with you later. Get to the cave."

His fierce eyes stayed on Ewen as that gentleman went off alone on the path they had taken Alasdair. It was hard for him, with bound hands, to climb the steep escarpment, but somehow he managed it in a casual sort of way that irritated Black Fergus almost beyond endurance. As the soldier reached the cave mouth, the four clansmen emerged and seemed prepared to argue his right to proceed. They got a roar from Fergus that made them step aside, and Ewen went into the arched opening. The men settled themselves among outlying rocks and boulders, to keep watch. One laid his gun ready to hand, in a most hopeful manner.

And Black Fergus stood alone, his back against a pine tree, his fingers tapping the hilt of his sword. He was not watching his clansmen settling by the fire again, to continue their interrupted meal, nor was he giving any attention to the fine cattle he had so newly acquired. There was a baffled frown on his weather-beaten face, and he was gnawing his lips. Suddenly the harassed chieftain said aloud, *"Why* was he shouting about ox-tails?"

7. *WORDS OF HONOR*

Fenella had made a very interesting discovery, for although her brain was now a mere fraction of its normal size, it functioned with remarkable clarity. As she went in long slow strides across the courtyard, she was wondering how to leave the castle without being seen. She had never had much to do with toads, and was unable to recall the general attitude toward them. Did people like them? Keep them for pets? Deride them? Throw things at them? Or fear them as they did snakes, and kill them! She must take no chances. She kept carefully to the shadows as Ewen had taught her, and tried to remember if there was any sort of gap or hole in the lower edge of the castle gates, where a very small creature might squeeze through. She wished with all her heart that she was already outside Kinrowan. And the discovery took place.

She found herself outside the castle.

"Well, ho!" said Fenella.

To experiment, she wished herself back by Hudart's door. Nothing happened. She sat there on a stone, under the arch of a fern leaf, and thought about it. And it came to her that she had made the last wish quite idly, and not with all her heart.

"Ho," she said, again.

And thought some more. Remembering how she had suddenly found herself inside the bailey-walls, after losing her senses by the hawthorn-well. She must have wished to be there, with every strength of her returning mind.

It was obvious that she could not travel the whole countryside, looking for Alasdair, by walking. It would take far too long. From the conversations she had heard by Hudart's fire— and especially those last words of his that had been called after her—she knew there was little time to spare. If the sun rose before she could be released, there was no hope for her. And she did not much like being a toad. It restricted her.

If Alasdair has gone to the Spaewife, she thought, I must go there first of all.

She shut her beautiful eyes and wished. She could feel, with slight annoyance, how her sides swelled as she took a deep breath. It crossed her mind that she must look quite revolting. Actually, she just looked like a toad taking a deep breath.

Then she was gazing at a tiny white cottage, on the far bank of a shallow river.

The Spaewife's home had only one window, and a door. It had no chimney at all, and was made of large stones so that the walls were about three feet thick. It looked very cozy. Fenella crossed the river by some easy stepping-stones, for she did not know whether toads could swim. She was wise not to risk it. She scrambled up on to the doorstep, and shouted loudly. Her heart sank at the thin squeak that emerged from her mouth.

Yet someone heard it. A head lifted behind a clump of thrift, and a large, and rather fat, drab-colored creature flopped up on the farther side of the step. It blinked copper eyes at her.

"There's no one in," said the second toad.

Fenella jumped about six inches into the air.

"Oh!" she exclaimed. "Are you real?"

"Certainly," and it sounded offended. "I'm no' a fake like you!"

"I beg your pardon," said the girl.

It moved its head from side to side, and began to flick its tongue in and out of its huge mouth. She had no way of telling what these signs meant. For though she wore the shape of a toad, she had not the mind of one.

"Don't be angry," she begged, "I'm in a bit of trouble."

"I see that. And I'm no' angry, I'm thinking," said the toad.

After a moment or so, it louped a little nearer. It said, "Madam's out after herbs. But anyways, I doubt she can help you. She's no witch. And you, my dawtie, have run into some of the old true sorcery!"

Fenella explained. And the toad listened to everything with great interest. When she told it how urgent it was to find Alasdair, it said, "He's no' been here tonight. Ye'd best start looking otherwhere."

And it gravely wished her luck, and flopped away.

Fenella sat quite still in the moonlight, and started thinking again. And she remembered Ewen.

"Fool that I am!" she said, in her small clear voice. "I know that one better than Ranald knows him—and I know where *he* will go!"

She wished with all her heart.

And she was sitting under a tussock of high-stalked heather, on a hillside that overlooked the Glen of the Pines. The moon was lying near the edge of the far mountains, and the air had that cold bite that heralds the coming dawn. Fenella began to make her way slowly down to where she saw men moving about a fading fire. She hoped Alasdair would be among them.

She just managed, with one frantic leap, to get out of the way of his pony's big clattering hooves, as the young man made his spectacular entrance to the Glen.

Now, Alasdair was having a very bad dream. He could not remember going to bed and falling asleep, yet he was dreaming most vividly that he lay on stony ground, and that his head was resting on rough warm wool instead of the linen of his pillow. He felt rocks loose under his hand. And he opened his eyes on darkness, and one patch of moonlight. He felt sick and dizzy, and his head was spinning. He moaned dismally. And whatever was under his head stirred, and moved away, so that he suddenly found pebbles against his cheek. The boy blinked feebly, and tried to lift his head. But a stab of pain shot from his temple right down through his whole body, and he cried out.

A large dark shape loomed over him, and he gave another yelp of sheer fright.

"Hold your noise!" said a vaguely familiar voice.

It came to Alasdair with a shock that he was not asleep. He

put a feeble hand to his forehead and found a lump there as big as a hen's egg. His exploring fingers could feel it throbbing. He focused his eyes on the shadowy figure, which had moved away a bit, and said, "Is that you?"

It snorted, which jarred his aching head like a blow.

"Don't!" he mumbled, and then in surprise, "Am I dying, Ewen?"

"I don't know *what* you think you're doing!" said the other. "And nor do I care!"

Alasdair struggled to collect his wits. He managed to get up on to his elbow, though waves of faintness and nausea swept across him with the effort. He dug his fingers into the loose stones, and bit his lip hard. He was gasping for breath, but said in a whisper, "Why are you angry?"

A controlled voice from the darkness told him, "Twice to-night I have been disarmed, and each time through your fault."

Alasdair muttered an apology. He wracked his throbbing head to remember these disasters. All that came to him was the fact that, for all his present manner, it was on Ewen's knee he had been lying recently. Alasdair had long given up any attempt to follow his soldier's thought processes, and made no effort to do so now. He said, "I can't recall—except—there were some faces looking up through deep water! A boat by the shore—rain and lantern light—"

He shook his head, and the sudden pain made him cry out again.

"It hurts," he said, childishly.

"It would. Why don't you lie still? You had a knock on the head."

"Who did it?"

"You did. You fell off your horse, playing the fool."

Alasdair thought this over. Out of a slowly revolving mist came a dim memory of the night's happenings. He could hear again the shrill laughter of the Bocan. Fenella's gentle voice. The accusing words of Ranald. And then he conjured up the ride across the hills—and the fire among the pine trees—the swords—

"Black Fergus!" he ejaculated.

The other made no comment. And Alasdair shakily gathered his legs under him and tried to get to his knees, and so to his feet. But he felt as weak as a newborn mouse, and his limbs would not obey. He held out his hand toward Ewen.

"Help me up," he said.

There was a slight pause. Then the soldier said flatly, "My hands are tied."

Alasdair sank down again, and tried to digest this piece of information. His mind was not moving quickly, and it took a little time to work it out. Two things emerged—Black Fergus was not the person whom Ranald wished them to find—and, if Ewen was disarmed and bound, they were certainly in serious trouble. He peered across the cave at his companion.

The place was not as dark as Alasdair had thought at first. The moonlight through the entrance caught the crevices and jutting rock surfaces, and lit them whitely, making black pools of shadow behind them. The cave was not very large, and bent around a little to where Alasdair was lying. There was only one way out of it. Here and there the roof arched up to about twelve feet, though in other parts it was too low for a man to stand upright. At its widest it was not more than twenty feet across.

Ewen was standing against the pool of moonlight. His back was turned, but even his stance looked defensive. Yet Alasdair had no intention of blaming him for anything. This long silence was only caused by the slowness of his mind in taking in the situation. He forgot that what he had there was a very touchy Highlander. And Ewen suddenly swung around and said explosively, "Well, speak! Call me what names you please! Do you think I am not ashamed? You rode off like a fool—and like a fool I followed you! I should have known—I should have waited—"

Surprised, Alasdair blinked at him. And the soldier said in a tone that few people would have expected from him, "Will you not even speak to me?"

"Give me the chance, man," said Alasdair.

In the tense silence that followed, he took it.

"Anyone can make a mistake," he said, "I never stop."

There was no malice in Alasdair.

"Don't distress yourself, Ewen," he said, and shivered violently, and added, "What will happen to us, now?"

"We wait Fergus's pleasure," said Ewen, very low.

Alasdair's bump was throbbing worse than ever, and he put his hand up to it, and informed Ewen of the fact that he had a severe headache, was bitterly cold, and as weak as water. Ewen said he was not surprised.

"It's not so long before daylight," he added. "There's a cold wind, too."

He went to the cave mouth, and stood there for a moment, silhouetted against the sky, in the jagged opening. Then he ducked. For there was a loud bang from somewhere outside, and a puff of dust and splinters rose from the rock by his shoulder. He backed into the cave, and said crossly, "Fools! Do they think I'll charge out with both hands tied!"

He came over to Alasdair, and looked down at him. "Could you manage, do you think, to unfasten me?" said he.

"With one hand?" Alasdair sat up, feeling giddy.

"Use your teeth," the other man told him. "And don't go biting me!"

He dropped to his knees, and turned so that Alasdair could reach his wrists. But, as the boy had feared, it was not going to be a simple task, for the thin cord cut deep, and the knot was fast. While he was was picking at it, trying not to hurt Ewen, Alasdair said, "Why did Hudart send us to Fergus?"

The other man laughed. An ugly sound, without mirth.

"He was being clever," said he, harshly. "It was none of Ranald's doing—I see that, now. It was just that old idiot adding some grace notes of his own. And I had to be clever, too! Heaven help me, I was a bit too clever this time!"

He fell silent, and Alasdair was worried. The boy was used to thinking of his Highlander as a cool-headed creature, and his occasional emotional upheavals always came as a surprise. Alasdair bent his head to the cords. Just for a moment he thought he had set his teeth in the wrong substance, as Ewen flung him aside with a swing of his shoulder, and turned on his knees, and said in a fierce whisper, "Get your head down! Pretend you're dying!"

"What?" said the boy, quite bewildered.

His fleeting bout of self-abasement quite forgotten, the other snarled at him softly and furiously. "Alasdair! Do what I say! Down," and he spoke as though to a dog.

The young man subsided on the stones and shut his eyes. He wondered if Ewen was over-tired—

"Speak to me, Alasdair!" said the soldier, loudly, and in tones of anguish.

Alasdair's eyes opened wide, and he said confusedly, "But you told me—"

"Ssh!"

A burly figure darkened the cave mouth. Alasdair saw it, and shut his eyes again. And Ewen, his light voice blurred with grief and despair, was saying, "Chief! Black Fergus! For the love of God, let me have some wine—some water—anything to bring back a spark of life to him!"

And footsteps came across the cave, crunching over loose pebbles and rubble. Alasdair could tell by the sound of breathing, the click of a sword-hilt on a belt, the smell of rain-soaked wool, and the brushing of a heavy fold of material, that someone was stooping over him. He could almost feel the searching gaze. Then he heard Ewen say, with shockingly convincing pathos, "Sir, he is dying. He's as cold as ice, and lies so still."

Fergus said, in his slow and rather beautiful voice, "He doesna look so near his end. There's plenty color in his face."

"A bad sign in his family," said Ewen, quickly. "They all look so at the last."

"Indeed?" Fergus sounded intrigued by this. "Is that true?"

And then Ewen said something that grated on Alasdair's ear. He said it very clearly and proudly, too.

"I give you my word of honor."

Alasdair stiffened. He heard Black Fergus move away, saying something about a possible remedy, and he opened his eyes and looked at Ewen kneeling beside him. Fergus had gone outside the cave, and there was a murmur of voices there. The boy said in an accusing whisper, "Your word of honor to a lie!"

The reply came so softly that it was scarcely more than a breath.

"Only mine, not yours."

And Fergus was coming back to them, with a leather bottle in his large hand.

"Let me give it to him," said Ewen. "You'll not get a drop between his lips, and you'll hasten his end. Just cut the cord at my wrists—"

A low rumble of laughter interrupted him. The chieftain said, "Do you take me for a fool?"

And he knelt beside Alasdair opposite Ewen, and lifted the boy's head and put the bottle to his mouth. Alasdair swallowed a mouthful of raw fierce liquid rather abruptly and choked, and gave a croak of disgust. He looked into the dark-bearded face of Fergus, and saw the narrowing of the bright eyes. The chieftain let Alasdair's head fall to the stones again, and lifted those eyes to look straight at the other man.

Alasdair looked, too. He was miserably ashamed for his companion, caught out and openly forsworn, but Ewen seemed unconcerned. He held Fergus's gaze for a moment, and then murmured something about a suspicious nature, and got to his feet. Fergus stood up also. He said scoffingly, "I think the lad will live! Your anxiety deceived you!"

Then he prodded Alasdair with his foot.

"Come on, sit up, you!" he rasped. "You've play-acted long enough—and with little skill!"

The young man sat up, so fast that his head reeled. The chieftain grinned down at him, and held up the leather bottle.

"One sip has swift results!" said he. "Has it given you strength to answer some questions?"

While Alasdair was still trying to see through the mist that had swirled about his eyes, Fergus went on, more roughly, "You are brother-in-law to Kinrowan."

"Is that bad?" said Alasdair.

"For you it may be fatal!"

There was no amusement now on Fergus's heavy face as he stared down at the boy, yet he wore a grin that was most alarming. He said, "How did you know where to find me tonight? Only my own men knew we would be in the glen here—and not one would let slip the word. Not under torture. Who told you?"

"Kinrowan's bard," said Alasdair. "He knows a lot. He's a sort of seer! And he does things with handkerchiefs—"

The chieftain took a step back, looking startled, and he crossed himself and strode over to Ewen.

"The boy's wandering in his wits!" he told him.

"I did warn you—"

"I suppose it's a sure sign of doom in his family!"

He grabbed the other by the shoulder and swung him around to stare hard into his eyes.

"No more lies, you!" said the chieftain through his teeth. "I've little time to waste, and I'll have the truth—if truth is in you!"

Ewen said steadily, "We were out riding for our own amusement, and saw your fire in the glen. How could we tell who you were? We came down to greet you in friendly—"

Fergus snarled at him.

"Shouting about ox-tails! Shouting my name, he came charging! Also, if you can remember your own lies, you told me that you came here to find me! You must lie more skillfully—tell me a better tale—!"

It was irresistible to Ewen's daft streak, though he knew what would follow.

"Ox tale?" said he.

The chieftain let go of him, and hit him a back-handed swipe across the face that cut his lip on his teeth, and hurled him against the wall. Fergus took a pace after him, and then turned abruptly and went to stare at Alasdair instead. The boy was trying to get to his feet, and Fergus shoved him roughly down again.

"I have a long-standing debt to pay Kinrowan," he growled, "and I think the time is here to do it."

"My brother-in-law is not so barbarous that he enjoys these clan-feuds—" said Alasdair.

"He will, when I send him what I leave of you!" said Fergus, darkly.

He put his hand down toward the sgian dubh at his knee. Alasdair stiffened a little. But, unexpectedly, it was Fergus who recoiled. He had seen something in the shadow nearby, and he said in deep distaste, "I hate toads!"

Alasdair looked where he was looking, and now he, too, recoiled.

"So do I!" he cried. "Kill it!"

"Ugh! I couldn't!"

The chieftain moved away rather quickly, and Alasdair managed at last to get on his feet.

"Fergus," he said, sincerely, "we came on you by mistake—nothing more. We meant you no harm—nor do we now. Let us go."

He got no reply, and went on in a scurry of anxious words,

moving nearer to the burly man as he did so.

"I cannot stay longer in this place! I have to go to the Spaewife of Kinrowan—as I should have done long since, if I had not been sidetracked! There's a lady in great peril! Chieftain, let me go!"

The cattle reiver threw him a look of unwilling admiration.

"Losh!" said he. "Here's yet another tale! Romantic and chivalrous, too. A lady in peril, is it—?"

"Do you doubt me?"

"Have I reason to do otherwise?"

Alasdair lifted his handsome head, and stared at him loftily.

"I do not lie," he declared, in stiff tones. "My honor means more to me than my life."

"Hm," said Fergus.

He rubbed his beard thoughtfully, and seemed suddenly uncertain of his next move. Fergus was not a brute at all, though the present circumstances did not show him at his best. The boy's sincerity had had its effect. He said, "A lady—and in danger?" And then, "Yet I owe Ranald a damage!"

"Can you pay it with a girl's life?" said Alasdair.

There was a pause.

"No," said Fergus.

He paced a little way toward the mouth of the cave, and, in the glimmer of moonlight spilling through the opening, Alasdair could see the long line of his draped plaid, and the eagle's feathers springing like horns from his bonnet. He turned again and said to Alasdair, "Will you fight me for your freedom? Sword to sword, and a promise of release if you best me?"

"Fight?" said Alasdair. "I?"

Fergus was instantly abashed and much distressed. He growled confusedly that he had forgotten.

"I'm a fool!" he said. "You have no sword-arm!"

"He has," said Ewen softly.

The man had stayed very quiet and forgotten during the previous exchanges. Nor did he move now, as both the others turned to look at him. He was not at all his usual dour and guarded self. With his coat in rags, blood on his mouth which he could not rub off, his hair falling over his eyes, unarmed and bound—he had a sort of excited eagerness about him, and he was smiling. It occurred to Alasdair, with some surprise, that he looked rather charming. When he spoke again to Fergus, there was a lilt in his voice that usually came there when he was happy about something. He said, "I'll make a bargain with you, sir. Fight me, and—whoever wins—let Alasdair go free. Whoever wins—I will stay. You'll have something to send to Kinrowan."

Fergus stared at him in silence for a while, then he grunted, disbelievingly. "You'll stay to face my men, if you kill or disable me? Am I to take your word for that!"

"If you will," said Ewen.

Alasdair suddenly found his tongue, and cried to Fergus to pay no heed.

"He's mad!"

The chieftain glanced from one to the other of his prisoners. From his expression he thought they were both mad. And Ewen said, "Don't be such a fool, Alasdair. This is not just a matter of your life or mine—there is Fenella. Go and find her."

"I won't let you sell yourself so!"

"You canna stop me. And the girl may be in hazard now."

He walked without haste to Black Fergus, saying no more. And the reiver searched his face as though he sought the answer to some question there. Then he nodded suddenly.

"Come then," said Fergus.

To his dismay, Alasdair heard his own commanding protest emerge as a wail of apprehension. He coughed and tried again. He said he would not permit his henchman to make so one-sided a bargain—

"You," said Fergus, "will pledge me your precious honor to stay here in the cave until one of us returns to set you free."

"I will not."

Alasdair hurried over to Ewen, and put his hand on the man's arm, but before he could say anything, that one gave his own orders. He said very coolly, "Get to the Spaewife with all speed, boy. I don't doubt Fergus will spare you one of your own horses! I'll hurry this matter one way or another—to set you free the faster."

While Alasdair still wracked his aching brain for a way to dissuade him, Fergus came to the young man's other side and said compellingly, "Have I your word?"

Caught between a pair of minds more stubborn than his

own, Alasdair said stupidly and in confusion, "Yes, but—oh, well, yes—I suppose—"

Ewen smiled. And Fergus clapped the boy on the shoulder in a rough sort of good humor.

"Fine!" he said. "Then you are bound in honor here, till the word comes for your release."

And he turned away, and said over his shoulder to Ewen, "I'll get you back your sword."

As he reached the cave mouth he paused and waited there for the other to catch up with him. There was the bang of a gun outside, and Black Fergus gave a yell of fury.

"Careful, you fool! You nearly got me!"

He marched out of the cave, and Ewen followed laughing.

8. *THE FIRST FAILURE*

After a nerve-racking, toad's-eye view of events in the Glen of the Pines, Fenella had wished herself into the cave. Now she was crouching there on a ledge, hidden in a pool of blackest shadow, waiting for the right moment to announce her presence. The brief glimpse unwittingly shown to Alasdair and Fergus had not been very encouraging.

She was annoyed with Alasdair. Kill the toad, indeed! And he had behaved like a fool in the Glen.

After the uproar of his arrival there, her heart had been in her mouth until she knew he had not killed himself. She had sat wringing her little four-fingered hands in helpless dismay. She thought that Fergus had conducted himself with admirable restraint, on the whole.

Now she peered down into the gloom of the cave to where Alasdair leaned dejectedly against a butt of rock. There was a weary and hopeless look about him that touched her heart. And yet, wing or no wing, she felt quite illogically that it was he who should be risking his life for her now, and not Ewen.

That brought her mind back to the soldier, and she gave a little hop of desperation. Something must be done quickly,

before it was too late. Ewen was in deadly danger. Fenella had
no idea what skill he had as a swordsman, but, however brilliant, she was sure he was in no condition to do himself justice.
Besides, with that absurd bargain, he had set his life at stake
whatever happened. She made a toadlike noise of irritation.
She was well aware that both Ewen and Alasdair had been
acting in a fog of misinformation—but she had a strong desire
to knock their heads together.

She called down to Alasdair now, and heard her own voice
falling 'ike dropping water through the cave.

"Alasdair! Alasdair! It's I—Fenella!"

She saw him give a great start and spring away from the
wall, looking all around the place, and she cried urgently, "No,
don't look for me—please!"

He halted, in amazement.

"Where are you, then?" said he.

She said she was on a ledge, and he put his hand to his
head and asked how on earth she had got there. She told him
she had jumped. He moved a little toward her voice.

"Wait!" she said. "I must tell you—you're going to have
a bit of a surprise when you see me," and added anxiously,
"Is it near sunrise?"

"Just on," said Alasdair.

His attention was distracted by the sound of men's voices
shouting from some distance away outside the cave. He took
a few quick paces toward the entrance, and spun around to her
again to say excitedly, "Fenella, you're here! And safe! There's
no call now for Ewen to risk his life!"

And he ran to the mouth of the cave, and as loudly as he
could, he shouted down into the little valley, "Hey, there!
Fergus!"

The moon was quite gone. A cold gray foretaste of dawn
was touching the sky in the east. Down by the water the campfire had been replenished, and Alasdair could see the close
cluster of men near by. Someone gave another shout, wild and
high.

"Fergus!" yelled Alasdair, again, "Black Fergus!"

Fenella took a couple of her short, four-legged jumps, and
she plopped neatly on to a boulder jutting lower down the wall.
She sent her clear little voice pleading through the chilly air.
It was so near to sunrise now.

"Turn to me—look at me! Oh, Alasdair, just for one moment—"

But he was hitting his hand helplessly against the rock beside him, and all his attention was for the activity in the glen. Even the four men who had been guarding the cave had now gone down to join the rest, and to watch what was happening. Alasdair's voice cracked as he shouted again for Fergus—for Ewen—

"You must look at me, Alasdair, and quickly! Before the sun rises. Oh, it won't take two seconds. Turn and look, and say my name!"

There was no way to reach his mind. He thought Fenella was safe, there in the cave behind him, and that only Ewen was in danger. The fire in the valley flared high, as someone heaved a fresh branch on it. Now he could see the clansmen in a wide circle, leaning eagerly forward, and with two moving figures in their midst. He saw the burly Fergus, and the whirl of his arm with the great broadsword in its fist. He saw Ewen turning warily on his own axis, and the other moving around him in a deadly way. Then the light lifted over the horizon, and it was dawn.

Alasdair heard a sob from the girl behind him, and half-turned distractedly to her. But his mind was elsewhere, and he did not query her distress. He said, "They can't hear me through the din they're making. I would go down—but—I gave my word!"

And he looked at Fenella for the first time.

She was standing near a seamed and splintered rock. Standing very still, with her head lowered and hands clasped at her breast almost as though she was praying. She was wearing the dark-green riding-dress, as he had last seen her, but she had wrapped the fine veil about her head so that her face was hidden. And she had folded her plaid over the veil to hold it in place, and to shadow her features completely. Now she asked him in a most calm and steady voice, "Is your word more valuable to you than his life?"

"It has to be," said he, miserable but certain.

He looked down into the lightening valley for a moment.

"I can't break my word for any reason whatever," he went on. "I would give my life for him. But not my honor."

"He gave his for you," said Fenella.

Alasdair remembered all too clearly how that giving had shocked him. He said stiffly, "That was his affair. Each man has his own standards."

Then he shot a quick look around the cave, and back to the girl. Something had been nagging at the back of his mind all the time, and now he said, "How did you get in here without us seeing you?"

"I—crept through the shadows."

"And never spoke."

"I was afraid. I'm afraid now," said Fenella.

"Of what? Not even Fergus, I think, would lift a hand to harm you."

"I wish I knew you better," said she, very low, "I wish I knew your heart."

At last she had his full attention. But a shadow chose this moment to cross the mouth of the cave, and the young man spun around to face it. He rapped out a challenge, "Who's there?"

The shadow gave a startled leap into the air, and a thin squeak. Then it said, "Alasdair! How you startled me!"

And Hudart came into the cave.

The old man looked frailler, and thinner, and more ungainly than ever. But he moved quickly to Alasdair and put both hands on his shoulders.

"You're not hurt?" he queried, anxiously. "Oh, I feared for you, my heart! It would have been all my stupid fault if any—"

Then he saw Fenella, and the words died away on his tongue. He stood gaping at her for a moment, and put Alasdair aside, and went across to her. At close range he searched her veiled face, and his own twisted with grief.

"It's happened," he whispered.

"Yes," she said, "the sun rose."

"I hoped to protect you from this, but you ran away—"

"I thought I could find—"

And now Alasdair himself broke into their low-voiced colloquy. He said in a goaded and impatient way, "I can't stand waiting here like a helpless child, while Ewen fights for us! It's beyond bearing!"

And he shouted from the cave mouth, "Ewen! Come here, will you!"

Hudart was shaking his head anxiously, and now he said to Fenella, "Wouldn't you know he'd embroil himself in a duel! I saw it as I came through the Glen—but I didn't know what to do. I can't even stop a dog-fight, though I'm told a bucket of cold water—"

Alasdair was still shouting furiously for his henchman. And Fenella lifted her head in a proud and graceful movement and she said, "I can stop them."

Hudart held out thin hands as though to hold her back.

"Oh, my dear—"

But she went past him and stood at Alasdair's side, looking out into the growing morning. The pool glinted bright in the first rays of the sun, with Kinrowan's cattle standing about it. Nearby, the circle of men had closed in a little, and they were silent now. It was harder to see the two that they were watching, for they masked them from view. But from inside that ring came the sudden flash of a sword.

"Don't," said Fenella, as Alasdair opened his mouth to shout again, "you may distract him."

She went out of the cave, and the boy caught at her sleeve.

"Come back!" he said, vehemently. "There are men on guard, though why they haven't had a shot at me already—"

"No one is on guard," said Hudart, coming up behind them. "That's how I got in unseen."

"Let me go," said Fenella.

He tried to argue. Telling her she was wild and headstrong—forever running into danger. He said she did not know what she was doing, and would get hurt.

"No one will lift a finger against me now," said she, rather sadly, "you may be quite sure of that."

And she slipped from his hand, and made her way down the steep and rocky gully. Alasdair took a pace after her, and then backed even more hastily into the cave again. An angry flush ran over his pale skin. He snapped, with an ominous ring in his voice, that no one ever paid the slightest attention to anything he said.

"Hudart, go after that tiresome wench," said he, "and make her come back!"

The old man shook his head, without even looking at him.

"She will stop the fight," said the bard. "Heaven send she is not too late already!"

"How will she stop them?"

"Ah—she is nearly there—"

But Alasdair turned his back, and went into the darkness of the cave. He slumped himself down on a boulder, looking extremely sulky. He sounded it, too, as he growled, "I don't care what they do! *Any* of them!"

Hudart still did not lift his troubled gaze from the Glen.

Fergus had been biding his moment. He knew his men were waiting expectantly for the finish. They had nothing against Ewen personally, but their hearts were with their chieftain, and they were perfectly aware that he had the other at his mercy.

At any other time, the contestants might have been fairly evenly matched. Though Fergus was the heavier man, and slower, yet he had a far longer reach and he was ten years younger. He was also a very good swordsman. Ewen might have leveled these odds by his greater experience and his coolness. But he had been tired before the duel began. He was stiff, too, with the exertions of the night. His left arm felt as though it was on fire, for Fergus had struck through his guard quite early on.

From the start, Ewen had made little attempt to attack, saving his energy for the more passive task of defending himself. Twice he had thrown himself wide open to the other's blade—to end the matter quickly, as he had promised Alasdair. But this curious proceeding merely made Fergus suspicious, and slowed down his fighting. So Ewen was forced to a straightforward combat. It was only a matter of time. With every moment that passed, the sword in his hand seemed heavier and more cumbersome. Fergus, apparently quite unwearied, was plying with faster thrusts and slashes. Ewen wondered if he would be slain outright, or merely maimed.

In fact, Fergus would probably have been content to disarm him yet again, if he'd thought about it. But he was a person easily carried away by excitement, and he was filled with battle-lust. He knew after the first few minutes that he had the upper hand, and would have finished the fight, bloodily, some time back, if Ewen's lowered guard had not twice confused him. The man should have yielded by now, wounded as he was, and laid his life at the victor's feet. Had he done so, Fergus would have been generous. But now—

Fergus narrowed his eyes along the gleaming length of his sword, and circled like a big cat, measuring his distance, and preparing to beat down the other flagging blade and go in for a death-thrust.

There was nothing charming about Ewen now; he looked dogged and grim and hard-pressed. He was breathing in ragged gasps, and his face was drenched in sweat so that his darkened hair was plastered flat to his brow. He was in his shirt sleeves, the left shoulder ripped, and stained with wet and spreading crimson. He flung up his sword as Fergus cut at his head, and heard the swish as the other blade disengaged and came in like a snake, lower down. Just in time, Ewen parried the deadly stroke. But, while he was still recovering balance, the chieftain sprang to one side and came in again with one of his powerful over-cuts; Ewen jumped back, but a little too slowly, and his opponent missed his head by so small a margin that the watching men gave a concerted gasp, and a groan.

Fergus drew back his lips. He felt a savage pleasure in his own strength and skill. The ring of clansmen crouched a little in anticipation. They knew the end was very near. Fergus put all his weight behind his arm and brought his sword down straight across Ewen's blade so that he forced it to the ground, and then he lifted his own again at immense speed and lunged.

Fenella stepped between two of the watching reivers, and called aloud, and threw aside her plaid and veil.

Fergus saw her face across Ewen's shoulder, and his stroke went wide. He stumbled and crashed to the ground, hitting his head with a shocking thud against an outcrop of low rock. There was a wild uproar from the circle of men, and they broke and scattered—some one way, some another. Disorder reigned in the Glen; but Ewen, with the point of his sword jammed in the earth, was leaning on it, head bent and gasping for breath. He did not even turn yet, to see what had saved his life by a hair's breadth. He did not even care; he was just glad of a moment's breathing space.

Back in the cave, Hudart let go of the rock he had been clutching, and looked in surprise at his own toothmarks on his other hand. He was trembling, and his knees shook together as though they had no muscles in them. He now gulped a few times, and turned slowly to look at Alasdair who was only a dim shape in the gloom, huddled disconsolately on his boulder.

"Don't you care what has happened?" said the old bard.

"No," said Alasdair. "What has?"

Hudart glanced back over the valley. He said, "Fergus's men are away."

They were. They were all over the place. Some on ponies, some on foot, they were getting out of the glen as fast as they could go. Some shouting and calling to one another, a few of them in white-lipped silence. It was like an ants' nest when the top is lifted. The cattle caught the general panic, and began to mill about, lowing excitedly. But no one had time for them.

In just one place there was stillness. A girl was quietly folding her veil about her face. A man had turned to watch her, still with hands clasped on the hilt of a sword that was stuck in the earth at his feet. And another man was lying on the stony ground nearby. The girl finished what she was doing, and then went and stooped over the fallen man, who was stirring now, and groaning. She said something to the other, and turned away and started to come up toward the cave.

The man with the sword called to the fast-scattering clansmen, and one or two paused to look cautiously at him. Then two of them went to him, and hesitated, and bent to hoist the fallen man between them and carry him to where a few horses fidgeted restlessly. Fenella had halted halfway up the hill.

And then there were only cattle in the glen. The reivers had gone and left them there forgotten. The man with the sword slid it into a scabbard that he took from the ground, together with a deerskin coat. And he came up to the girl, and they climbed the steep gully rather slowly together.

Hudart put his arms around Ewen as the mercenary came to the cave mouth, and held him for a moment.

"You're alive!" said the old man, rather weakly.

"I'm fine," said the other.

Alasdair now jumped to his feet and ran over to him and grabbed the nearest shoulder. Ewen gave a grunt of pain.

"Do be careful!" said Hudart.

"What?" and then Alasdair saw, and said in dismay, "Ewen! Your arm's torn to ribbons!"

"My sleeve," said Ewen. "Don't exaggerate. And you should see Fergus!"

"Did you kill him?"

The soldier laughed briefly. Hudart, who had seen how nearly it had been the other way around, led him over to a smooth rock, and let him sit there, and took his coat from his unresisting hands. Alasdair watched them, frowning. Then he said, in rather a curious voice, "Who won, Ewen?"

"Fergus, I think, in another moment. He had me. But he fell and bashed his head, and his men took him away."

He suddenly lifted his own head and looked full at Alasdair. A sort of scornful anger came into the bruised and dirty face. He said, heavily, "I didna break my word again, if that concerns you! I waited down there till they were all gone. If they'd wanted me, they could have had me. Yet the fight was not truly ended—it was stopped."

Alasdair turned away. He felt he had, rather unfairly, been put in the wrong, but could not quite see how. And he saw Fenella come very quietly into the cave. She went to Hudart, without a glance for the others. The boy looked back at Ewen.

"How did she stop you?" he said.

"You leave me be," said the soldier, "I'm tired."

Alasdair, baffled, crossed the cave to Fenella.

"How did you do it?"

Still without a word or look, she lifted her hands to her veil and drew it closer around her face. She moved nearer to Ewen, and touched his shoulder.

"Let me do something about your arm," she said, "it must be hurting sorely."

Biting his lip, Alasdair glared around at them all rather hopelessly. He said, "Why can't any of you answer a simple question? Fenella, what have I done to offend you? Why won't you look at me?"

"I'm trying to put off the moment when I must," said she.

Poor Alasdair, entirely in the dark and strongly resenting the fact, caught her hand and pulled her around so that she had to face him.

"Stop treating me like a baby!" he flared. "What's this great mystery you're making! What are you feared to tell me? Let me have the truth and stop baiting me so! Fenella," he said, pleadingly, "what do you hide behind that veil?"

There was a little silence. Ewen shifted as though he would rise to his feet, and changed his mind and slumped back. But his eyes were watchful on Alasdair. So were Hudart's. Fenella

stood straight-backed and very slender, and she said steadily, "I am hiding myself, Alasdair. Only myself—as I am,
now."

Her voice shook a little, and when she spoke again there
was a lost and forlorn note in it. "Truly, I am still me, under-
neath the rest. Oh—try not to turn from me!"

She put her hands to the veil.

Hudart had been biting his knuckles again. Now he took a
pace forward and said in a sort of breathless gabble, "Alasdair,
listen to me—there's an old rhyme—never knew its meaning
till now—"

And then, in a musical monotone:

> "Fail her once, for pardon sue:
> Fail her twice, ye both shall rue:
> Fail her three times, never then
> Shall ye see her face again."

And Fenella drew aside her veil and looked at Alasdair.

There was a long and heart-searing silence in the cave.
Hudart was watching the girl, now, and his eyes were full of
tears. Ewen's stern look never left Alasdair. And Alasdair—?

With slowly whitening face, he stared at Fenella. He lifted
his hand as if he would shield himself from what he saw. He
licked a suddenly dry mouth, and horror grew and grew in
his mien and bearing. He tried to speak and failed, and tried again.
This time he found words.

"Oh—loathsome—"

And made a choked sound of revulsion, and ran from the
place as though it was accursed.

Fenella watched him go with her great round golden eyes.
Then she started to cover her face again, and said in a dull
little voice, "Go after him, Ewen. Stay with him."

"When he gathers his wits," said Hudart, "he will break his
heart."

And the soldier said, "God help him, has he got one?"

All the same, he came to his feet with an effort and a grunt,
and went to the cave mouth with one hand against the rock for
support. He moved rather blindly, and so struck his shoulder
against an outjut of the archway. He then leaned on it, clutching
it, with his eyes shut, and Fenella ran to him.

"Wait! Of course you can't go!" she cried. "Oh, Ewen, forgive me! I had forgotten your arm!"

He said it was nothing to bother with. But his face was white under its sunburn and dirt. And Hudart came and put an arm around him, and lent him a strength that was quite surprising for so old and frail a person, and took him into the bright sunlight, and eased him down on a tussock of turf. With one hand still on his shoulder, the bard took a small bottle from his pocket, and gave it to him. The younger man, rather thankfully, took a gulp or two of the contents, and then said that he thought he was tired.

"You'd best tie up my arm," he added, to Fenella. "It's not much of a wound, but I'd be better without it. It's making me as useless as a girl."

He gave her the wicked look that she knew well by this time, and she rewarded him with a small and shaky laugh. Then she gently tore back the sticky red shirt sleeve, and laid bare his upper arm. In alarm and horror she saw where the broad blade of Fergus's sword had plowed through the muscle and then torn free at the side, leaving an ugly and gaping wound. There was little she could do, except try to press the edges together and bind them in place. But just as she was about to attempt this task, she gave a little gasp and snatched her hands away.

"Oh, can you bear to be touched by me!" she said pitifully.

"Do you intend to be rough?"

"You mistake my meaning!"

And he meant to go on doing so. He said, "You'd better not be *too* rough, unless you want me flat at your feet! An unladylike revenge for a few gibes."

She shook her head speechlessly, and sniffled. Then she took a deep breath, and lifted her hands to her veil, and said more steadily, "I shall have to use some of this. Look away, Ewen."

"Why?" said he.

The girl looked down into his eyes. Then she took off her veil. She tore it, and made a pad which she soaked in the cold water of the burn beside them, and then very carefully she bathed the wound. And she told Ewen to hold the pad in place while she tied a long strip of the fine silk around and around to keep it there. The bleeding slowed, and almost ceased. Ewen had kept quite still under her ministrations, and all the time he talked to her in his softest voice—soothing her hurt, as she was doing for him.

"I saw you when you came first to Kinrowan," he said, "as pretty as a rose. And I saw you after you gave me my life just now. Do you think I would ever turn from you, or find you loathsome?"

Hudart had seated himself farther down the hillside, with his hands locked around his crooked, bony knees, and he was watching them with a very loving expression. The soldier was still soothing Fenella with words that he spoke sincerely.

"It was a brave thing you did," said he, "to walk into that crowd of caterans. And braver still to do the thing you must have hated—unveil your face and see a score of reckless men turn tail and flee. I know what that cost you, m'endail."

And he added, so low that it was hard to hear, "It's a terrible thing to have men recoil from you."

The girl had thrown the shortened veil loosely around her face, and he looked up at her, and saw the gleam of olive-green skin behind it—the inhuman outline. And he said, "Don't hate Alasdair for what he did. For saying what he said. He's very young still—more so than his actual years. He has seen so little."

"If he lives to a hundred," said Fenella, hopelessly, "he'll never see anything as horrible!"

"Well, I'm not so old," said the man, "and I've seen things just as horrible."

Fenella choked on a laugh and a sob, both at the same time, and she took a fistful of Ewen's sun-bleached hair and tugged it gently. She said, "That remark might soothe a man, but it has no comfort for a woman!"

He touched the bandage, which she had just finished, to test its security. Then he glanced over at Hudart, and asked how he had found the cave.

"I knew it was here," said the bard, "and I knew Fergus was here. I came to find him, really."

"How did you guess we'd be with him?"

The old man looked at him with slightly raised eyebrows, and he flushed a little.

"You knew I'd do something daft," he said, plaintively.

Then he got to his feet, and Fenella went and fetched his

coat, and helped him to put it on. It was not much of a coat by now, but it was better than nothing.

"You must have that hurt seen to properly," she told him, "as soon as possible. It needs a doctor."

He lifted her hand to his mouth.

"You are the bravest, and the best," he said. "Alasdair must learn to look more deeply."

The girl put both hands to her face, and gave a little cry. And he turned and started on the long scramble down the gully. Hudart called after him to bring Alasdair to the well in the hawthorn-wood. And Ewen said certainly, if he could catch up with the stupid boy.

"After twilight!" cried Hudart.

Ewen waved his hand, and went down into the Glen among the clumps of pine.

Hudart turned from him, to find Fenella leaning against the rock and sobbing stormily. As he hurried to her in some alarm, she caught at his jacket with trembling hands, and said, "My face has changed! I felt it happen when Ewen said what he did. It was like a mask being lifted! Oh, Hudart, have I my own face again?"

She raised her veil, in a turmoil of fear and hope. He let his brown eyes travel compassionately over her face, and shook his head.

"Not quite," he told her.

She sobbed aloud, and he lifted his voice a little. "Not quite. Only half! Your chin and your mouth and nose are yours again. Though the eyes and the brows—! My soul," he said, "I do not understand it! The rules are quite clear for this sort of thing—such a spell is only broken by the recognition and acceptance of the one who loves you. The one you love. This— this *half*-lifting—"

Fenella gave him a trembling smile that lit the corners of her pretty mouth like sunshine, and even glowed in her poor bulging eyes. She said, "Oh, there are different kinds of love, Hudart. And strong, for all their difference."

She stared out across the glen, and away to the far mountains. She drew a long shuddering sigh, and wiped her eyes with her hands like a child.

"Alasdair knows too little," she said, "and that is my grief. And Ewen knows too much and that is his. I weep for us all!

Oh, Hudart, I can't bear to be seen by anyone! Let us stay out on the hills while day lasts. Where there will be only you and the birds, and the deer, to look at me."

She took his hand and clung to it tightly, and the old man nodded.

"We'll do just that," said he, soothingly. "I left my pony up there behind the pines, well hid. He'll take us to some quiet place where we can bide till twilight comes. We can do with a bit of peace and quiet for a while."

9. PEOPLE WITH PROBLEMS

Alasdair lay in the heather and watched Ewen looking for him. The boy had not gone very far. Guessing he would be followed, and determined not to be found, he had wriggled deeply into a patch of strong heather clumps, and lay well hid. He had, however, a fairly clear view down the glen.

His mind was in a ferment, not only from the pain of his throbbing head, but from shame and misery. When he had first crawled into his hiding place, he had sobbed uncontrollably for a while, and even now fresh tears kept springing.

It's small wonder they all despise me, he thought to himself, I behave like a bairn.

And still he could not stop crying. Through a haze he saw Ewen come down from the cave and begin to cast about in the glen and the surrounding hills. Alasdair knew what he was seeking, and just about what he would say if he found it.

"I won't take any more of his gibing," muttered the boy, and then in a sullen flush of rage, "I'll kill him if he comes near me!"

He came very near. So close that another pace would have set his foot on Alasdair's hand. But he stopped and hesitated, and went off at a tangent. And Alasdair released his held breath. It did occur to him to wonder how he would set about killing his swordsman, anyway. At least the tension had stopped his tears.

When Fenella and the old man came down into the valley, he put his head into the crook of his arm, and kept it there until she and the bard had gone out of sight up the hill into the pine forest. He could not bear to look at the girl again. He could scarcely bear to think of her. He gave a choking little cry, and suddenly fell asleep. Like a bairn, indeed.

Ewen went on searching for him.

The soldier did not notice when Fenella and Hudart went away. He was too busy casting around the vicinity. When he decided at last that Alasdair was nowhere near, he was quite exhausted. He went down to the pool, and lay down flat, and washed his face and hands. He drank some water, and waited until his labored breathing grew easier. His arm was hurting him, and he felt rather peculiar. When he heard a movement in the bushes nearby, he got up so slowly that he would have been an easy mark for any enemy. But it was only Alasdair's pony, who whickered when he came to it.

"Fergus's men feared to take you," said Ewen, aloud, rubbing its nose, "lest you are infected with your master's taint of witchcraft!"

He was perfectly right about this. Not one of those reckless cattle raiders had dared lay his hand on anything belonging to Alasdair.

"I wonder if they left mine," said Ewen, "and for the same reason? Yet they didn't mind handling me! But it could be on my garron that maggot-brained boy has galloped himself off."

It was mostly a sop to his own weariness that he decided this must be why he had not found Alasdair, and he climbed on to the pony's back, and set off up the wooded hill. He thought he would probably see the boy somewhere ahead as soon as he came out on the open moor.

But he saw no one at all. The long rolling slopes of heather were peopled only by deer, who were away like the wind when they sighted the horseman, by some flights of mournfully crying peewits, and a couple of circling and unheeding eagles. Ewen pulled up and wondered dispiritedly whether to ride back to the Glen of the Pines. He also wondered if Alasdair had man-

aged to get more speed out of the garron than he himself had
ever succeeded in doing, and galloped off to the Spaewife.
Sighting his weariness, he set heels to his mount, and went to
seek him there.

Ranald of Kinrowan had spent a tiring night, too. He also
was searching. He had gone out with a dozen picked men,
thinking Ewen and Alasdair would be easily found and brought
in. He knew they had taken horses, and he ranged widely and
fast—but had no glimpse of them. They should have been
going quietly to see the Spaewife, he kept thinking, in growing
anger. Where, in fact, *had* they gone?

Baffled, Ranald went back to the castle for a further con-
ference with Hudart. Only to find *him* gone, and the rush basket
on his hearthstone empty. Inquiries at the gate revealed that
the old man had ridden out some time earlier with a big cloak
around him and a bonnet on his head. As if he meant to go
far, the captain of the watch said. No, there had been no sign
of a toad anywhere. Then the officer said he had tried personally
to dissuade the bard from going out at all on so chilly a night.

"But you know what he's like?" he said to the Chief now.

And he looked uneasy, though he was a big fellow, and not
one to be cowed easily.

"He looks *at* you, and *through* you, and far away," said he,
"and the hair lifts on your neck, as though a door had opened
behind you, and a cold draft blowing. He does it to frighten
people!"

"He doesn't do it to me," said the Chief, shortly.

"Well, he wouldn't," said the captain. "You gave no orders
to detain him, Kinrowan, and he has always been privileged.
We saw no harm—*I* saw no harm"—he accepted full responsibility—"in allowing the old fellow to go."

Ranald said the castle was rapidly becoming like an ale-
house, where anyone might come and go at their pleasure, at
any hour of the day or night. He brushed aside the pained
protests.

"Did he leave no word at all for me?" he demanded.

The officer struck himself on the forehead.

"Fool that I am—he did! He said you were not to worry."

Ranald gave a very angry laugh.

"Did he tell you any way of stopping me!"

And he took from him the command of the night watch.

Ranald was not often unjust, but when pushed he could be as unjust as the next man.

He went to Agnes and said despairingly, "They're all away!"

And left her to a sleepless night, and the hardest task of all—to wait. And he collected his troop again and rode off, to make a line of riders across the hills between Kinrowan castle and the Glen of the Pines. At least, he thought, he could intercept Alasdair if he did try to reach Black Fergus. But this attempt was made too late. By that time, Ewen had led the boy on to his secret paths, and the trackers saw nothing of them. This was not the fault of the said trackers. There was a great deal of ground to cover, and the moonlight was treacherous.

Ranald dared not go to the Glen of Pines itself, remembering Hudart's stringent warning. It galled the Chief greatly to let his enemy get away with any cattle, but he valued the safety of Alasdair more than that of a few stirks. In any case, he comforted himself that it would be quite easy to fetch the beasts back, later—with interest.

He managed to rouse the rest of his countryside to an absolute ferment. Beasts and birds scattered far and wide. Innocent crofters, and tacksmen, and shepherds ran from their shielings, with snatched-up weapons in their hands, fearing some war had broken out. A few individual poaching parties were interrupted, though Kinrowan had no time or inclination for reproach or retribution. In the end, he gave up and went gloomily back to the castle in the dawn.

The deer and the owls and foxes went quietly about their business again. So did some of the bolder poachers.

Ranald went around by way of the cottage at the ford. But the Spaewife was still from home. He did think for one moment that he had found Fenella on the doorstep. He picked up the creature between his hands, and it shot out a long tongue at him. He eyed it with slight misgiving, and said tentatively, "Er—Mistress Fenella—?"

His men glanced nervously at one another, and one of them volunteered the information that it was a male toad. The Chief said sourly that he hoped the man knew what he was talking about. But he set the creature down rather quickly, for he had thought himself that it was bigger, duller, and wartier than Fenella had been.

The toad went off into the herbage, and Ranald left a man sitting in its place on the step. He had instructions to send the Spaewife, as soon as she came back, straight up to the castle. That was all Kinrowan could think of to do, at the moment, and he went home to breakfast.

He missed Ewen by moments. That gentleman pulled up his pony in the shelter of some trees, and watched the Chief and his troop ride away. He also saw the smokeless cottage, the closed door, and the man on the step. He sat down and waited for half an hour. Then he got some writing materials from his pocket, and began to compose a letter. It did not take long. He fastened it securely into the headband of his garron's bridle. Then he tied the reins up, turned the beast's head uphill toward the castle, and gave it a hearty open-handed slap on the rump. It set off eagerly for its stable and breakfast and Ewen envied it. His own men would take charge of the beast, when they knew it had come in riderless. And the first thing they would do would be to examine the headband, where he had taught them to look for possible messages.

He watched the horse go clattering out of sight toward the dark bulk of the castle on the skyline, and then he turned and went back to the hills, where he faded himself rather skillfully into the landscape.

Over a hearty breakfast, Fenella's father looked amusedly at his host. He thought Kinrowan was looking the worse for the festivities of the previous evening. And yet, they had not gone on so late as all that. And they had been fairly restrained, as such affairs usually went. He had been pleased to hear that his young daughter had risen at dawn this morning and gone out with a hunting party. She had a good deal more stamina than the Chief of Kinrowan, he thought proudly.

He would have had a frightful shock if he'd been able to see his young daughter at that moment.

Yet she was sitting quietly enough, beside a little hill-loch, watching Hudart fishing.

They had made a small and surly fire from bracken and twigs, and the old man had cut a long hazel-rod. From one of his many pockets he produced a length of line, and some beautifully carved fishbone hooks. He found a bright blue feather that had drifted on to a bush, and a scrap of soft rabbit-colored fur caught on a thorn, and he assembled all this and cast out over the still water where the fish were rising. He had great skill. He made his mock fly dance and bob and drift. Indeed, it did everything but buzz for him. And they cooked their breakfast, two trout apiece and an extra unknown but delicious, fish for Fenella, who was hungry.

Now they were fed, they settled down to wait until the evening, when they would make their way to the well in the hawthorn-wood.

"Even if Ewen fails to find him," said the bard, "yet the boy may come there of his own accord. To seek the Bocan again, and ask his help for you."

"He may not wish to help me," said Fenella.

"Well, no. The Bocan never wishes to help anyone, but he might be forced—"

"I meant Alasdair."

The old man made a tutting noise. And then said severely that he could not see why Fenella had any sympathy at all for such a self-centered creature.

"He's as thoughtless as a month-old baby," he stated, sadly. "And with no sense of responsibility at all."

"He's had small chance to learn," said the girl, in a very gentle voice. "Everyone treats him as though he is a child. Never expecting him to behave like a grown man. Why, they even speak to him in the sort of tone they would use to a bairn! And as for his soldier—!"

"Oh, Ewen does not handle him well," agreed Hudart. "He'd do better to let the boy take the lead sometimes. But he's Alasdair's guard and it bores him, I think, for who would harm the lad anyway? He just saves himself bother by keeping Alasdair under his thumb."

Fenella smiled, and said, "I love Ewen very much. But I would give a deal to see Alasdair challenge him one day."

Hudart smiled too. He said it would certainly make an interesting episode.

Then he looked long and thoughtfully at the girl. Her attention was far away, for the moment, but she had taken off her veil, and this made the old man glad, for it meant she did not mind him seeing her face. She trusted him, and his affection for her.

It was such a strange face to see. Her forehead was bronze-green, with knobs here and there that were dappled with red and gold. The color darkened in the folds that surrounded the bulges of her truly lovely eyes. Lovely—though not with the beauty that many would envy. Not humans, anyway. Topaz-yellow, they were, with thin bright lines radiating from the centers, and they shone dazzling in the sunlight. Below her eyes, the brown and green faded into the fair skin of a very pretty girl. Strange face, indeed. But not loathsome, thought the bard—not loathsome, once you got used to it. He wondered at Alasdair.

And by now Alasdair was wondering a bit at himself.

He had wakened about noon, to judge from the position of the sun, and he was hungry. Yet the thought of food revolted him. The lump on his forehead was very sore to touch, and he had a splitting headache. His mouth was dry, and felt as though it was full of heather. Alasdair went down to the pool for a drink.

He recoiled from the reflection of his own face in the water. White and drawn, and with swollen eyes, and dark shadows under them—a stiff and bulging brow, on which a great bruise was vividly colored. Also, which was more interesting of all, a fine, soft stubble over his chin and cheeks and upper lip, which made him look very different from his usual self. For the first time in all his life, Alasdair had need for a razor.

He lay still and tried not to think about Fenella. And the more he tried, the more he thought. He stared at the water until his own reflection faded, and he saw only her face there. Her face as it had been by the well-side—and as he had last seen it. He shuddered. There was a thorn of anguish rasping at his mind that reminded him of all he wished to forget. Fenella's kindness. Her brave and generous attempts to help him. The reproaches she had never made. The revulsion she had never shown. Her gaiety—youth—beauty—all blotted out, now. And then the memory of what he had done, when she begged for his aid—the word he had used—

"Loathsome—"

He spread his wing wide across the thin gray bent by the loch-side, and put his head down among the soft feathers. But he neither saw them, nor felt them. And he found he could not shut out the voices in his mind, nor find any ease in tears. Instead, and to his surprise, anger was growing in him. And a desire for constructive action. For the first time, it did not

occur to him to seek help from someone else. There had to be
something he himself could do. He sat up, and folded his
wing—and again without his usual, shrinking consciousness
of it—and the set of his face changed and strengthened. This
greatly added to his already extraordinary good looks, and
would have astonished all who knew him. The brother of Agnes
was growing up.

Looking around, he saw among the debris of rapid departure
a small bag lying on the ground with oatmeal spilling from its
mouth, left there by one of Fergus's fleeing clansmen. Mixed
with cold water, the meal would make a boring but sustaining
sort of gruel, which would keep him from the pangs of star-
vation during a day on the hills.

For Alasdair was not ready to face anyone. He had still
some thinking to do. And he remembered the place where it
had been his custom to seek refuge away from the world of
people. Beinn Ard, the highest mountain in the district, whose
lofty head lifted over all lesser hills and was usually swathed
in a veil of mist—but this thought brought a memory to Alasdair that made him shake his head to drive it away. He rose
and collected the bag of oatmeal, and set off at a fine swinging
pace to find his refuge.

Ewen had found a refuge, too. Not one he would have
chosen, given any alternative, but it was all he had. He was
under a thick clump of furze. The wicked thorns had completed
his disorder, enlarging the tear on his sleeve so that a long
swatch of deerskin hung loose, and decorating his cheek with
a couple of raw scratches. His hands were stinging, and the
last few hours had done nothing for his wounded arm. He had
a great desire for three things—sleep, food, and that Ranald's
men would go away.

He buried his head deeper in his arms as he heard them
coming close. Though, in fact, his tanned skin and sun-streaked
hair were so like the color of his coat and the withered lower
branches of furze, that he was not easy to see even had they
known he was there. After a while, the search party moved
off. And Ewen was relieved. He had no wish to be taken to
Ranald. It would be unfair of the Chief to blame him for obeying
instructions, but Ewen felt strongly that he would nevertheless
be blamed. It did not occur to him to inform Ranald of the
night's events. Ewen was a person who liked to cope with

things his own way, and without aid from anyone.

He wondered, as he began to pick the thorns from his hands, if his note had reached his men.

It had just done so.

In the general turmoil at Kinrowan, no one had thought to mention the arrival of the garron for some while. Then a word was tossed casually to one of Alasdair's following, who went off like a hunted stag to tell Calum. And Calum dispatched his nephew to search the horse's headband, where Ewen might have put a message. It was not many minutes before the sturdy Neacal came rushing back with the scrap of parchment hidden in his hand.

Alasdair's half-dozen clansmen were no kin at all to Ewen. But they were loyal to their mercenary leader. Dour and difficult as he could be, they had a sort of love for him, and they were his to command. Calum read his note with frowning concentration. He was the oldest of the six men, a heavy-bodied, slow-moving person, and by no means as simple as he looked. He was a good fighter, and could think for himself if the need arose. He had another talent, also, most unusual for a man in his position—he could read, and write. His father had been foster-brother to Alasdair's father, and had learned his books with him, and passed on the knowledge to his own son. Carefully, now, that son deciphered Ewen's note. The spelling was extremely erratic.

"God be thanked," said Calum, deep in his beard, at last. *"He's* alive—or was when he wrote this, and the ink is still damp—and if that one lives, Alasdair will not be dead!"

He glanced around to be sure that only his own men were in ear-shot, and read the note to them.

"Send Nikal. Sekret. Furce-brake on Slev Bueey."

Perfectly clear.

Neacal left the castle with a group of herdsmen who were going to collect some cattle; and he left *them*, unobtrusively, as the road wound between some trees. He then made his way by devious routes, and mostly on his belly, over a good couple of miles, until he came out behind the furze-brake on Sliabh Buidhe. He started to search through it, looking and listening for some sound or movement. But he saw and heard nothing at all. Until a hand suddenly shot from some ferns, and grabbed his ankle. He came down full-length with a crash that winded him, and reached for his knife.

"Hold still, you fool!" said Ewen.

Neacal obeyed, knowing the voice, and turned his head sideways on the ground to look at him. He took in the appearance of the other, and concern replaced his surprise. He said, in a fierce whisper, "Where is Alasdair? Why have you brought me here?"

"He's fine," said Ewen, "and I just want your clothes."

The younger man blinked, but he made no argument. He took his captain's word for Alasdair, and without question. He meekly stripped off his few garments, and helped Ewen to change into them. Nor did he comment on the stained bandage around the mercenary's upper arm; he was just very gentle in putting the rough shirt and leather jerkin over it. Then he wrapped his kilt around Ewen's waist, and belted it there securely, with the goatskin pouch hanging from the belt containing all the personal wealth Neacal had ever had—one small silver coin—and he was happy to let Ewen have it. Lastly, he slid his little black stocking knife into the right knee of the woolen hose, and knelt to garter it safely there. He surveyed his captain thoughtfully for a moment, and nodded; and only then did he start to dress himself in the discarded clothes of the other. He did not put on the torn and bloodied shirt, however. He rolled it tightly and tucked it into his breast.

"Someone might notice and question me," said he.

"Someone will notice, anyway, if they see you in my clothes!"

"I can't change them, Ewen, for I have no others," said Neacal, simply. "What shall I do when I get back to the castle? Go to my bed?"

Ewen laughed, wished he had not, and put the back of his hand to his cut lip. He said, somewhat inaudibly, "You won't *go* back to the castle, tomfool! You'll lose your silly self in the hills, and not let Ranald's men find you. They're all running themselves ragged, looking for me and for Alasdair—"

"We looked, too. All night," said the other. "But Calum thought some of us must stay always at Kinrowan in case of a message."

"Bless his thick ugly head," said Calum's captain.

"He'll be waiting now to know—"

"He can wait."

Ewen looked into the anxious eyes that were fixed on him,

and added more kindly, "If you stumble over Alasdair any-where, tell him to come to the well in the hawthorn-wood as soon as it's dark. If Kinrowan's men lay hands on you—say nothing to them at all."

He settled his sword at his side and flicked his fingers at Neacal. That very patient young man gave him a last doubtful look, and went off among the thick whin-bushes that covered the whole slope. Ewen strolled away in the direction of Kin-rowan.

Halfway there, he passed a paddock where some young heifers were grazing peacefully. He opened the gate and drove them out, and, to their surprise and excitement, took them on with him.

After about a mile, when they came out on the steep road that led up to the castle, he was heartily sick of his active and cheerful charges. But he chevied them into a gallop. It was peacetime and daytime and the gates of Kinrowan stood open. They went through in a cloud of dust, and a chorus of indignant yells. Men busy about their duties, women carrying baskets of laundry or buckets of water, children and dogs and hens—these and the heifers went milling around the bailey-court to-gether in a fine clamor. And Ewen slipped through a doorway, and left them to sort themselves out.

If anyone had had time to notice him, or identify the tartan he wore, they would only think that one of Alasdair's tail had got himself involved with some stray stirks. He went watch-fully, however, until he reached Alasdair's small suite of rooms in the tower.

Calum was there, pacing to and from the window rather impatiently. When he saw Ewen, he leapt forward and caught hold of him. Luckily not by the left arm, but so abruptly that the soldier staggered.

"Where is he?" demanded Calum, steadying him.

"Not here?" said Ewen.

"He has not returned."

And Calum looked the other up and down, and let him go, frowning, and said, "What are you doing in Neacal's clothes?"

And then he looked more closely into his face, and added, "You've been hurt."

"I'm tired," said Ewen.

He went and sat on the bed, and then dropped his head flat

against the dark-green velvet cushions.

"Tired," he said again.

Calum went over and surveyed him, still frowning heavily. After a few moments, Ewen opened his eyes and said if there was anything he particularly hated, it was people looming over him. Then he roused himself with an obvious effort, and told the other man all that had happened—or most of it. Calum thought it over for some time.

"We must tell Kinrowan," said he, at last.

"No!" Ewen's eyes opened again, and he scowled at the man sitting near him. "Ten to one he would hold me here, and I must find that cursed boy."

He yawned and rubbed a hand across his face wearily.

"Let me sleep for an hour," said he, "and then you can find me some food, my soul, and I'll be off again."

"Well, you can't sleep here," said the sensible Calum. "Not with the Lady Agnes coming in and out every ten minutes, to see if he has come back! Nor in your own bed, for that same reason. You can have mine, and no one shall disturb you there."

Ewen told him to go away, and mumbled that he felt quite unequal to climbing the steps to the upper tower. But when Calum came and stooped over him, and offered to carry him there, he groaned and rolled off the bed and on to his own feet. He said something about fidgety old hens, and then smiled at the unruffled Calum.

"If we meet anyone," he said, "hold me up!"

They did pass a man as they went from Alasdair's bed-chamber into the passage outside. And Ewen leaned heavily into Calum's arm, and let his head fall forward, and covered his face with his hands. The fellow eyed him coldly, and said it was a fine time of day to be helpless with drink—and caught Calum's forbidding eye, and hurried by.

In the round room at the tower top, three of Alasdair's men were waiting for instructions. Receiving them, one went to stand guard at the door, one at the foot of the stairs and one tore off to the gate to bring immediate word of any new developments.

Calum let Ewen drop on to his own straw pallet in the little turret at the side of the room, and covered him with a couple of plaids, and then stood back and surveyed him thoughtfully. As soon as he was sure his leader was asleep, a matter of minutes only, he knelt down and found the wound which he had guessed was there. It seemed an excellent opportunity to do something about it, so he sent for hot water, and ointment, and clean clothes, and a needle and thread. His knowledge of surgery was limited but sound. Ewen woke up while it was being applied, and cursed him feebly. Calum told him to hold his noise unless he wanted them to send for Ranald. Ewen fell back into something between sleep and insensibility. This made everything easier, and Calum finished his task quickly. Then he calmly disobeyed his captain's orders, and stretched the hour he had asked for into two, and then to three. He did something else that would have disturbed Ewen, had he known— he sat and watched beside him.

Agnes and Ranald had a very wearing day, too.

The lady of Kinrowan, mindful of her baby that would come in the spring, and determined to remain calm, called her women and threw them and herself into a perfect frenzy of small chores. They washed things, and dusted things, and polished and mended things. Agnes even fetched out a great length of blue cloth and started on the making of a new gown. But she was unable to concentrate on any one thing for long. The castle living quarters began to wear an air of chaos.

Ranald ranged the district in search of the missing ones. But found no hair or hide of them. He wondered gloomily if they had *all* got themselves bewitched. Turned into swans, or toads, or worse and now flying or louping beyond reach of human aid. He did not, wisely, mention these thoughts to Agnes. He was a very worried man. And his anger was growing too. It was just as well he could not know his quarries were all fast asleep.

Alasdair had wedged himself deeply into the overhanging and exposed roots of a huge oak on Beinn Ard. Taking refuge from a confusing world in a sleep so profound that not even the distant shouts, near or far, of Kinrowan's search parties could reach his tired brain, Alasdair was, for the moment, at peace.

And Hudart was dozing, an old man's succession of catnaps, with Fenella's strange head against his knee. He had wrapped his cloak around her, to keep out a chilly wind, and she was happy in some faraway place of dreams, with a glow on her cheeks and a smile on her lips. They had found a little hollow down by the river, full of soft grass and wild strawberries. Hudart's pony had been turned loose some time before, away up on the hills where he would be easily found and distract anyone that Hudart thought might be looking for them. No one came near the hollow. Only a wild stag and three does, who looked at them and fell to grazing without fear. The old man and the girl slept so peacefully.

Calum had thought his captain peaceful, for a while. The hard lines of Ewen's face had relaxed, and he looked defenseless and vulnerable. Too much so. For he turned his head suddenly, and said something about a foreign battle that appeared to have distressed him greatly. Calum caught the words "heavy losses—resigned command—bad leadership above—" Then Ewen said very clearly and brokenly, "I shouldna have come back so near to home—it has all caught up with me, and Kinrowan will not let me stay—"

"Be done with your havers," said Calum, softly, "Kinrowan likes you well."

Ewen started to tell him something about a well, and a song—fragments that meant nothing to the man who listened. And all the time, his eyes were shut although there were tears on his cheeks. And Calum hushed him into peace again, as gently as any woman might have done. The mercenary might not have sought, or wanted, friendship, but it was with him in the tower of Kinrowan.

The only thing that Ranald found at all cheering, the livelong day, was that his missing beasts were found. A good way from the castle, he ran across a man from his neighbor's land, who told him they were in the Glen of the Pines, and the reivers of Black Fergus long departed. No, said the man, there were none of Kinrowan's people with them. This information lifted a small corner of the cloak of gloom that had fallen over the Chief. By then, he was badly in need of some encouragement.

10. *THE SPAEWIFE*

As the sun drew near to its setting, a thought struck the Lady Agnes.

She could bear no more of her autumnal spring cleaning, and her remaining guests were beginning to eye her askance; so, when the thought came, she put down her needle and went to Ranald, who had descended on the castle for food and fresh horses.

"The well!" said Agnes, running to him.

"Eh?"

The heat of the fire and the large meal he had just eaten were making him feel stupid; and his normally controlled temper was fraying badly.

He had raised Neacal on a hillside, not long before, and had a long and irritating chase to catch him. Then, when they had done so, and found he was not the man they had hoped from his dress, he had refused to speak. He just stood looking at them dumbly. He was a literal-minded young man, and his captain had told him to say nothing. So he said nothing, not even to tell his captors that he had been ordered to say nothing. In the end, and forgetting it was not one of his own men,

Ranald had boxed his ears—and apologized instantly, before Neacal could retaliate in kind, or challenge him to fight. It had been most galling.

Kinrowan longed to lay hands on Ewen or Alasdair. Even old Hudart and the girl were beginning to come under his displeasure. It would have sent him half out of his mind to know that one of the culprits had been sleeping for several hours under his castle roof.

"The well in the hawthorn-wood," said Agnes, patiently, "where Hudart sent Fenella in the first place. You must remember! They described it. And there was the Bocan—"

"Of course I remember."

"Well, they might go back there."

"Where?"

Agnes sighed. She sat down beside her husband in front of the fire, and she filled his wine cup—but only half-full—and said it all over again in slightly different words.

"Oh!" said Ranald. "Good heavens! We might find some of them have gone back to the well, now!"

"How clever of you. Indeed we might. Shall we go and see?"

He got rather reluctantly to his feet, and called for horses, and a dozen men for escort.

But there was a bit of trouble when he told the men where he was going. They said they did not want to go near that place.

"The Standing Stones!" exclaimed one.

"And daylight going."

"The Cairn—!"

"The Black Keep!"

"The well—and the darkness coming down on us!"

It was a tribute to their affection for Ranald that they finally agreed to go. And then it was on the strict understanding that they could stay out of the wood. And they still muttered nervously to one another as they jingled and clattered after the Chief and his lady.

As they went, the cold air roused Ranald, and he said suddenly to Agnes, "This coil is all my fault. I was never cut out to be complicated, and should not have tried."

"It was myself and Fenella—"

"I ought not to have agreed! We should just have shown Alasdair where she was sitting in her wee basket."

Agnes sighed deeply.

"I wanted so much to rouse his wit and courage," she said. "How could we guess it would all go so wrong? We missed our mark."

"It dodged!" said Ranald, wryly.

He brooded for a while, slumped wearily on his horse, then said half to himself, "That devil's mercenary! I'll swear it's he who muddled our simple plot beyond saving!"

And, to his wife, "If I could have caught them! But they took to the heather as though they'd been born outlaws! I wish I'd tracked them with dogs!"

"Darling, they might have bitten them."

"With my blessing," said Ranald.

They went around beside Kinrowan loch, and over a pass. It was a longer way to the well than the one the others had taken the previous night, but easier for the horses. And they came at last to the black ruin by its own secret water, the Standing Stones on the slope, and beyond them the hawthorns. And here their men halted and looked at them pleadingly. One said, "We shall be within calling-distance, Kinrowan, if you need us."

Ranald did not reply. He lifted his wife down, took her hand in his, and began to climb the hill. The men, looking ashamed, started to follow. And their Chief turned on them, and ordered them back. Then he saw their faces, and relented. He said, "It's better that we two should go up alone. If we take a clanking great war party, we scare away those we have come to find. No blame to any of you, but stay here and out of sight among the fir trees over yonder. I know you'll come running if either of us should call."

So Ranald and Agnes came together to the well.

It was getting dark under the trees. The sky was wonderful in the west, with great sheets of red and gold spread across it, and shafts of fire slanting down between bright clouds. The hills had turned to copper and purple where they were brushed by the sunset. The grim Stones cast long black images of themselves along the ground, and the Keep was like a great and savage broken tooth carved out of ebony. But the blackest place of all, when they reached it, was the inside of the well. Ranald looked in, and there seemed to be a cold wind blowing up out of it, that smelt of damp and decay and ancient peril.

He held Agnes away as she also tried to look in.

"Nothing to see," he told her, "and it smells odd."

She went and sat on one of the nearby boulders of rock, and pulled her plaid more closely around her.

"I keep remembering Fenella," said she. "So fine and pretty! If she must be a toad forever—which God forfend!—will she creep off and hide, and never be seen again by any of us? Or will she come back, trusting us to love and care for her?"

She covered her eyes with her hands, and Ranald went over to her.

"Surely she'll have the sense to come to us," he said.

And he gave her his handkerchief. She mopped her eyes and he added, glumly, "Soon her father will be dissatisfied with the lies I've told him! He'll be asking some very difficult questions."

He was looking at his wife, and Agnes had her wet eyes on the splendor of the sunset, out beyond a gap in the trees. So that neither of them saw the person who came down from the high hill behind them, and moved silently to the well.

Agnes said, "Duncan has a right to your answers, my darling."

"Every possible right," agreed Ranald, "but will he believe what he hears?"

"No," and Agnes gave a small bleak laugh. "He'll think she has run off with Alasdair—or Ewen—"

"Either way, he will not be pleased," said Ranald.

The master and mistress of Kinrowan brooded on their responsibilities. The person who had gone over to the well was now huddling shapelessly on the edge of it, almost indiscernable in the dark shade of the hawthorns; and keeping so still and quiet that it might have been a low-hanging branch across the coping.

"Who could guess," said Ranald, at last, "that they would all go quite out of their minds? Even Hudart. What possessed him to tell—?"

And Ewen strolled casually into the clearing.

Had he seen Ranald and Agnes, he would have left again at about ten times the speed, and remained unnoticed; for he

moved very lightly and softly, despite his stocky build, and
the green-and-blue tartans of his kilt, and the long shoulder-
plaid he had acquired from Calum, merged with his background. But he did not see them, and came out full into the
bronze light of the sunset. He had come over the brow of the
hill, and down through the hanging wood, and for all his caution
he had seen no glimpse of Kinrowan's horsemen in their hiding place by the shore, and was deceived by the stillness of the
clearing into thinking it empty. But Ranald saw him well enough,
and the Chief could move fast, too.

Before Ewen knew he was near, Ranald had his arm in a
grip of iron. And after one convulsive movement, the soldier
stood perfectly still. Kinrowan was in no gentle mood, but he
would have been appalled to know just what he was doing, for
it was Ewen's left arm he was clutching and shaking.

"Where is Alasdair?" he demanded.

The other looked at him rather hazily, and the sweat stood
out on his face. He found it difficult to speak. Unfortunately,
Kinrowan had recently met the same sort of reaction from
Neacal, though from a different cause, and was not prepared
to take it calmly.

"Curse you, answer me!" he roared, and tightened his grip.

Agnes had come across to his side, and now she said pleadingly, "Ewen—please—what has been happening? We're half
distraught!"

Yet, distraught or no, the lady of Kinrowan had a quick
eye. She caught her breath.

"Ranald, let go of him!" she said.

Reluctantly, he did so. And the other man put up his right
hand and covered the top of his wounded arm. Ranald looked
at him, and then took a step back. And Agnes said, "Dear
Ewen—he didn't know you are hurt—"

"I'll speak for myself," interrupted her husband. "I did not
know, and I'm sorry—but I still demand an answer to my
question. Oh, come, man, don't just stand there!"

Ewen recovered his tongue and said hoarsely, "I am still
looking for Alasdair, and so—by your leave—"

And turned, rather shakily, to go.

Ranald shot out a hand, but did not touch him; instead, he
gave a roar that startled the other into stillness.

"Don't dare go off!" snapped the Chief. "You can't possibly

be under the impression that I'll let you from my sight again!"

"You can't hold me," said Ewen.

"That's your considered opinion, is it?"

"You've no right. I am not your man."

"You are my prisoner," said Ranald.

"Take me, then!"

Ewen's hand flashed to his sword, and Ranald, goaded, threw back his plaid with one wide shrugging movement, and his own blade was half-drawn when Agnes stepped between them.

"Give me patience!" exclaimed the lady. "Will you two never be done squabbling! And at such a time! I think you're the worst-tempered pair in the kingdom!"

They gave each other a sideways and rueful glance. This she saw, and it spurred her indignation. She said, "I regret interfering with your amusement—for I know you enjoy aggravating one another—but save your energies now to deal with more pressing matters!"

Ewen said, in unusual meekness, "My lady."

And Ranald slid his sword unobtrusively back to its scabbard. He looked at the other man, more charitably, and said, "Who hurt you? Fergus?"

"We had a small disagreement," said Ewen, "and he was better at it than I. But he's away home now, and he left your beasts—"

Ranald said he had them back.

"Where have you been since you escaped Black Fergus?"

"Looking for Alasdair," the soldier gave him a wicked glance, "and sleeping at Kinrowan."

Ranald stared as though he'd said he had spent two years in Elfland.

"No one saw you—"

"I'd changed my clothes," said Ewen, with glinting eyes, "so of course none of your people would look—"

He was avenging Ranald's torturing grip on his arm, and Ranald knew it. But the Chief was a generous man, and gave him his small victory.

"We found Neacal," he said. "We knew you must have his clothes. They *should* have looked! Why did you change?"

"To fool your lot," said Ewen, unworthily.

Agnes eyed the two men with some fear of further hostilities.

Then a small movement by the well caught her eye. She looked into the gloom there, and gave a stifled scream, and put both hands to her mouth.

Both the men swung around to follow her gaze. But Ewen's sword was out first, and he gave a shout of anger, and plunged across to the well.

"Uruisg!" he shouted. "Monster!"

"Be careful!" cried Agnes.

And the sun, which had been showing a last red sliver on the rim of the hills, dropped below them. Above its grave the clouds were still brilliant orange and scarlet; the after-glow remained, but twilight moved rapidly over the beautiful land. The figure on the well-coping got to its feet, and threw back its muffling cloak, confronting Ewen calmly. It said in a cool, sweet voice, "Don't be afraid of me, sir. I will not harm you."

Having disposed of him, the Spaewife turned and bowed her head politely to the others.

"Beannachd, Kinrowan," said she, "and blessings on you, too, my lady."

She smiled at the stunned faces of her hearers.

She was tall and old, with hair as red as fire. Her pale, freckled face would be beautiful if she lived to her century, and that was not so far away now. She was clothed in what seemed endless layers of green wool, home woven, and over it all a gray-green tartan cloak, where the pattern had faded until it was like a blurred pattern of leaves. Her feet were bare, and she stood like a queen watching Ewen sheath his sword, and Ranald's look turn to relief—and she held out her hand to Agnes, as that lady came running.

"Oh, Marjorie," cried Kinrowan's wife. "It is you! I feared you might be—!"

"The Bocan? No, this is my night for the well. He never comes when I'm here, my lady, for we've a sort of arrangement. From sunset till midnight I sit alone and speer into the water. Sometimes I can see the future writ there—but only if I say no word at all to anyone till after the sun goes down."

"Look now," said Ranald. "Ease our minds, Marjorie, or let us know what worse we must face!"

The Spaewife drew Agnes down to sit on the well, and seated herself beside her.

"You are in great trouble," said she.

They told her, Agnes and Ranald between them. For Ranald had known her all his life and trusted her. And she had been one of the few people in Kinrowan, with Hudart, who had been good to Agnes from the start, and stayed faithful when the others had turned on her. And Ewen listened, hearing a good deal that he had guessed, and some things he had not.

"I knew nothing of all this," said Marjorie, "I've been away after the herbs."

She brooded over the tale for a while, her chin in her palm. Then her green eyes, deep under the shadowed sockets, turned on the soldier.

"*You* know more than you've told," she accused him. "Why do you keep it from Kinrowan, who is not your enemy—and the Lady Agnes, who has a right to hear. Be done with your nonsense, man! You act like a child, with a grudge against the world. Worse than young Alasdair!"

Ranald gave Ewen a stony look. Not for anything would he have shown a sign of sympathy. For the Spaewife had spoken to Ewen as though he was a tiresome baby, in the very tone he used to Alasdair. But the mercenary merely said quite calmly, "I don't know where Alasdair is at the moment, ma'am. Nor do I know the whereabouts of Hudart or Mistress Fenella. This I'll tell you," he added, with deceptive gentleness, "the Lady Fenella is no longer a toad, as when you last saw her—except just her face!"

He got the horrified reaction he expected. And said that was all he knew, when they tried to question him further. He was perfectly aware he should tell them that Fenella and Hudart were coming to the wood this evening, and of their hope that Alasdair would do the same. But he had a strong wish to see that young man himself, and alone, before any of the others found him. He feared their gentleness to the boy would soften him further, and Ewen meant to be sure Fenella was freed from her present fate before long, if goading Alasdair could bring it about. Also, though it was unfair to blame Ranald for the present pain in his wounded arm, Ewen was not by nature a very reasonable person. The Spaewife's remarks had not helped, either.

Agnes was begging her to use her double Sight, but the old woman said, "I can see nothing at all but a veil. The girl—has she a veil about her head? Is it the veil of death?"

"Och, it's just a veil!" said Ewen, impatiently.

Then her eyes widened, and she came to her feet with a speed astonishing in so ancient a woman. She was staring at Ewen, with a sort of blankness settling across her gaze, as though she could see more than just his face. The twilight had come, and the shadows were gathering quickly around them all. In the east the sky was already donning its cloak of indigo. Westwards, the little red clouds were turning gray. Ewen stood dourly under old Marjorie's look, and said, "Don't try to frighten me. I'm no' easily scared."

"I am," she said, under her breath, "I am hearing a piper playing—and the tune a lament."

She caught her breath. No one else spoke, and after a moment she went on, "For some clans, I have heard, a piper plays before a death—and the piper is not human. Have you heard that tale?"

"I've heard many tales," said the soldier, without interest.

She went over and looked at him more closely.

"Listen," said she. "Can you hear? The words are singing out of the tune—"

Agnes shivered, and the Chief moved closer to her. For them there was no sound in the wood but the soughing of the wind in the trees, the far cry of a blackbird in a panic at being up so late, and the bright sound of the burn. But the Spaewife was saying slowly, as though she quoted what she heard, "'A mhic an eilean, theirig thusa a' chadal—' Is that for you?"

Ewen said steadily, "If I knew, I wouldna tell."

She nodded to him.

"Hold the knowledge, then," she said.

And she put a hand on his breast, and said very gently, "This much for your comfort, m'eudail. You shall have your heart's desire."

"I trust you have the true Sight," said he, flippantly.

And she turned away. She went to the edge of the clearing and looked out over the darkening water in the valley for a few minutes, and then said, without turning; "Kinrowan, send word to your men down there. They are in terrible peril if they stay from home one hour after the sun sets."

"I'll send them back," said Ranald.

He joined her at the edge of the wood, and cupped both hands to his mouth. But before he could shout, the Spaewife put her own hands on his, so that he lowered them and looked at her. She held his eyes.

"Send a messenger," she said. "I charge you, Kinrowan—send that man. Take my warning!"

Something passed between them—a look—a thought—and Ranald turned to Ewen.

"Will you go, captain?" he said. "I ask you as a favor."

He got a very suspicious stare in return, and then Ewen said slowly, "I'll carry your message, if you also will leave this well, and let me wait here alone."

"We'll arrange that when you return," interrupted the Spaewife. "It shall be as you wish, my dear."

Ewen moved unwillingly to the edge of the slope; and the Spaewife went to him with outstretched hands.

"Leave your sword here," she said, pleadingly. "You must carry no weapon for this errand. Life or death, soldier!"

"Rubbish," said he, and took a pace out of the wood.

Her voice rang out behind him.

"Will you not trust someone besides yourself—just for once! Do you fear Kinrowan's men will harm you? He shall call to them before you go down. Surely, for so short a time, you can trust yourself to us?"

He stood hesitating, and looking around at them all. The Spaewife gestured to Ranald, and he lifted a shout that echoed over the hill slope and the loch—calling to his men that he was sending instructions to them, which they must instantly obey. And Ewen's eyes kept roving from face to face, most uneasily. Then he unbuckled the broad leather sling, and let it slide from his shoulder, and he gave his sword to Ranald.

"Three times!" he said, oddly.

"And the sgian," said the Spaewife.

He drew the little black-hafted knife from his stocking, and she took it from him. No one spoke again, and he went down to the hidden troop of men. The three on the hill watched him, until Ranald said quietly, "What are you about?"

"Hush," said old Marjorie.

Ewen reached the fir trees, and went out of sight into their gloom, and she turned to Ranald and said urgently, "Now, Kinrowan! Call to your men to take him!"

"What?"

"Do what I say," her voice was high and wild. "Make them

hold him fast. His death, otherwise! Now! Now, Kinrowan! Call your troop captain!"

Ranald glanced at Agnes, and she gave a small nod. And he shouted again, and louder than before, "Doughall! Hold that man! Let him not escape!"

A distant yell came from below the trees, and Ranald added a rapid addition to his orders, "Don't hurt him!"

Then he turned to the Spaewife, and his face was exceedingly grim.

"That is the first time I have set my men on one who was unarmed and a friend," said he. "Is that what you wanted?"

"I want him safe," she said.

"He was right not to trust us," said Kinrowan, bitterly. "I'd rather not have done this. What shall I do with him now?"

"Take him back to the castle with you," said she. "Let him not set his foot outside tonight. Kinrowan, I have not done this idly. His life is at stake."

"Mine, too, when he gets free," said Ranald.

And Agnes came soft-footed to them, and said in a strained voice, "If Alasdair needs a sword, he is unguarded now."

"Be at peace," the old woman told her. "If he comes here, I shall do my best to help. If he doesn't, not twenty swordsmen could be of any use to him."

"Do you think he may come here?" said Agnes. "Oh, then may we not stay? Must we just go back to our waiting? I know you are wise, Marjorie—but it's so hard—"

The Spaewife stroked her shoulder comfortingly.

"I will send word—or bring it myself—as soon as there is word for you to hear."

With that assurance, the lady of Kinrowan looked a little less anxious. She cast one long look back at the well.

"There is evil down there," she said, shuddering.

The Spaewife nodded. And Agnes went down to the waiting horsemen with her husband, who had fallen into a brooding silence.

Left alone, old Marjorie went over to the well. She laid Ewen's sgian dubh carefully on the rim, and then she turned toward the steep braes above, where the night was beginning to light its stars one by one, above the brow of the hill.

She called softly, through the gathering wind, "Come out of hiding—they are all gone away."

11. *WAYS INTO DANGER*

Fenella was glad of the twilight. Even if they should meet anyone, who would cast a second glance at a face that was masked in the kindly darkness as well as in a veil? A little spring of hope had risen in her heart, too, for she was a gay-spirited girl who found it hard to be depressed for long. She felt things must take a turn for the better soon.

Hudart said nothing to dampen her, but feared she would be the worse hurt if her hope proved false.

They had done some more fishing, and were both reasonably full, though a bit tired of singed trout. And they were as fresh as any two people could be who had slept in snatches through the day in the open air.

They went up the river until they came to the loch that fed it, and they then branched off on to the moors, and came at last to the high hill that looked down on the Standing Stones and the ruined keep. Here they adopted very stealthy methods. Hudart patiently taught the girl some woodcraft—how to move silently on dead leaves and twigs, and how not to trip over loose stones. He found her a way whereby she could hold her skirt close to her, and so prevent it catching and clinging. He never once mentioned elephants or herds of bullocks. And, after a bit of practice, Fenella found she had acquired a sureness and ease of movement she would not have believed.

So now, down through the hanging wood she came again. And this time she came lightly and gracefully. She was almost sure Alasdair would be waiting there, ready to take the spell from her with a kindly look and word. So she was smiling as she moved from twisted roots to clumps of heather, and then to outcrops of rock, and along the narrow ledges, and slid down the gullys. Ahead of her went Hudart, moving as easily though slowly because of his lameness, and the girl restrained her desire to hurry, in case he realized how he was holding her back. He knew it well, though, and loved her kindness. Then suddenly he halted and lifted a warning hand. Fenella almost felt her ears prick forward to listen to the voices that could now be heard some distance ahead. A soft murmur of several people talking together.

Hudart put his mouth close to the girl's ear and whispered, "Stay here. I'll go and see who they are."

She clutched his sleeve.

"Do be careful! And—come back quickly."

He nodded, and slipped away through the black shadows, like a shadow himself.

She stood still, but her hands were clenched nervously, and she tried not to think that there were eyes watching her from among the hawthorns, and unseen malice lurking. Then she started violently, as she heard someone shouting in the clearing ahead. The eyes seemed to retire a little, as though that deep shout had alarmed them. Yet it was a voice she knew. She gave a sigh of relief. And Hudart came back, shaking his head, and saying softly, "Ranald and Agnes and Ewen—and the Spaewife herself. But dear knows what they're all at!"

And then they heard the old woman calling, "Come out of hiding—they are all gone away."

Hudart took Fenella by the hand and led her to the Spaewife.

As soon as she saw the face of the tall woman, Fenella knew she was one to be trusted. And Marjorie put three fingers of her right hand to the girl's veiled forehead, and gave her a blessing. Then she said, "I knew you were somewhere near, poor little one," and to Hudart, in deep reproach, "How could you let these things happen, Guardian of Kinrowan?"

"Bard of Kinrowan," said he, quickly.

"Call it what you will, but the luck of the house was in your keeping."

"I retired long since! Why, I've been expecting a replacement any—"

"Huh!" said the old lady.

She saw how Fenella was not heeding them, but looking with growing disappointment all about the clearing. And she put a hand on the girl's arm and said, "He is not here, mo chridhe."

"We told Ewen to bring him—"

Marjorie shook her head.

"He never found the boy, nor will he—now. If Alasdair comes here, it will be of his own accord. And better so."

She looked from one of them to the other.

"You know more of this than I do," she said. "Is it likely he will come?"

"He might go first to your cottage," said Hudart. "It's what we told him to do—at least, not exactly *told* him, but—"

"I know. Kinrowan and his lady explained," said the Spae-wife, dryly. "A very involved bit o' strategy! No wonder it went wrong. Suppose he does go to seek me at home?"

"Well, he must realize you are not there," said the bard, "unless he's a bigger fool than I take him to be! After that, he may come here. Marjorie," he added, impatiently, "we can only wait and see!"

Fenella said in a sorrowful little voice, "*I* am to blame for that—strategy! I meant it well, but it has put everyone to such trouble—"

And she went rather quickly to the place where the trees thinned away, and stood with her back to the others. All the same, she heard only too clearly the next words of the old woman and the old man.

"Will he be looking for help for himself—" said Marjorie, "or help for the Lady Fenella?"

"I wish I knew."

"If he does not come, he will torture himself forever about her."

"Perhaps he enjoys doing just that!"

And Fenella put her hands to her head.

"Oh, poor Alasdair," she murmured.

A flight of birds went over the crest of the hill. Their long necks outstretched, and wide wings making a throbbing noise as they rode the wind. The wild swans. Homing for the night to some quiet water, where they would know no fear—no scorn.

"I wish he need not be so tested!" she cried, aloud.

This brought the eyes of the others around to her, and she held out her hands to them in appeal.

"I don't want him hurt anymore!"

"My darling, you cannot spare him everything," said the Spaewife.

Fenella pointed to the cairn, away down to the left at the place where the hill leveled toward the loch.

"What is that?" said she.

The Spaewife started, and put a hand to her lips. And Hudart said, "That? Why it's only—"

Marjorie stopped him, with a tiny gesture that was unseen by the girl. He let his voice trail away, and turned a puzzled look on the Spaewife. She drew herself up, as though she had made a decision, and she moved toward the girl, and said slowly and impressively, "It is an entrance to the Sithean."

Hudart's jaw dropped. But Fenella's eyes were only for the cairn.

"Are you crazed!" said the bard, under his breath.

The Spaewife shook her head. There was a smile on her mouth, partly of guile, partly of amusement, and mostly of tenderness. She stood watching Fenella until the veiled head turned to her.

"I thought it might be," said the girl, "and that's where I shall go."

"No!" cried Hudart.

Marjorie made a hushing sound at him, and he stared at her as though he could not believe what he heard. And Fenella went on, lost in her own thoughts, "I can be safe there, and forgotten. No human eyes will look on me again. And Alasdair need not torture himself with concern for me."

"Aren't you afraid of the People of the Hill?" said Marjorie. "If you go to Them, They will never let you leave."

"I'll be better off with Them," said Fenella. "They won't scorn me or turn from me. They are used to strange creatures about Them, or so I have heard. And They are not human, either!"

Hudart made a sort of gulping protest, which the Spaewife quelled by raising her clear voice above it.

"You are right, my heart," said she. "That is where you must go."

"But, Marjorie—!"

"Hudart, be quiet!"

"I will not!"

The bard went quickly to Fenella, and his lined face was twisted with distress. He said, "Don't listen! Do *not* listen to her! This is utter and final madness! There is naught inside that cairn, my darling girl, save dark and empty tunnels, twisting through this hill like a great rabbit-warren—leading into—"

"The Sithean," said the Spaewife. "Into Elf-land."

The old man rounded on her crossly.

"Nothing of the sort!" he snapped. "And you know it! What are you at?"

And then, to Fenella, he said, "You will come back with me to Kinrowan. The Chief and his lady will care for you there. And there may be something I can do to sort out all this coil—if I have time to think—"

While he wrung his hands, and groped for further arguments, Fenella turned to the Spaewife.

"Will you point me the way into the hill?" she said. "I have made up my mind."

The two women, the young and the old, went down the hill together. Hudart followed, shaking his head and muttering.

It took a while to reach the cairn, for old Marjorie went slowly. But at last they came to the great stone mound.

Seen close to, it was more blurred in outline than it had seemed from farther away. Thin grass grew over it, and heather in the crevices. It was indeed more like a gigantic molehill than anything else.

"The entrance is at the far side," said Marjorie, "and well hid."

Around they went. In one place was a tangle of briar and bramble wrapped around a dead alder tree that was lying against the cairn. No scrap of earth still clung to its long-dried, pitifully reaching roots. The Spaewife caught hold of a handful of the trailing spiky stuff.

"Come, child," she said. "Pull—and never mind the scratches."

Fenella pulled. And the tangle lifted. There, below the slant of the dead tree, that had been acting as a sort of curtain pole to the festoons of thorns, was a battered little door set into the cairn. Made of oak, gray as the alder, with huge rusty hinges and a wooden latch.

"There!" said Marjorie. "The wooden door that is not made of wood. The wooden latch that is not wooden, either. The hinges that are not iron. The gateway to the Sithean."

Fenella looked long, then she drew a shaky breath, and gave the other woman a nervous glance through the folds of her veil. Old Marjorie smiled reassuringly; and Fenella put her hand on the big latch, and it clicked upwards easily as though it was often used. She stooped to go under the alder tree, and then, at the very last, she hesitated.

"What will I find in there?"

Hudart, coming up alongside Marjorie, was minded to tell her. But he caught a warning in the Spaewife's eye and said nothing. The old woman considered Fenella's question carefully; then she said, "You'll find what will seem to be a narrow, dark, and low-roofed passage leading into the hill. With many other tunnels opening into it from all sides. Smelling airless, and dank, and cold—"

Hudart nodded vehemently, and she glanced at him without expression, and went on, "At first you will see naught of the bright lights about you—the jewels glinting in the carven walls—the thin gold pillars—and the soft grass underfoot, all starred with flowers. You will not have the scent of summer in your nostrils, nor will you hear the sound of singing—not at first."

"Nor ever!" said Hudart, but he said it under his breath.

"It takes a while to grow used to magic," said the Spaewife.

Fenella swallowed. It crossed her mind that she had never in all her life had so much to do with magic as she had during the last twenty-four hours, and it seemed as strange to her as ever. She said, "And Those Ones?"

"They will be there, my child. With Their bright eyes, and Their beauty. And the white deer running with Them. Though again, for a little time, you may not see anything of Them."

The girl sighed, and turned again to the low doorway; and the Spaewife leaned forward to lay a hand on her arm.

"Fenella," she said, very earnestly, "you must promise me one thing. Promise on your soul! Go only a short way in. No more than fifty feet. Then sit down by the side of the path, and wait."

"Wait for what?"

The older woman seemed to hesitate. Her eyes clouded, and she bit her lip as though unsure of what she was doing. And then she said, "Just wait. It's a matter of magic—and of life and death. Wait there until you hear someone calling your name."

"I'll try to be brave," said the girl, rather tremulously, "but I had hoped Those Ones would accept me at once—and that I would not be alone. I wish the darkness and the waiting will soon be over!"

"So do I," said Marjorie.

She put both hands around the girl's face and kissed the veiled forehead, dim in that dim light.

"All the luck that you have go with you, my bird."

Hudart and the Spaewife watched her while Fenella went through the little door. It closed. And the two old people were alone in the night and the wind. Marjorie shivered, and the bard gave her an accusing stare. He pointed a thin finger at her, and said, "You've sent her into the old mine workings! Where the ancient men once dug for tin. The tunnels run twisting and turning for miles—honeycombing the hill here—are you from your wits!"

The Spaewife had recovered her usual calm.

"I have set it on her to stay near the door. She will obey, and not go wandering. If Alasdair comes, I'll send him in to bring out his lady from the Sithean. If he does so, surely he'll set his love and protection about her always! And so win back her beauty, and find his own self."

Hudart remained unconvinced.

"We've taken too many chances with her safety already," said he, "and I'm going now to fetch her back!"

"Wait—oh, wait! If you do that, you take from her the last chance of happiness she may have. If the boy does fail her," said Marjorie, "I'll fetch her back myself, poor little soul."

They went from the cairn and climbed the hill slowly together, toward the hanging wood

It was dark in the clearing, when they got there. For the crest of the hill cut off the light from the deep sky with its gathering clouds, and stars and its round yellow moon. The thorn branches twisted together to make a further screen for the place and its mystery. There was a little scurry of rain now and then in the cold wind. The Spaewife gathered her plaid around her, and shivered again.

"I hope I've done the right thing," she said, at last.

Hudart did not answer, and this seemed to worry her. She glanced at him once or twice, and then said; "Could you not make some small charm to hasten Alasdair here?"

"No," said he, bluntly.

There was silence for a time. Light began to filter through the thorns as the moon went further up the sky. A stag belled from the distance across the loch, and from even further away another answered his challenge.

"Why not?" said Marjorie, at last.

Hudart faced her, throwing out his hands in irritation.

"I've told you, over and over again—I *must* not! I've retired!"

"You could try."

"What about my pension?"

The Spaewife gave him a sharp and scornful look. She said, "What are you, to think of money at a time like this?"

"It *isn't* money! I've never told you before," he said, "but it's just a little drift of warm air that laps me around when the weather's hard. It keeps my old bones cozy—"

She said in obvious disbelief, "Does Ranald grudge you firing, that you must look to magic to warm you?"

"He grudges nothing. But all the peats on the moor could not keep out the cold. They might send on me, if I ignore Their wishes."

There was another long silence. The Spaewife began to walk to and fro on the stony ground, hugging her elbows, head bent as though in thought. Finally she stopped in front of Hudart and said, "No one has been sent to replace you. Is it truly meant that the house of Kinrowan should lie unguarded? And with such trouble gathered?"

Hudart did not reply. He kicked nervously at a heather tuft, and examined the palms of his hands for no reason. He cleared his throat, and stared up through the thorn branches to where a very small star was glittering overhead. He said, weakly, "It would be better for Alasdair to come of his own will."

He did some more fidgeting and muttering, and then he burst out, "I'm no good at such things and never was, and so I tell you! It will come to nothing, Marjorie! I could try the worm-spell—"

"Do," she said. "It's pretty, anyway."

The anxious lines of her face relaxed their tension as she watched the old man go over to the well, and start peering about its flat stones, and the moss and lichen there. She sat down on a boulder, and huddled into her plaid. After a moment or so, Hudart gave an exclamation of triumph. He took up some tiny thing between his finger and thumb and set it carefully on the coping.

The moon had risen a little more behind the hill, and now its pale light began to filter into the clearing from above. Hudart cast a glance at the Spaewife, and went and stood in the brightest patch of moonlight. He groped among his many and well-stocked pockets. Then he laid a white handkerchief over his left hand, and mumbled something, and snatched it off again. On his palm now lay a small spray of rowan. Marjorie clapped softly, and he bowed, smiling proudly. Then he hesitated and said, "Have you seen me do that before?"

"No, no," said she, and quite untruthfully. "It was very clever. Why do you need the rowan?"

"For courage," he said, seriously. "To protect my soul from evil. Now for the spell—if I can remember the words."

He returned to the well-side, and crouched down, staring toward the tiny thing on the coping. And a thin shaft of moonlight just touched him—the old man with his white hair and hunched back, and the thin hands moving in circles. He began to sing, in his sweet voice that had never lost its own magic whatever else had failed its possessor.

> "Commence to shine, ye gentle worm,
>   Start ye to glint and glow;
>   That Alasdair may stop and turn,
>   And move toward us now."

From the top of the well's edge gleamed a spark of light, so small that the Spaewife blinked several times to be sure it was really there. It was, and as steady as a little candle, unflickering in the wind.

"Charming," said she. "And now, will Alasdair come?"

"Oh, my dear Marjorie, I've scarcely started!"

He touched his palms together very slowly, three times, and then crossed his wrists so that his hands were back to back. He sang again, and a bit more loudly:

> "Let no one douse ye, worm o' mine,
>   Let not your lantern fail,
>   Until the lad shall come in time
>   Here to the hawthorn-well."

The old man was so intent on the song and the glow-worm, that he neither saw nor heard any sign of the slim figure that came down through the trees, and halted at the edge of the clearing; like a wild creature that fears to be seen, but wishes to approach. Yet Marjorie both heard and saw, and she put a finger to her lips, and beckoned with her other hand. The newcomer hesitated, and then went lightly and soundlessly to her side.

"Ssh, my dear," she whispered.

She took his cold hand and held it. Hudart was rubbing his white hair until it stood up in wild wisps, and humming snatches of tune, and mumbling various combinations of words. He gave an irritable groan.

"This is a very long spell," he said. "And it's many years since I tried it. I can't remember exactly—"

"Might it be having some effect already?" called the Spaewife.

"No, no, of course not! Nothing will happen until I get right to the end."

He dealt himself a sharp tap on the forehead, and gave a pleased exclamation; and he sang again, rather quickly in case he forgot the words before he could get them out.

> "If ever spell had power to charm,
>   Or I have power to spell—"

A little quiver of excitement came into his voice.

> "Turn now your light, my bonnie worm,
>   As green as any jewel!"

The person who stood by the Spaewife now leaned close to her ear to say in a low whisper, "What's he doing?"

"The dear knows!" said she.

Hudart knelt bolt upright, his glittering dark eyes fixed on the little light.

"Oh, come on, worm!" he said, impatiently.

The light went suddenly and quite unmistakably green. Hudart was delighted. He said over his shoulder to Marjorie, but without sparing her a glance, "We're getting there! Another four verses, and that wretched boy should be on his way here— that is, if it works at all!"

"He *is* here," said Marjorie.

Hudart cast an absent look across the clearing, but immediately turned back to his task.

"Nonsense!" he said. "Now, listen to this—"

And he went on singing:

> "Oh, worm of glow! Oh, glow of worm!
>   Ye little winsome joy—"

He then stopped abruptly and said, "Who's that man?"

"Dear heart," said the Spaewife, patiently, "pull yourself together. Alasdair has come of his own free will."

The bard stared at the young man beside her, and shook his head wildly.

"It's not himself but his fetch!" he cried.

He shrank back as Alasdair crossed to him, and lifted shaking hands to ward him off. The boy laughed and leaned over to pat his shoulder.

"Is that a ghostly touch?" he asked.

Hudart scrambled to his feet, and he laughed too, though rather shakenly; he rubbed his chin with his fist, and looked across at the Spaewife with a rueful expression. But that kindly lady did not even smile at his discomfiture. She said, "I'm sure the worm-spell helped a bit."

"It did," agreed Alasdair. "For I heard you, and it guided me down the hill."

The old man nodded to them, understanding and appreciating their good intent. Then he saw that Alasdair was looking at him with a mixture of eagerness and uncertainty.

"Where is Fen—?" The boy stopped, gulped, and then said, "Where is Ewen?"

The Spaewife answered him. "In a dungeon by now, I hope—and in chains!"

He stared at her, aghast, and stammered, "A—dungeon? But—did Fergus come back then, and—?"

"No, no," she assured him, quickly, "Ranald has him, and in friendship only. No dungeon." Then she looked at him piercingly, and said, "It is the Lady Fenella for whom you should be troubled. Ask about her."

Alasdair turned his head away.

"I hardly dare to," he said, very low.

The face of the Spaewife softened. The light was clear enough now for her to see Alasdair's beautiful profile, and the soft, dark curly hair that clung to his strong neck. She also saw how his left hand clenched and unclenched tightly. And she smiled. During the last two years, since he came to Kinrowan, she had thought of him as a young lad—now he had the look of a man. She wondered if it was just the lack of a razor, or had the years caught up?

"Oh, do look!" said Hudart, unexpectedly. "The glow-worm is crawling on to my hand!"

"Don't tease it," said Marjorie.

The old man gave a delighted laugh. He said the little creature had grown fond of him, and he could keep it for a pet. He wondered what glow-worms ate—

"You're distracting me!" said the Spaewife.

"But it's interesting."

"Not to me. Not just now!"

Hudart sat on the side of the well, rather grumpily, and looked at his new friend for sympathy. But it was hard to tell what it was thinking. It just glowed.

Marjorie touched the arm of the silent Alasdair, and said, "Do you care what happens to Fenella? Do you mind at all?"

His head came around, and he met her eyes with a flare of anger.

"Of course I care. Do you take me for a monster?"

"What would you do to help her?"

His left hand went across his body, to clutch at the folds of his plaid.

"Whatever a one-armed man may dare!" said he, fiercely.

And then his face changed, in rather a horrible manner. It became fretful and bitter, and all the fine lines softened and weakened. It was no longer the face of a man, but of a sullen child. And words poured from him, in a flurry that he seemed unable to check.

"Oh, what is there that *I* can do!" he cried. "Other men can go boldly to defend the things they care for! Yet I must always walk with meekness, taking any affront—knowing I can't challenge it. I've known this a long time, but now the full meaning of it comes to me!"

He turned away, and dropped down into the heather, and lay biting his lip, and screwing up his eyes. Marjorie watched with compassion, but she said in a very stern voice, "Has it ever occurred to you that others may carry burdens? Perhaps heavier than yours, though they may be less easily seen?"

He dug out a smooth stone from the peaty ground and tossed it away to clatter among other stones, and then he said sulkily, "If a thing can be concealed, it can't be much! Nor can it be mocked or pitied!"

"It could corrode and destroy."

And the Spaewife went and stood over him, and said in a commanding way, "Alasdair, get up at once!"

He gave her a startled look.

"It isn't a sword that Fenella needs now," she exclaimed, angrily. "It is love and courage and intelligence. Even a wild swan has these! They love once, and if their mate should die, they live lonely all their days."

Alasdair had started to get to his feet, and now he paused on one knee, and stared at the ground.

"But who could love Fenella—as she is now?" said he.

Hudart's head came up abruptly, away from the creature he had been cajoling. And the Spaewife drew a long hissing breath of shocked surprise. There was a silence in the thornwood clearing. During it, Alasdair rose, and brushed the clinging scraps of heather from his side. Marjorie found her voice.

"You must judge for yourself what she is, of course," said

she. "But at least it is your duty—if no more—to bring her back from the Sithean."

"From *where?*"

"The Elf Hill. She has gone into the Hill. She will never get out, unless someone can find the courage—"

Alasdair was not listening. He interrupted, harshly, "What's she doing there? Ewen was guarding her—"

"Not now, he isn't," and Marjorie was equally harsh. "She has gone to the Hill alone. Into great danger once again—and for the same reason. For your sake, Alasdair."

"How do I find her?" he demanded.

His eyes had gone as fierce as a hawk's, as they glared down at the Spaewife. Tall as she was for a woman, she was not as tall as he—not when he stood so straight.

"In spite of what she is?" said Marjorie.

"Because of it!" he said, in the crossest possible way. "She has no sense at all! What *for* would she go crashing into the Hill!"

His mouth tightened, and he said, "I'll get the little wretch back, though she had the face of Medusa!"

The statement was received with mixed feelings. The Spaewife put up her hands to her mouth, and looked at him over the fingertips with fathomless eyes. Hudart sat bolt upright on the side of the well, and let the glow-worm roll gently out of his palm to a soft bed of moss where it lay glowing green. And from the black circle of the well itself came a shrill burst of laughter.

The Bocan scrambled over the coping. Hudart leaped up and backed away. And the Bocan hunched himself there in a shapeless heap, still laughing.

The Spaewife rallied first.

"Why are you here? This is my night," she said.

"You've lost your turn!"

And he wagged a fat finger at her, and gave her a revoltingly arch look of reproach.

"You forgot, you silly. woman! We made a pact that you should have your place here only if you stay in it. You promised not to go more than ten feet from the well. You've been all over the place tonight. Prying and speering after my secrets. The hill is mine, and well you know it! My people would drive you off—but I have respected your small power of Sight, having so much myself."

She looked at him with loathing.

"I did promise, but—"

The Bocan cackled triumphantly at her. Then turned his pale little eyes on Alasdair. The young man shifted uneasily, looking unsure again.

Most of his life had been lived so close to sorcery that it was hard for him to be anything but nervous in the presence of one whom he thought to be a most powerful wizard. He stood frowning.

"There's the lad with the wing!" said the Bocan, sneeringly. "And still ruffling his poor feathers, is he? And—oh, Hudart, you should not venture out so late, at your age, and with your many infirmities!"

He shot a malicious glance around the moonlit clearing.

"Where's the soldier?" he said. "Has he run away—from what he knows I know? And the pretty girl? Oh, my!" he mocked Alasdair. "What will you do without those two to look after you?"

He had gone too far.

"I'll manage!" snapped the boy.

And he strode to the well, and glared at the Bocan, and said furiously, "You slimy boggart! Did you send her into the Sithean?"

The Bocan cowered away from him. "Into the Sithean—?" he echoed, in alarm.

"If she's there, it's by your doing! Tell me how to find her," growled Alasdair, "or I'll wring your flabby neck!"

It seemed he had forgotten he was addressing a sorcerer. And now the Spaewife suddenly saw the danger looming in front of the boy—a danger she had set there. She hurried forward, and cried loudly, "Alasdair, he knows nothing of Fenella! *I'll* show you the way into the Hill."

And saw by the gleam in the Bocan's eyes that he knew the power of the weapon that had come into his hand. He showed long yellow teeth in a grin.

"She is not in the Hill, now," he said, softly.

Marjorie gasped. She clutched Alasdair frenziedly.

"I saw her go into the cairn!" she said. "Oh, I promise you—"

"Through the cairn she may have gone," said the Bocan, "but the People of the Hill have taken her to Lochlann."

"What do you mean?"

The Bocan gave a high-pitched giggle, and rolled his eyes up at Alasdair.

"Taken her down into Lochlann," he repeated, glibly. "Once you go inside the Hill—whichever door you choose—there are roads and pathways there that lead to all the other places of magic. Tir Sorcha, the land of light—Lochlann of the waters—"

"She's in none of them!" said the Spaewife, angrily. "You're lying, Bocan."

But he kept his eyes on Alasdair's distracted face, and said deliberately, "I've seen her in Lochlann, not half an hour ago."

And he pointed into the deeps of the well.

"Down there."

Alasdair started forward, and the Spaewife tried to hold him.

"He's lying!" she cried, again. "There's nothing down there of magic! Only the water from the hill, and an entrance to the ancient working of the miners—"

"Have you ever been down to see?" said the Bocan, and giggled.

He peered closely at Alasdair, and said with deliberation, "She's held under the black waters of the loch. Weeping, too, and that one is not a lady that cries easily! Yet," he added, unctuously, "she is lucky, for there are others of her sort there. Web-footed ones—warty ones—finned ones, and cold of skin—things that are neither fish nor frog nor human—things to welcome her as their own kin—"

"Not for long they won't!" said Alasdair.

He set one foot on the coping, and was aware of the Spaewife tugging at his sleeve. He disengaged his arm, but not ungently.

"Alasdair—Alasdair—she is in the cairn!" cried Marjorie, in despair. "Just inside the doorway and waiting to be found—"

But he was not listening. He was armed in mind to meet danger, and he swung his feet across the well-coping, and began to scramble down the wet and slippery rocks that carried the burn water steeply into the well. It was very difficult for a man with only one hand. After a few slips and slithers, he lost his balance and splashed down into the icy water.

The Spaewife gave a cry of alarm, and the Bocan chuckled in his fat throat. But after a moment, Alasdair's head emerged from the water, and he shook the hair back from his face and he grabbed the rocky wall and looked about him, blinking the wet from his eyes.

After a few moments, he noticed a jagged black opening at the side of the well, by the gully. A hole that a man could crawl into, on hands and knees, with its step worn smooth and slopping from the passage of many people over the years. He could vaguely discern the beginning of a low tunnel beyond. Alasdair pulled himself across the water, and managed to scramble up on to the flat stone. He caught his breath, and then began to crawl into the darkness of the hill.

Above, in the open air, the Bocan was laughing excitedly. He put out a greedy hand toward the little green glow among the mosses at his side. But, whatever Hudart's worm-spell had failed to do, it had done something to the glow-worm. It bit the Bocan. And he screamed, and thrust his finger in his mouth and sucked it. Old Marjorie looked at him with angry eyes.

"I never thought you a real monster until now," said she. "Oh, did you truly find the girl?"

"Truly," said he.

He opened his eyes till they were quite round.

"My people have her safe," he said, with pride. "Did you think anyone can walk into my stronghold, and sit on a pile of stones, and not be noticed?"

Then he yelled loudly at Hudart. The old hunchback was making his halting way out of the wood on to the first downward slope of the hill, toward the cairn so far below.

"The mound is sealed!" shouted the Bocan. "No one can get in now, by that door! It is too late!"

Then he broke into a squeal of absolute terror. The Spaewife had snatched up Ewen's dirk, and now came swiftly at him with the little weapon glinting wickedly in her hand.

"Ahh!" shrieked the Bocan.

And jumped into the well.

There was a loud splash; then a wallowing noise as a heavy body spluttered its way to the dark opening in the rock below. Then silence.

The Spaewife sobbed aloud.

Hudart limped back into the clearing, and over to her side. He said with strong disapproval, "So! The girl is in the Bocan's hands! The lad has gone straight into his stronghold. And the soldier, according to you, is in a dungeon! I don't think you've been very clever. Had you asked my advice—"

The Spaewife was already upset. She cried, "Go and advise someone else!"

And gave him a shove. He was very near the well. There was yet another splash.

Marjorie put her hands over her mouth hard, and stared in dismay. She leaned over the coping and called, "Are you all right? Come back up here!"

There was no reply from the well, nor any sign of the hunchback.

The Spaewife sank down despondently on the coping-stones. She looked at something under her hand, and took up Hudart's little spray of rowan. With an almost absent-minded movement, she dropped it into the water. Then she straightened her shoulders, and said aloud, "I must call out Kinrowan."

She half-rose, and then sat back again. It had come to her that Ranald's arrival with his men—the first sign or sound of a rescue party—would spell death to the three who were in the Bocan's hands.

"There must be a way—"

And then she seemed to freeze. Her head tilted as though she was listening to a far sound. Yet there was only the wind in the trees, and the burn chuckling down its gully into the well.

"The piper—" she whispered.

Her mouth felt suddenly dry, and there was a chill in her heart that made her tremble. And still she listened. And slowly formed words with her lips, not quite speaking them aloud.

"A mhic an eilean—" And then, "Son of the island—come thou to thy rest—"

She looked down at the small black knife in her hands. And grief settled like a shadow over her face. She bent her head and sat waiting quietly, as though she had glimpsed destiny.

12. *THE PRISONERS*

A party of horsemen was making its way over the moors toward Kinrowan castle. It had bunched itself together rather too closely for comfort, which was making the ponies uneasy. And, with one exception, every man in it had just three fervent wishes— one, that the Chief had not ridden ahead and out of sight with his lady—two, that they were safely under the familiar roof of home—and three, that Ewen would hold his tongue.

By riding fast they were doing their best to remedy the first of these wants—though two people on good horses can go more speedily than thirteen on heavy garrons. And they probably would have made a strong bid to tackle the third problem but for Ranald's strict command. They were forbidden to lay a finger on the soldier, and no one could think of any way to gag him otherwise. He was not even tied, though Kinrowan had hesitated whether to fasten his ankles to the stirrups. But being unable to look Ewen in the eye anyway, he had finally left him free, and ridden away quickly from that disparaging gaze. The orders left with his men, however, were firm enough. They were to keep the reins of Ewen's horse, and to maintain a strict guard on him.

The men would much rather have been riding well out of ear-shot, but as it was they kept together for company as much as for duty—and were enthralled, against their better judgment, by what the mercenary was saying.

He had a dreadful store of blood-curdling tales. And he lifted his voice clearly above the jingle and clatter of his escort, and their few half-hearted attempts to drown his words in song. He made every gruesome point strike home to the minds of his hearers. Drawing freely on memory and imagination, he peopled every rock they passed, every stretch of water, every tree or tussock of grass, with a fine variety of boggarts and bocans, carlins and kelpies, and some that no one, not even himself, had heard of before. Ranald's men were heartily sick of him. They kept glancing nervously back over their shoulders, and to either side.

One of the horses stumbled, and the troop leader said loudly, "If any man falls out, the rest will not be waiting!"

This cast an added gloom over the party, and Ewen's mouth curled a little.

Then they were forced to slow down. They had reached a place between two hills where the ground was soaked into being a deepish bog; the only place firm enough for the horses' feet was a winding track, marked with white stones, not a yard across, but quarter of a mile long. On either side, the treacherous ground was grown over with bog-myrtle, cotton-grass, and thin tall reeds. Six men rode ahead in single file, the last leaning back to clutch the reins of the lead horse. Behind Ewen came the six others. They let the nervous ponies pick their way carefully. The attention of the escort was about equally divided between the unreliable nature of the immediate landscape, and the revolting climax of the tale it was hearing.

"—sucked every morsel of marrow from his spine," said Ewen, with horrible emphasis.

Then he screamed like the pipes of war, and threw himself sideways off his horse, and vanished among the bog plants and reeds. There was some splashing and then silence.

Complete confusion ensued.

The horses caused most of it. Worried already by the squelchy ground under them, and by the nervousness they felt through their rider's hands and knees, this yell was the last straw. The leaders leaped forward wildly, trying to bolt and tossing their heads, start-eyed. Those at the back, not sure which way to run, sat down or tried to jump over their leaders, or swung off to the side, and felt the bog deepen, and reared and whinnied. The riders, cursing freely, held them and calmed them, and rode them back on to the causeway, heaving them out of the wet ground with difficulty. Then they started to consider their missing prisoner.

The wind was rising. Black clouds were scudding, fast and malevolent, over the face of the moon. Some dead trees stuck up from the bog nearby, leaning together companionably, and the men had been hearing some curious things about trees. Then there was a rock looming on the hillside not far away— it had a look about it—was it a rock? It was impossible to take the horses off the causeway, and no one felt any great urge to search the bogs on foot, and maybe find himself on his own— among those reeds perhaps where an odd sort of ripple ran. After a while, and a useless reconnoiter of the near places where a man might be hiding, they decided Kinrowan's anger was less to be feared than a minute more of this eery spot.

Fenella was getting apprehensive, too.

She had found a place, not far from the door of the cairn, where the wall on the left curved outwards a little, making a shallow bay. A small pile of stones had been left here by water coming down the slope of the floor, and here she sat to wait for the coming magic and the People of the Sithean. It was damp and dark and cold.

The air smelt ancient, seeping through the tunnels from who-knew-what deserted and long-unlighted caves.

"Oh, no! It's the Elf Hill!" said Fenella, aloud, to give herself courage. "It's only that I'm not accustomed yet to the scent, and the sounds and colors—"

She shut her eyes and waited for these lovely things to drift into her senses. It did not surprise her much, however, to find that she was crying. Gradually a chill sense of terror swept over her. She sat bolt upright, hands pressed against the wet stones, and her eyes searching uselessly this way and that in the thick darkness, her ears strained to catch the slightest noise.

And she heard a muffled laugh.

She leapt to her feet. It was no good—Sithean or no Sithean—magic or none—dank darkness or bright jewels—she was going back to the open air. She ran down toward the unseen doorway, and screamed wildly as she heard other running footsteps; and several pairs of hands grabbed her and held her tightly. Then her own veil was wrapped thickly about her mouth, cutting off her cries for help.

She made a hopeless little struggle, and, for the second time in two nights, she sank down into converging blackness. And she was tossed carelessly over a ragged shoulder, and carried deep into the heart of the hill.

Behind her the door was barred with heavy baulks of wood jammed into sockets at either side. The cairn was sealed.

The ruined and roofless great keep was built of massive stones piled high into the air without mortar. Only their own weight had held them in position so long. They were stained with the rains of years, and blackened by the marks of fire. On their jagged tops, silhouetted against the stars, were clumps of weed carried by the birds who built nests in the ruin.

In one wall below there was a huge fireplace, with a nearly obliterated coat-of-arms carved above it. All that was left now was an eagle's outstretched wing, and part of a sword, and one word—"Honor"—nothing more. No one could read it now and say which chieftain had built his fortress by the shore, or which of his sons had surrendered it to destruction. Only the flagstones of the now-uneven floor, and the discolored blotches that smeared them, might have told a tale of defeat and treachery—but they had no tongue.

Black stumps here and there on the walls showed where once the floors had been of higher levels. People had lived here, laughed and slept, and quarreled and had their day. Now there were owls in the cracks and crevices, foxes and martens made their dens in the rubble on the ground, and humans far more savage than they had made the place their stronghold.

Opposite the fireplace was an arched doorway whose lintels were blackened by the flame and smoke of long ago. But the door was quite new, and strong, and had a latch of twisted bronze. In the third of the walls there had once been another door to a part of the fortress now utterly fallen away, and the doorway itself was nothing but a shapeless hole. Yet it was impassable. For a grille of thick metal bars covered it, making a barrier between the ruined hall of the keep and the world outside.

It was not at all a pleasant place. Even the red flicker of a pine torch in a cresset on the fireplace flank gave it no air of comfort.

Alasdair was fiddling with the latch on the door. He had been at this for some time, although it had long been borne in upon him that it was a useless task. He could not open it.

When he'd first gone crawling through the tunnel from the well, he had been so hedged about with anger that he had no thought of fear. But the anger had cooled and the fear had grown, the farther he went into the hill. At last he had found he could stand upright, though still he must bend his head under the arch of the roof. In the dark he stumbled constantly over rubble, and heaps of earth that had silted down through the cracks in the rock, and the places where tree roots had broken through into the tunnel. He felt suddenly weighed down with the knowledge of the hill above him, and all its solid mass, and age, and heaviness. Panic began to grip him.

For a little while it was touch-and-go whether he went crawling ignominiously back the way he had come, and so out into the well—to confess failure and cowardice. He stood trying to fight off his fears.

If this passage leads into the Sithean—he thought, and if the girl can venture in there—I can certainly go and get her out again!

And he went on, stumbling blindly through the dark, feeling his way with his hand along the rough wall. The smallest sound—water dripping—a stone rattling away under his foot—made his breath catch in his throat. His heart was beating very loudly and quickly. Alasdair was most unhappy. He kept remembering the way he had hidden in the Glen of Pines, and watched Ewen looking for him. He wished he had not been quite so successful. It would be nice to have the soldier with him now. He also remembered how often that same swordsman had suggested teaching him to use a blade left-handed.

Why did I refuse? he wondered. I must have been fey!

It would be nice to have a weapon now.

Ahead of him he heard a grunt, and a scuffling noise. He froze against the wall, and held his breath. Something was moving there in the dark. But after a few moments it seemed to have gone away. The boy crept forward with great caution to the place where the last sound had seemed to come from. And found there was a hole in the wall, about two feet high and not quite so wide.

"Whatever it was," he said to himself, "it wasn't human." This reassured him—until he thought it over.

It had, in fact, been a badger.

Once he came into a place where the walls opened outwards into quite a large cave. Cold air blew through it from some hole that could not be seen in the darkness. And there was a rushing sound of water from one side. Alasdair edged his way around the outside wall with the utmost care, fearing a chasm might be the water's path. It was a horrible place. There was a fetid smell; and a great cluster of bats, who lived there, suddenly took fright and flew about squeaking. This terrified Alasdair into forgetting everything and running blindly until he crashed into a rock-face, and winded himself. Just beside this was another tunnel entrance, and he hurried into it to escape the bats. They whirled around for a bit and then hung themselves up again and went to sleep.

Alasdair was going deeper and deeper into the hill, though he himself had no way to tell if he was even in the same passage all the time; there were so many side-turnings out of it, and it twisted so. Any of these other openings might have led him to disaster, for the hill minings were full of traps and pitfalls, but he was lucky. And every path ran into the heart of the hill— except one. It is unlikely that he would have found this one for himself.

It opened out of a broad gallery where once the miners had worked a rich seam of ore. And before he came anywhere near it, Alasdair walked into trouble. He walked into a ring of extremely hostile ruffians who were waiting for him.

These men were so used to the old mines that they could find their way through them at high speeds and without noise. The Bocan had given them their instructions, and Alasdair had actually had one or two behind him and ahead since his first ten minutes in the passages.

Now they held him, twisting his arm behind him until he feared to hear the bone crack; until he cried out in pain. Unlike Fergus's cattle thieves, these had no fear of a wing. They laughed at it.

They marched him through a maze of tunnels, into the broad gallery, and so to a narrow passage, square-built in blocks of stone. At the far end was a stout door; and they pushed it open, and threw Alasdair into the hall of the ruined keep. And they left him there, and slammed the door, and went to report to their master.

The boy had searched frantically for a means of escape. Without two hands, no one could have climbed the walls or the chimney. The bars over the broken doorway were immovable. The latch on the other door was fastened from the outside. Alasdair had found, however, some flint and steel and a twist of tinder, laid carefully on a battered wooden stool, and he had set light to a torch on the wall. It smoked abominably, and smelt awful, but it was better than the cold gray moonlight that set an even more haunted look on that ancient, unlucky fortress.

By the torchlight, Alasdair could see other things.

Several stools, and a tree trunk that was halved and set on strong wooden legs to make a bench. A table of rough planks. A pile of rotting straw at one side, and some torn and stinking pieces of cloth lying tangled there, as though it had been used as a bed. Varying lengths of wet rope. A few cracked bowls on the table. He wondered how often this place was used as a prison.

It was almost a relief when the Bocan came.

The door creaked and moved, and Alasdair sprang toward it. But the Bocan slid in while it was still ajar. There was a brief, unsoothing glimpse of faces beyond in the passage— tangles of unkempt hair and beard—ragged, half-clad, savage-looking men—and the door was shut. Alasdair looked at the Bocan, who cowered away from him slightly and said, "Be careful! Stand back! If you touch me, it will be your doom!"

"It could be yours!" said Alasdair.

He took a pace toward the other, and the Bocan gave a shrill cry. There was a shout from outside, and the door opened again and a brutal face looked in.

"Well?" said the Bocan to Alasdair, with deep venom. "Shall

my men tie you? Or will you speak courteously with me, and keep your hands—your *hand*," he amended, grinning, "unbound?"

There was little choice. Alasdair turned from him and went to the barred gap in the other wall, and stood there looking out; at a level stretch of ground, heaped with the fallen stones of the castle; at the steep drop to the loch beyond. Behind him, the Bocan was muttering to his man, who went away again. Then the gloating voice rose, and Alasdair knew he was going to be baited.

"You're trapped," said the Bocan, "and the Spaewife gave you plenty warning, so it's all your own fault! There's no way that you can escape from here, for it's my dungeon as well as my keep, and I've held many others—some for ransom, some for vengeance—and none has ever broken free!"

He went over to the great empty fireplace, and turned to peer at Alasdair again.

"I have been lord of this stronghold for many a long year," said he, with pride, "and many a man has come here to call me chief and master. Kinrowan would be glad to know of it," and he laughed loudly. "Does he think Fergus MacIaian is responsible for every stirk that he loses? Does Fergus think that all his go to Kinrowan's hands? Why, every chief and lordling for many miles—each thinks the others have raided him—and my people eat well!"

Alasdair did not reply, or turn, and the Bocan adopted a reproving tone.

"Do speak to me," said he. "I am, after all, your host."

"Where is Fenella?" said Alasdair, unmoving.

"Who knows?" said the Bocan.

And this brought Alasdair around fast enough.

"You said—!"

"I said she was somewhere in the hill. No doubt she is so. But just exactly where—at this precise moment—"

The young man almost choked with resentment. He said, thickly, "I'd like to kill you!"

The Bocan chuckled.

"You have not the means," said he. "The touch of a feather is no threat. There is my magic to protect me—and my men outside that door! I have also two strong hands. You can't harm me, my hero!"

He sat himself down in a high-backed chair, that had one broken arm and some tatters of velvet clinging still to its sides and back. Here he slumped comfortably, dangling his short legs in their sheepskin wrappings. He folded his hands across his stomach and showed his yellow teeth in a broad, pleased smile.

"I do hope you've taken that in," said he.

"And I," said Alasdair, "hope you will take this in—that the stroke of a swan's wing can break the leg of a man! It's not a helpless bird, not a meek one!"

This thought had just occurred and it startled him. He was so used to thinking himself disabled and unarmed.

"And why should I fear your magic?" he added. "What more can you do than has been done already? I would rather be a swan—a toad—than crawl to you."

Again it surprised him, to hear himself say it. A sense of power began to grow in him, and angry excitement. This the Bocan saw, and it disturbed him greatly. He half-rose in his chair.

"I'll call my men!" he gabbled. "And then—there's the lady—Fenella—"

This had some of the effect he hoped. It halted Alasdair.

"What of Lady Fenella?" he said, fiercely.

"If you ever wish to see her again—"

"How can I?" snapped the young man, scowling at him. "If I am held here by you and your ruffians—and she is with Those of the Sithean—"

The Bocan blinked.

"The Sithean? Oh, ah—yes, of course. Yet I can bring her out of Their hands and into mine, if I so choose. I—I have dealings with Them."

But his eyes slid nervously sideways as he said it.

"I have sent my men to Them, even now," he hurried on, "asking that she shall be handed over. Telling her you are here. Giving her your message—your appeal for help—"

"My appeal!" cried Alasdair. "My appeal for help—to a girl!"

The Bocan tittered at him.

"Oh, forgive me?" he said. "I took you for the sort of person who begs help from everyone!"

Then he shrank back into his chair as the young man advanced on him. He raised his flabby hands and waved them warningly.

"I'll call! I'll call!" he yelped. "Remember what I said! Your life is in my hands, mo bhalach, and I'm not forbearing by nature. I've no great liking for you, anyway. So far I have only spared you as bait!"

Alasdair stared at him. The Bocan gave another of his nervous, high-pitched cackles of laughter. His ugly little eyes were bright with malice and fear. He repeated his last words, looking into the puzzled eyes of Alasdair.

"Just for bait. Or—a bribe. To make the young Fenella easier to handle. So that she will obey me."

He drew a deep breath, and said loudly, "So that she will stay here as my bride."

The shock on Alasdair's face annoyed him, and he shouted angrily, "Why not? Why not, then?"

It annoyed him even more to see that handsome head go back as Alasdair began to laugh. It was a sound not often heard in that grim ruin. And the more insulting as it was perfectly sincere amusement. The Bocan heaved himself to his feet, shaking his fists in frenzied rage.

"Stop it! I'll call in my men! I'll have you tortured to death!"

"Your bride!" said Alasdair through his laughter. "Are you crazed? Can you see Fenella as your bride?"

"Can you see her as yours?"

Alasdair stopped laughing. He tried to say something and failed. He turned his face aside, muttering that at least she was human.

"Much good that will do her—among humans!" And the Bocan sat down again, glaring at him. "Will they accept her as one? Are you sure that you do?"

A confused sort of struggle was going on inside Alasdair's head. After a few moments, he lifted a straight gaze to the gloating face of the Bocan. He said in a cold voice, "You want me to humble myself, to beg you for mercy. I'll do so. I'll offer you my life—my service—anything—if you will release the girl, now. Not bring her here—"

"I had not imagined you in so chivalrous a light," the Bocan told him, softly.

"Gibe away. But I want a civil answer!"

The Bocan drew up his knees in the big chair, and hugged them.

"It's for you to be civil," said he. "Surely, my prospective servant—and that *is* your suggestion, is it not?—must prove very civil and sober, and submissive."

The alliteration pleased him, and he cackled.

"There was a condition to my offer," said Alasdair.

"Yes. But what if the lady won't accept such a sacrifice?"

The young man's temper slipped again, and he said forcibly, "She will not be asked! Nor brought here at all! If you can take her from the Sithean, as you say, you'll set her free in the world again. Not bring her to this foul lair, to be mocked by a repulsive, venomous and disgusting brute!"

Not very tactful. The Bocan's face went dark-crimson, and his thick neck swelled alarmingly. He banged his hands against his chair, and gave a shrill yell. The door creaked open, and Alasdair turned quickly to face the new threat.

Fenella came into the keep, and the door was shut again.

She walked dazedly and blindly, with outstretched hands. Her veil had been wound so closely around her face that she could see nothing. Alasdair ran to her, and took her hand, and said in a tone of the utmost censure, "You are the maddest girl I've ever met! How do you get into these situations?"

She gasped aloud. She had been loosening her veil, and now she held it more tightly against her face. Through it she stared at Alasdair. It was only a few minutes ago she had recovered consciousness, and she wondered if she was still in a daze of faintness. He was the last person she had expected to see. But it was certainly Alasdair, and his hand was warm and strong on hers.

"I—well, I just went into the cairn—" she faltered.

"A place people avoid! Yet you walked in there without a thought!"

"I *did* think," and she rallied slightly, to defend herself.

"Ha!" said he, and then he added, with a sort of boyish curiosity that brought a little smile to the girl's pale lips, "What was it like in the hill?"

"Dark," said she, simply.

And she went and sat down rather dizzily on one of the stools. She had not yet noticed the Bocan, for Alasdair was between them, and her recovering mind was concentrated on him, and on his presence here in the hill.

"Did you see Those Ones?" he asked.

"I saw some tattered and brutal-looking men, when I stopped being—"

Then she noticed the Bocan, for he yelled at her in fury, "My clan! Outlaws—escaped thieves and gallows-fruit! Land-less and leaderless men, who have taken refuge here. Fine fellows, mine, but unused to gentle company."

"They can be nothing much," said Alasdair, "to take *you* for a leader! A decent thief would be ashamed!"

The Bocan began to shout something at him, and broke off suddenly. He went rigid in his chair, and then yelled at the top of his voice, "Ciod tha sin!"

The others turned to look where his pale eyes were staring—at the door. And after a moment, Alasdair said, "Well, *what* is it?"

The Bocan had got to his feet, and now he lifted his paws in a curious gesture toward his head, and shook them there very quickly, as though there were waves coming from the inside of it—waves that carried sounds to which he was lis-tening. The lids came down over his eyes, and his big mouth hung half-open. He looked more revolting than ever.

"There's a stranger in the hill—" he slavered.

And his voice rose to another bellow.

"I feel him in my mind! Walking the tunnels of the hill—coming closer—coming near! Where are my men? Stop him! Ah—ah—they fear him! Why? Why? Why should they be afraid?"

His eyes sprang open, and he licked his lips, and a horrid look of pleasure crossed his face. He lumbered quickly over to the door, and turned there to say to Alasdair, "It may be your soldier. I hope so. I'd like to get him into my hands. He'll be hard to break—and yet I know how to set about it!"

"You won't get the chance," said Alasdair. "He's safe at Kinrowan."

"Pity!" said the Bocan.

He gave a whinnying sort of screech, and the door opened. He shot through as soon as the aperture was wide enough, and Alasdair got there too late to stop it from closing. In fact, he jerked his hand back only just in time to prevent it being crushed. Fenella gave a small cry of alarm, and Alasdair surveyed her rather ruefully, and spoke in gentler tones.

"My grief!" said he. "I've led you out in a fine reel!"

"I chose to dance," said the girl.

He eyed her nervously for a moment, and then went over to the Bocan's chair, and put his hand on the rotted velvet of its back. He said, "Fenella—I'm not very good at saying— but I'm sorry—about everything—"

She waited rather hopefully, but he said no more. Nor did he look at her again. She gave a soundless sigh, and went across the littered flagstones—with the green stains of rain and damp on them, and those other stains, less innocent—and she sat down on the long bench. She said gravely, "Was it nice, being a swan?"

He stiffened, but did not turn.

"No one has ever asked me that," he said.

"Perhaps they feared to," she told him. "But I am sure they wished to know—those who—love you."

And now he did look at her. With a sort of eagerness to share a cherished memory.

"It was fine," he said. "To be free! With no memories to torture the mind—nothing to regret—"

"No wish to be human?" she asked.

"We never thought about it, until Agnes found us and made us remember!"

He swung away to the fireplace, and struck his hand hard against its surround, and cried bitterly, "If only she had let us be!"

Fenella rose and went across to him in a swift, graceful movement, and her hands were outstretched—but not to touch him. She stopped before she reached him, and let her hands drop to her sides. He had leaned his head against the damp, gray stone, and she just stood looking at him for a moment or two. Then she said, very gently, "Were your brothers sorry to go home? To lift twenty years of grief from your father? To begin their own lives as men?"

She thought he had not heard. But at last he straightened himself slowly, and said, "I was thinking of myself only," and then added, apparently to the blank stone in front of him, "You make me feel ashamed."

She took a very small pace closer.

"It's not so terrible to have a wing," said she. "And it's such a beautiful one."

And still he would not face her.

"Is it?" he said. "I think it's grotesque! Beautiful on a swan perhaps—"

"If you think it grotesque, you make it so," said the girl. "You have such a great imagination."

She was teasing him, and it brought his head around quickly. A slow and unwilling smile curled the corners of his mouth, and affectionate amusement dawned in his eyes. He said, "You're laughing at me without unkindness! And it doesn't rankle. That's something else no one but you can do."

Then he added, casually, "You should never leave me for an instant! If you married me—"

"Alasdair!" she whispered.

"—you could be always veiled," said he.

She gave a heart-stricken little cry, and covered her face with her hands. He, breaking off abruptly, stared at her in surprise, and then said anxiously, "Have I offended you?"

She dropped wearily into the high chair.

"So near!" she murmured. "So near—!"

Alasdair was honestly unable to think what he had said that upset her so. He stood in front of her and wrinkled his brow.

"Don't be afraid," he said, "it wouldn't be difficult. I'm sure I could get quite used to the veil in time."

There was a funny little sound from the girl, half a laugh and half a sob. She gasped, and then said, "Alasdair, tell me the truth. How dreadful is my face?"

"Have you seen it?" said he, cautiously.

She nodded.

"I looked in a pool."

"Well," and he was choosing his words with care now, "it isn't exactly dreadful—just unexpected."

She cried out, and then jumped up and ran to the barred gap in the wall, and put her hands on the bars and her head on her hands. She was in much the same attitude as that adopted by Alasdair a little earlier at the fireplace. And, as she had done then, he took a few paces toward her. But he stopped sooner.

"Er—Fenella—I—"

"Don't speak for a minute!" said she, in a muffled voice.

He bit his thumbnail, and looked at her in some perplexity. He was perfectly prepared to apologize most humbly, as soon as he had some idea of what had distressed her. But before anyone could say any more, the door flew open. And the shrill yell of the Bocan echoed into the keep, "Throw him in there! Trespasser! Spy!"

Someone hurtled in, to crash full length on the flagstones. The Bocan came flouncing in, and the door slammed shut.

"I might have guessed," shouted the Bocan, furiously, "that *you* would be the one!"

13. *THE WAKING OF THE SWAN*

The man on the floor lay quite still. He looked like a bundle of broken sticks, thrown down carelessly and abandoned. His limbs sprawled as awkwardly as though they were disjointed, and his head was half-hidden under the high twist of his shoulders and back. He was clutching a handful of golden leaves.

Fenella gave a cry, and ran to kneel beside him.

"Hudart!"

Almost at the same moment, Alasdair reached him, and he dropped on his knees and lifted the old man to lie against his breast. The young people looked at one another in dismay, over the white hair of the bard; and through the fine silk veil that hid her face, Alasdair saw Fenella's eyes glinting jewel-yellow, and the curiously inhuman shape of her forehead. But he did not truly notice these things at the moment.

"Is he—?" Fenella's voice was only a thread of sound.

"I don't think so," said the boy.

And the Bocan said, "No. Death is not for him and his like!"

And he went to the little group on the floor, and stood looking at them with strong antipathy.

"Only stunned," said he, "and serve him right! He frightened my men, by telling them he saw their end coming near! When

they found courage to seize him, they were less gentle than
they might otherwise have been!"

Alasdair looked at him. And there was neither anger nor
hatred in the boy's dark eyes now. Only a sort of contemptuous
wonder. And it made the Bocan flinch. Alsadair said, quietly,
"You must be very proud of your people's courage."

The old bard of Kinrowan stirred, and opened his eyes. He
blinked at Fenella, and then at Alasdair, and smiled a little.
And he saw the Bocan. He made a feeble attempt to rise, and
Alasdair got to his feet and lifted the bard with him. Hudart
was so light and frail that it was no effort, even with one arm.
He led Hudart across the room to the bench, and let him sink
down on it. And Fenella ran to sit by his side, and put her arm
about him.

"Oh, my two dears—" said Hudart.

The Bocan was muttering and glaring, and now he broke
out, pointing a finger accusingly at the old man.

"You!" he snarled. "Prying out the secret ways into my
keep! You were always a sly, tricky fellow—but you've taken
too great a chance, this time! It's easier to come in here than
to get out again."

He set his arms akimbo, and added sneeringly, "Well? This
is my stronghold. You've found it. Do you like it?"

"There's a shocking draft," murmured Hudart.

"No roof," said Alasdair.

A faint smile crossed the bard's tired face.

"One can feel that," said he.

The Bocan bared his great yellow teeth. He was not used
to this sort of thing. It was so seldom anyone found anything
amusing about his residence.

"The place grows on you!" he shouted. "And I can turn
people into moss and lichen—so they grow on it!"

Hudart laughed. And the Bocan marched over to the big
chair by the fireplace, and threw himself into it, where he
huddled and glared. He wracked his brain for some gibe—
some sting—that would bring his prisoners to heel, and to a
proper appreciation of their position. He said suddenly, "You
with the wing—you have told the lady what honor I pro-
pose—?"

"Hold your tongue!" said Alasdair.

He spoke with such authority that he got a quick look from

Hudart. But the Bocan was annoyed. He opened his mouth to say so, and Alasdair spoke first, standing between the Bocan and the others.

"Let us have no more of your silly threats," said he. "You must let these two go."

"Must? That's no word to use to me! You're over-bold, and it's a change in you! Yet watch your manners, boy. I've warned you!" and he tittered, and grinned at them all. "You have come walking into my territory," said he, "like silly flies to a web. And you have just their chance to evade the spider! It's madness to irritate me, when all you have and are lie at my mercy."

He got up restlessly, and padded over to the chimney-breast, and then to the table that stood near. He was striking the knuckles of his hands together, and grinding his teeth, as though he sought an outlet in violence for his rage. He picked up a dirt-encrusted wooden bowl, and threw it against a wall, so that it fell in two halves. And he brushed a couple of platters viciously to the floor, where they also broke. He scowled at Alasdair.

"I can treat you the same!" said he. "I need no bait—no bribe for the lady! Force will suffice."

And he turned his alarming face upon Fenella and said harshly, "Mistress, whatever I do with these others, you will stay here as the lady of the Black Keep."

Hudart gave a little groan, and clutched his hand tightly on the rowan spray. And Alasdair took a deep breath of rage, but Fenella spoke first.

"Are you joking?" she said.

The Bocan gave a howl of fury.

"How dare you! Never in all my—! I'll call in my men, and—! Oh, I'll make you pay for that—insult—!"

The girl rose to face him, but found that she was trembling. The murderous frenzy that blazed from the Bocan's pale eyes was most terrible to see. She put a hand to her face, and, seeing this, he gave a mad yell of laughter.

"Yes, yes, remember what you are!" he shrieked. "Few would take you! You'll be better off with me, hidden from the world and all its cruel sneers—"

"Hidden?" said Hudart, unexpectedly. "How long will this place stay hidden, when Kinrowan hears of its existence? He will bring the clan and smoke you out!"

The Bocan gave him a sideways glare of triumphant malice.

"Kinrowan!" he scoffed. "Will that fine gentleman dare to move against me, while you three are in my hands? Oh, I dare swear the Spaewife—poor Marjorie—will run to him. But I have hostages here. And he will not know whether alive or dead—or something in between!"

"I will stay," said Fenella. "I'll do all you wish, if you will not harm Alasdair and Hudart."

"Fenella!" cried Alasdair, in outraged horror.

But her eyes never shifted their steady gaze from the Bocan.

"Can you give Alasdair his right arm?" she said.

"I might," said he.

Alasdair marched across to Fenella and stood between her and the Bocan. And that one backed a little from the look on his face.

"You both talk rubbish!" snapped Alasdair.

"Yes," said Hudart, and caught the Bocan's glare, and added rather weakly, "Well, you do."

And he got stiffly to his feet, and limped over the littered floor to the girl.

"Nothing can ever be done about that wing," he said, "and that's all there is to it. Do you think the Lady Agnes has not tried? Do you think I haven't? It was stupid of me to let you think there was a chance—but I was hoping for another kind of magic. Don't be taken in again. The Bocan is not the great sorcerer you suppose."

"Be quiet, hunchback!" shrilled the Bocan.

Hudart gave him a curiously pitying glance.

"His malice is more terrible than his magic," said he.

The Bocan lost his temper. He ran lumberingly across to the door, and dragged at the great metal latch. He twisted it this way and that, forgetting in his rage that it could not be moved from outside. Forgetting even to call to his men to move it. As he chittered and mumbled to himself, Hudart went on speaking.

"A twisted mind that elects to live apart—desiring power over men who have mocked his ugliness—might find some elementary magic. To read men's thoughts—to put thoughts into men—"

The Bocan turned, crouched like a wild beast. He shouted something incoherent, and Hudart gave him a strange smile.

"Will you kill me, then?" he said.

There was a sudden silence, and the old bard was still smiling. Then the Bocan said, "Magic may not destroy magic."

"Exactly," said Hudart. "You dare not even try. For if I can die—so can you!"

Another silence fell. Fenella and Alasdair were held quiet by the battle of wills that seemed to be taking place. And at last, the Bocan said in a voice that hissed like a snake, and dripped venom like one, "Even though I cannot kill it, I can have your twisted body twisted more dreadfully! You jeer at my ugliness—what of your deformity!"

"I was not jeering," said Hudart.

And indeed, the old man was looking at him with sadness, standing awkwardly with crooked limbs and the hump between his shoulders—and there was great beauty about him as he pitied his enemy. Fenella felt a rush of tears, and she said sobbingly, "Bocan, I have offered—"

But the creature she addressed was half-insane with rage.

"There's no offering—no choice—no mercy for any of you, now!" he yelled. "The boy dies—not quickly! The hunchback will lie in chains here forever! And you—"

He shrieked with dreadful laughter. Alasdair moved quickly toward him, and he gave the wild yell that summoned his men.

"I am the Bocan!" he shouted, then. "My fortress is the haunted keep! My lairs are in the hill. In the Sithean! I am a sorcerer—Lord of the Hill—enemy to men—"

His voice had risen to a mad skirling, and his three prisoners stared at him in horror. There was certainly very little that was human about him at the moment. He screamed for his men again. He was foaming, and beating his hands against his sides.

"Not one shall escape!" he howled on. "Not one shall get out! Never get out! Nev—!"

His yell broke off in mid-word as the door was flung open. He shrieked again to his men.

But it was Ewen who stood alone in the doorway. His sgian was bare in his hand, and he stabbed it deep into the lintel beside him.

"Neither can you, Bocan," he said.

And into the sudden silence, his voice rang clear and cold, "You cannot pass the steel."

For a moment no one moved. Then the Bocan plunged

forward. Ewen stepped aside, and the Bocan slithered to a halt and stared at the dirk. Hudart said, almost whispering, "If you can, you prove yourself human. No sorcerer can go past it."

The Bocan looked back at him. Then he looked at Alasdair. He looked at the girl. He looked at the soldier. He put out his hand toward the black and guardless hilt of the little knife, and just before touching it, he snatched his hand away as though it had been singed. He stood hesitating and grimacing. Then he half-reached out again, and again drew back. He turned and stared at Ewen with swollen and bloodshot eyes, glazed from his recent fury. He hissed through loosened lips, "How did you pass my people?"

"You keep a poor watch on your tunnels," said the other, severely. "The only guards were outside here—they had even left torches alight to show me the way! And—you have fewer people than you did."

He looked so calm, thought Fenella, standing there easily as though he was in no sort of danger, and had not fought his way through to them. But she also saw the battle light, and caught her breath. He knew the danger well enough.

The Bocan suddenly gave a savage laugh. He said, gratingly, "You! Macrinan! Are you so brazen that you'll risk hearing again the 'Coirefuil'—the song of the price of blood!"

"Sing it to me later," suggested Ewen, coolly.

Hudart said something below his breath, and turned a searching look on him. And the Bocan gaped and spluttered, and then said, "Have you no shame at all?"

"Not when I'm busy, said the mercenary.

He then turned to the others, and said briskly, "Come now. While the men I scattered are collecting their friends and their wits—let us be going."

"You took them by surprise!" gabbled the Bocan.

"I did, indeed!"

Ewen strode across to him, and the creature shrank from him. The soldier put a hand on his shoulder and said forcefully, "Now you shall come for a stroll through the hill with us. Let one of your creatures lift a finger—and we'll test the strength of your magic against the keenness of my sgian! You are a hostage for—"

The Bocan turned his head as swiftly as an adder's strike,

and bit the other on the wrist. As Ewen slackened his hold for a second, the Bocan wrenched himself free and scuttled frantically across the room, over the hearth, and into the fireplace. He reached to the inner side of the chimney and dragged at a jut of stone—and a set of metal bars, like those which sealed the gap in the other wall, came clashing down behind the chimney-breast.

The Bocan began to dance up and down, grimacing in angry glee. He shouted, "There are many ways for me to leave the keep! That's slowed you down, a churaidh!"

"You look like a monkey in a cage," said Ewen.

The dancing ceased.

"You're in the cage, my buckie!" yelled the Bocan. "Try if you can get out! My men will be rallying now, and wanting you—badly! And where's your hostage? Go out to them, with your little black knife, and these three to cling to you and hamper you—an old man, a girl, and a one-handed changeling!"

Ewen's expression did not change. Probably only Fenella noticed the small tightening at the corners of his lips. The Bocan was looking pleased with himself. He said, "If I were merely human, I'd call my men in now, and that would be the finish for you all. But I am the Bocan! And this is how I mean to deal with you—"

He slowly widened his slack lips in a horrible grin, and said very slowly and impressively, "One life shall pay for all. Three shall go free from the keep. The fourth shall die. Decide which one. And send him out to me by that door—unarmed, and unresisting."

He pointed to the open doorway, with the knife in the lintel.

"We will be waiting," he said.

And then he swung the pointing finger toward the broken, barred, arch in the other wall.

"When those bars lift," said he, "you will know that my price is paid."

Alasdair had been watching and listening with a feeling of inertia that was only too familiar to him. Ewen had come, and Ewen was now in charge, and Ewen would tell him what to do, and when to do it, and Ewen would settle everything safely. Now he suddenly gave a gasp, and shook his head violently.

Ewen had done enough! Alasdair strode across to the fireplace
and spoke harshly to the Bocan.

"I've already offered you my life!" said he.

"How selfish you are!" said the Bocan, smiling dreadfully
at him. "Let those you love have some chance to show their
courage, too. And—take my warning—hurry your decision,
lest my men grow too impatient to abide the issue!"

He turned to the side of the chimney, and leaned his weight
hard against a sharp edge of the stone. And it turned on a pivot,
and showed a low black hole. The Bocan, cackling to himself,
dropped to his knees and wriggled rapidly through. When he
was out of sight, the stone swung back into place.

Ewen went over quickly to test the bars. But they were
solid, and hardly gave at all when he shook them hard.

"Can't we fight our way out of here?" Alasdair asked him.

The soldier gave him a brief glance, shook his head, and
turned away. Though not actually scornful, it was a look that
dimissed the boy as though he was of no importance at all. A
look that always galled Alasdair, but now roused a deep anger
and pain in him.

Men were gathering outside that open door, just out of sight
in the dark; the whispering and shuffling, clinking weapons,
and nervous muttering told of a fair number. The Bocan's clan
had rallied, whether or not he had gone to collect and rouse
them.

"Which way did you come?" said Hudart to the soldier.

"From the well. The Spaewife showed me—"

"I thought Ranald—?"

"He did, but I got away."

"Ewen," said Alasdair, "what did the Bocan mean about
the song of the price—?"

But Ewen had turned his back and was surveying the walls
of the keep. Alasdair glowered at him, and caught Hudart's
eye, and subsided a bit. But he was still feeling very cross.
The bard put his arm around Fenella, and drew her over to the
bench. They sat down quietly, and the old man said, "He will
not accept my life, I fear."

"Of course not. I knew what you were, from the first," she
told him, gravely.

"Did you, my darling? Fine luck I brought you all with my
meddling!"

Alasdair said bitterly, "I brought the ill-luck. And it's my right to pay for it."

"We're not listening to you," said Fenella.

"Then do so!" he snapped.

He came over and thumped himself down at her side. He told her it was useless to argue. And while they argued, Hudart left them and went over to Ewen by the doorway, where he stood listening to the uneasy movements outside.

"No way to get through?" said the bard, under his breath.

The other glanced at him, and said flatly, "None. Can you climb those walls—forty feet up and down again? Can she? Can Alasdair?"

Then he lowered his voice, and said, "I sent old Marjorie to the castle, to call out the clan. They will move fast. But they'll not attack until I give a signal that we're safe."

Hudart stared at him with anxiously furrowed face, and said softly, "What like signal—?"

"Hudart," said Ewen, "when those bars lift—and he *will* lift them, just so that you will know—"

He broke off for an instant, and then went on, very rapidly, and very softly, "Don't go far outside this place. He'll honor his promise, and let you from the keep—but outside he will be waiting. How could he let anyone go free, carrying the secret of his lairs? Go just beyond the bars, so that they can't trap you in this place, and wait for Kinrowan. The signal will bring him. And the Bocan's lot will have their hands too full to bother with you."

Hudart looked at him for a moment, and then let the lids fall over his suddenly sorrowful eyes, and bent his head.

"I understand you," he said, in a whisper.

Both men turned and looked at the boy and the girl, and the bard saw them through a blur, but Ewen was merely thoughtful.

Their argument seemed to have gathered force. Fenella had jumped to her feet, and Alasdair had grabbed her hand to keep her listening to his views. He was now saying, "Do not talk rubbish, girl!"

And she said in a tone of extreme exasperation, "My sorrow! How can a wing be worse than a toad's head?"

"Don't squabble," said Ewen. "The choice was made long since."

Alasdair turned on him, and said curtly, "By whom?"

Ewen lifted an eyebrow at his tone of voice, but he said mildly enough, "Who knows?"

And the young man jumped up and caught his arm—even at that moment he remembered to catch the right arm and not the left—and he said quietly, but biting off the words, "Ewen—listen to me. Just for once, you will take my orders. Is that clear? You will escort Fenella and Hudart back to Kinrowan castle. And I want no further argument with any of you," he ended.

"The decision does not lie with you," said the mercenary, rather wearily. "The Spaewife heard the piper—"

"*What* piper?"

Ewen shook his head, and Alasdair jerked at his arm impatiently.

"I'll accept no more of your protection," said he, "nor will I be treated as a child. I'm a grown man—"

"Good," said the other, and turned away.

But he found himself held and swung back to face Alasdair.

"Take me seriously!" demanded that young man, fiercely. "My father bought your sword and put it in my service. Now, in his name, I release you! Leave me, and go."

"If you dismiss me," said the mercenary, "you have no further right to command me."

Alasdair gave an exasperated cry, "Dhia! Can't you understand! I'm staying here because I am already maimed, and—"

"*I* am staying here," said Fenella, "because I am—loathsome."

"Mo bhroin! How you two harp on your small drawbacks!"

Ewen spoke explosively, and he jerked his arm free, and strode over to the fireplace and caught tight hold of the velvet chair-back, and it broke between his hands. He threw the rotten wood on the floor, and turned stormily on Alasdair. And that one said quickly, "Ewen, you know what I think about myself."

"And you know what I think about your thoughts!" Ewen had quite suddenly and unexpectedly lost his temper. "I've tried always to remember that you only had five years as a human being—and three of those as a baby—"

This took Fenella by surprise. She had not realized the soldier had so worked it out. Now he was rushing on, "It's time you showed a glimmer of sense!" he said, angrily. "It's not your fault you have a wing—and it's no' a virtue either! You make a stick of it, to break over people's heads. You're a coward, to hide from life with your head under your wing!"

Alasdair went over to him in a rush, and Ewen laughed at him harshly across the broken chair. The young man stared at him with narrowed eyes.

"If I had two hands—!" he said, between his teeth.

"I wouldna take your challenge if you had six! You're not worth the fighting!"

Fenella gave a choked gasp. And Hudart went to her, and put a hand on her shoulder to keep her still. She gave him a small nod. She would not interfere. And she remembered how once she had wished to have Alasdair challenge his swordsman. He did not seem to be having much success with it.

Yet he was not entirely crushed. He had flushed darkly at Ewen's taunt, but now he said in a very cold and level voice, "Are *you?* You can scorn people and fleer at them—and you're good at keeping secrets, but—what did you see in the well, Macrinan?"

14. *SON OF THE ISLAND*

The silence seemed stifling. Fenella made an abrupt movement and felt Hudart's palm press gently on her shoulder. She shrank nearer to him, clasping her hands tightly together.

Ewen, staring at Alasdair, said very bleakly, "You choose this way to challenge me?"

The young man nodded. He looked indeed as though he had thrown a gauntlet on the floor between them.

"Since you're so lofty about any other sort," he said coldly.

He had gone very white, and the muscles were ridged around his mouth. There was nothing unsteady or faltering about him, now. He was stern and quite uncompromising. And the most surprising thing of all was the glint in his eyes—the battle glint shining there. Seeing all this, Ewen's own face went as hard as stone. But there was no answering gleam from him. His eyes were blank and gray.

"I don't have to answer you," said he.

"Do you not? I have the right to know what manner of man wears my tartan."

This brought a slight derisive twist to the older man's mouth.

He said, "I wear it for my ability, not my character!"

But he was watching Alasdair all the time as though he faced a stranger. And one who held a sword. After a moment, he said, "Very well then."

But he seemed not quite sure how to go on. He shifted his weight from one foot to the other, still watching Alasdair. He took a long shaken breath.

"You have called me by my name," said he. "It's one I may not ever use myself, for I lost the right—twenty-five years ago—"

But he was not quite as impassive as he tried to sound, for he suddenly caught his lip between his teeth, and looked away. It cost him an obvious effort to bring his head around again and face his inquisitor.

Fenella said, under her breath, to Hudart, "Oh, he should not be made to speak!"

And only just heard the soft whispered answer, "It's his choice. Hush."

All of a sudden it seemed as though Ewen was a very long way away from them all, with a great gulf between. He looked lonely there. Alasdair felt his anger drain away, and put out his hand toward the other man. If the soldier noticed this gesture it only made him move further off in body as well as mind. He went to the fireplace, and stared at the empty hearth. Then he said, in a level voice, "When I was sixteen, I went hunting with some men of my clan. I lost them in a mountain mist, miles from home, and went wandering half the night—"

Fenella ached with sympathy. His choice or not, he had been brought to bay. Once more, the girl was looking back through time to a place that was far away and long ago.

She saw clearly the young lad running lightly on the hills, looking for his friends. The wet mist forming into drops on his face and his bright hair. A boy with a name. And then—the stumble on a steep brae, and him rolling over and over to the bottom—to the men who were suddenly all around him—to the hands that seized him.

"The clan that was a bitter blood-feud with mine," Ewen was saying.

Recognizing him they had been delighted, and hauled him off to their chieftain and dropped him at the old man's feet. A better prize than the deer they had been after.

"And fine they knew what *I'd* been after!" said Ewen.

For the boy was far from his home, in enemy territory, and they would not believe he had come alone. They asked many questions. And for a long time. In the end, the chieftain said, "They'll hide somewhere through the day, and drive my cattle tomorrow night. Where will they hide?"

Alasdair gave a startled exclamation in the smoky gloom of the ruined keep.

"Did he think you'd tell them that?"

"He described vividly what would happen to me if I did not."

Fenella could not keep silent. She said in a shaking voice, "Did they hurt you?"

"Scarcely," said Ewen, "for I told them."

"You couldn't." This was Alasdair, and with great conviction.

Ewen cast him an odd glance across his shoulder that was almost affectionate. He turned around, and set his back against the wall. Not just a creature at bay, thought the girl—but a man who would always prefer to face what was coming to him.

"I invented a hidingplace," he said. "An unlikely sort of a lair, a corrie with a rock at the foot shaped like a sleeping dog—and I described this in detail to the chieftain. I planned to escape while he was mustering his fighters—to get home—bring out the rest of my clan—I thought we could ambush the—"

He stopped abruptly, and put his head back against the stone behind him. It seemed wrong to look at his face then, and yet they did. Fenella saw him through tears. But Alasdair was watching him with great intensity. The mercenary went on speaking, but he hardly knew he spoke aloud. He was dredging deep into his own heart, for things that had been hidden there too long.

"They did not let me escape. They took me with them—to the place I had described! The stone like the sleeping dog—the corrie on the hill—the place where my men had chosen to hide. And they made me watch. And after—they allowed me to go. They let me go home—to tell them—"

To tell his people. To tell his Chief, his clan, the remnants of that betrayed hunting party, the kinsmen of those who had not come home.

"To tell them how I talked to save my skin. Because I was afraid," said Ewen.

There was utter silence then. Until Ewen said the words that none of the others would speak.

"Too strange a coincidence—to imagine a place that was real! Of course I must have heard them arrange it—and conveniently forgot that I had heard—"

"You are not sure of that!" cut in Alasdair, quickly.

"I've tried not to be sure. But in my heart I know—I know," said Ewen. "I was afraid to be hurt—and I saw my men die! I saw the faces of my people when they heard."

They had given him a boat to reach the mainland—and one hour's start. At the last, his Chief had looked at him searingly and said, "Return to the island when you die—if you die in honor, which I doubt."

And his son had bent his head, and gone into exile.

"I rowed over the Sound," he was saying, now, "and waited on the hill for those who followed. But they guessed what I'd do, and turned back. Perhaps because they wouldn't let me off so lightly—perhaps to give me the chance of an honest death—I don't know."

Fenella said in a very small voice, "Had you no friends to plead for you?"

"They were lying in a corrie, far away. And if they had sent their spirits, what could they say but that I was rightly judged—and guilty!"

He went on in a rush, as though he must say what he had to say even if it broke him. He was very near the end of his tether.

"I set a smear on the name I must no longer bear. Put a sword into the hands of enemies—a fleering song on their lips—!" And he laughed, a very desolate sound. "My men used to sing it sometimes, when I had command of mercenaries in the Low Countries long after. They did not know it referred to me! I sang it, too," he said.

Alasdair, still frowning intently, said—as a statement, not a question, "That was the song you heard in the well."

A curious thing happened then. It was a simple enough remark, but it smashed through the last of the soldier's defenses. He gave a small cry, and threw out his hands as though to show he was unarmed. His head went down. Though he still stood stiffly upright, he seemed to be lying in the dust.

Fenella shivered, but did not speak or move. Nor did Hudart. It was strange how they both knew it was Alasdair who must deal with this.

I am too old, thought Hudart, sadly. To me, Ewen is a hurt child. I would just hold him and let him weep. But that is not for now—not for here—

The girl was praying Alasdair would be grown-up enough to say no word of pity. She need not have worried. When he did speak it was in a cool, hard voice, "You came too near home when you came to me at Kinrowan," he said. "You would never come down to the castle hall, would you, when there were strangers there? You feared a word—a look of recognition. You stayed safe in the tower room, to gibe at me when I ran from the fear I had of people. I am not concerned with what you did when you were a child," said Alasdair, rather cuttingly, "nor am I ruled by your harsh Highland code. But your behavior to me was contemptible."

Ewen gasped a little, as though cold water had been thrown over him. And then Alasdair said, "If you had told me, I would not have let anyone hurt you."

Oh, we were right, thought Hudart.

He had needed someone to protect. But they had chosen Fenella, who was a strong one, and not in need of protection and so had embroiled everyone in unnecessary danger. And all the time, they had what they wanted right under their hands. Hudart remembered unhappily that he had once sung that song— the "Coirefuil"—and had noticed Ewen's face. And meant to say something to him, and had forgotten.

Now Alasdair was speaking again. "Tell me one thing more," said the young man. "Did you break your word to Fergus because you think your honor of no worth?"

The mercenary's head lifted a little. He would have gone to pieces, offered any pity or gentleness, but under Alasdair's hard questioning he rallied. He looked at the young man, white-faced but under control, and said steadily, "My word was given to your father. To protect you, at any cost."

"I should have known."

"Fergus did," said Ewen.

Alasdair gave him a small bitter smile.

"But I had not learned you then, my friend," and then he said, very slowly, "No—you have never let me be your friend. You are too arrogant—too cruel."

"Am I so?" said the other, very low.

"Worse! Far worse! You have kept the whole world at the length of your sword—for fear of a word of blame or scorn. And you called me a coward! You twisty Highland devil!"

Fenella slid a cold hand into Hudart's and waited anxiously the effect of this new challenge. Yet she had a good sort of confidence in Alasdair. Deep joy that he was not an ordinary kind of man—not one to make harsh, conventional judgments. Ewen, mouth set grimly, just stood listening to what was being said to him. This unexpectedly took a new turn.

"My poor Ewen," said Alasdair, "your own people did not treat you as cruelly as you have done. The past, I think, is paid for. But you are much to blame for your unkindness to yourself— and to those who have loved you."

This seemed to bewilder the other completely. He glanced around, and saw nothing but kindness on the faces of his friends. He said, haltingly, "But—what would you have done—if I'd told you—?"

"Perhaps—valued your trust," said Alasdair. "Perhaps grown up a little sooner! You have shown me clearly how much you've always despised me!"

He turned his head away quickly. But Ewen had seen the hurt on his face. The older man's look changed.

He said, "Alasdair—"

And stopped. And then he said very quietly, "Could you forgive me?"

Startlingly, the other laughed. Clearly and gaily, in that dark place.

"You were a fine one to jeer at the—the chip on my shoulder!" said he. "You—with a roof beam riding yours!"

He grabbed Ewen before he could take more than one pace backwards, and held him, saying, "Man, that was a small gibe in return for all that I've taken from you!"

His voice lowered to a sorrowful note.

"I know why you told that tale, Ewen," he said. "I know well what you're after."

"I am asking you for my release," said the mercenary. "As a favor."

"How can I hold it from you, my soul!" said Alasdair.

He put his head down for a moment on Ewen's shoulder, and turned away, and went rather blindly across the room. He stumbled a little among the rubble of burnt timber and fallen stones, and Fenella put out a hand to steady him. And he gave her a blank stare, and said, "I've been a fool about you, too!" And his face twisted, and he went away from her toward the barred gap in the wall, and said half to himself, "If you had ten heads, all hideous, you would still be my Fenella."

The girl's hands flew to her face.

There were sounds outside the door.

For some little while, now, there had been sounds; though none of the prisoners had noted them. They were getting louder. The muttering began to swell to a growl, like that of a pack of dogs impatient for meat. A flicker of torchlight showed through the doorway. And suddenly the Bocan was standing there, with his wolfish henchmen crowding behind him in the opening.

"Who is chosen?" said he, thickly.

But he was looking straight across the keep at Ewen, as if he knew.

"Unarmed," he said, with relish, "and unresisting! Or else—!"

"My word on it," said Ewen, jeeringly. His eyes moved to the lintel on the door, where the black hilt of his knife stuck from the blackened wood. The Bocan looked, too, and leapt back from it as if it had been a snake. He scowled at the soldier's scornful grin.

Then the mercenary moved unhurriedly toward the door, and Fenella ran to him. He paused, and looked at her searchingly.

And she nodded and lifted his hand to her face. She was fighting a mad desire to weep, and scream to him to stay—to hold him back. It would only distress him, not deflect his purpose. He needed her courage as well as his own.

She smiled at him.

"Slan leat, my darling," said she.

And left him.

Hudart had come up on his other side, and now he carefully tucked his spray of rowan behind the soldier's plaid.

"A safe return, mo chridhe," whispered the old man.

And Ewen said, in a voice as quiet as a sigh, "Give me what is dragging at your pocket there."

No one at the open door could have seen what happened next, for he had his broad back between those hostile eyes and Hudart. The bard reached into one of his many huge pockets, and took out a long wheel-lock pistol which he then laid in Ewen's hands. Alasdair looked at the soldier's face and saw only too clearly how desperately he wanted to take the weapon with him when he went out to the Bocan. And Alasdair, knowing him now, knew he would have done it without a second thought for the breaking of a word, if it would have helped his friends. But it would not. The first sight of it would bring death to them all.

Ewen lifted his eyes and caught those of Alasdair, and gave him one of his old mocking looks. He examined the priming of the gun, and handed it back to Hudart.

"Signal to Ranald—later—" he whispered.

Hudart nodded, and turned away quickly and went to the barred archway in the wall. Ewen looked at Alasdair again.

"Tell Ranald my sword is yours," said he. "Learn her left-handed or give her one day to your son."

He jerked his sgian from the door-post and held it out on his palm. And Alasdair went over and took it quite quietly and with no word of thanks or farewell. He just smiled into the dancing gleam in the eyes of his soldier. And Ewen said, very casually, "I've been from home too long."

And he was away.

The noise outside grew to a snarl—to a shout—and the door slammed and cut off the sound. And the echo of the slam went alone up the dark and broken walls of the keep.

Fenella at last allowed herself to weep.

"What will they do?" she sobbed to Hudart.

"Set him free to find his heart's desire."

"He would rather have gone fighting," said Alasdair, staring at the knife in his hand.

"Has he not?" said the bard.

He looked through the bars at the hills on the skyline very far away.

"Kinrowan is at the cairn," he said, as though he saw it written on the night sky, "and his men are out there among those rocks and ruins—"

The grille of metal bars began to rise. And Hudart gave a little cry, and said breathlessly, "Dhia! They have not lingered over what they did!"

Alasdair clutched the sgian tightly, and said, "I wish his people could know that he is home."

"Someone will," said the old bard.

The bars had risen so high now that he could stand upright in the jagged gap, and he lifted his head so that moonlight spilled down over his face.

"His father is long dead," he said, "and a cousin in his place—but the piper of the Sithean will be playing the lament for the Chief—so someone will hear, and know."

He held out one hand toward the boy and the girl.

"Come," he said. "Leave this ruined place to its further ruin."

Alasdair went to Fenella, and she averted her head.

"Don't!" he said. "I won't turn from you—ever!"

Then she did look straight at him, and she had thrown back her veil. He smiled.

"See? I'm beginning to like your little toad-face," said he.

"Alasdair," she was very patient with him, "I no longer have a toad-face."

"I didn't notice," he said, with perfect truth.

He threw back his plaid, and because he still held the sgian in his hand, he set his great white wing around her—comfort and security in the softness and the strength of the swan's feathers—and they went together out of the keep.

"Wait there," said Hudart, as they stepped into the open air, "till Ranald comes."

And he lifted the heavy pistol. Its report echoed from all the walls of the keep, and went out over the water, and sounded again from the hills beyond.

Hudart glanced back at the shut door on the far side of the dark hall. He said clearly and with a note of pity, "Now prove you are not human, Bocan!"

He heard a cry from the passages beyond the door. And saw a rush of men come up from the loch toward the keep. He leaned against the fire-broken stones, and stood listening. But not to the sounds of Kinrowan and his men sacking the keep a second time. He was hearing something from much farther away. After a few minutes, he said very softly, "Son of the island, go thou to thy sleep—"

And smiled, hearing the far, thin singing of the pipes.

GLOSSARY OF GAELIC WORDS
AND PHRASES

Beannachd leat . . . (ben-acht lett) . . . blessing on you.
Ciod tha sin? . . . (cut ha sheen) . . . what is it?
Garlach . . . (gar-lach) . . . spoilt child.
Leanabh . . . (len-uv) . . . baby.
M'eudail . . . (may-dell) . . . my darling.
Mo bhalach . . . (mo val-uch) . . . my lad.
Mo bhroin . . . (vroin) . . . my sorrow.
Mo chaileag . . . (chail-ag) . . . my girl.
Mo chridhe . . . (chree) . . . my heart.
Mo churaidh . . . (choory) . . . my hero.
Mo Dhia . . . (Yeeu) . . . my God.
Sgian . . . (skee-un) . . . knife.
Sgian dubh . . . (skee-un doo) . . . black knife, the stocking-knife.
Sithean . . . (shee-un) . . . the Fairy Hill.
Slainte mhath . . . (slawntu var) . . . good health, a toast.
Slan leat . . . (slawn lett) . . . good-bye.
Tir Sorcha . . . (cheer sor-a-cha) . . . Land of Light.
Uruisg . . . (oor-ishk) . . . water monster, kelpie.

A mhic an eilean, theirig thusa a'chadal . . . (a veek un ale-un, hoorig hoosa uh cha-tal) . . . son of the island, go thou to thy sleep.

My sincere gratitude to Mr. Hugh Macphee, of the B.B.C. Glasgow, and to Mr. John MacCormick, of the Island of Mull, for checking and correcting the above.

N. S. G.

Do you dream of dragons? Would you like to work magic?
Or travel between worlds in the blink of an eye?
Would you like to see faeries dance,
or the place where baby unicorns are born?

COME ON A

MAGICQUEST

In these magical adventures
for kids from eight to eighty from
Tempo/MagicQuest Books:

#1. THE THROME OF THE ERRIL OF SHERILL,
Patricia A. McKillip

*The Throme of the Erril of Sherill — a book of songs
more beautiful than the stars themselves — does not
exist. Everyone knows that. But if Caerles is to win
his lady love, the sad-eyed daughter of the
King of Everywhere, he must find the Throme,
and so he sets out on an impossible quest.
Here's magical adventure from one of the most
popular fantasy writers since J.R.R. Tolkien — and
there are beautiful illustrations and a
special bonus dragon story too!*

__80839-5 — $2.25

#2. THE PERILOUS GARD, Elizabeth Marie Pope

*Kate is lonely. Banished by the Queen of England
to the Perilous Gard, a remote castle in Scotland,
she has no one to talk to all day but the moody,
mysterious young man whose brother owns the Gard.
But when she follows him into the world of faeries
she must do battle with the queen of Faery herself
to get him out again! This romantic fantasy won
a Newbery Honor.*

__65956-X — $2.25

#3. THE SEVENTH SWAN, Nicholas Stuart Gray

*There is a fairy tale about seven brothers
who are turned into swans by their evil stepmother.
Their sister turns them back into men
by knitting coats of nettles — but she doesn't
finish the sleeve of one coat in time
and at the end of the story the poor youngest brother
is left with a swan's wing in place of one arm.
Did you ever wonder what happened to him after that?
This book will tell you!*

—— 75955-6 — $2.25

#4. THE ASH STAFF, Paul R. Fisher

*Mole is the oldest of six kids who were raised in a cave
by an old sorcerer in the magical land of Mon Ceth.
When the sorcerer dies, Mole must take up the ash staff
and become the group's leader.
This is the first of four books telling of their adventures
and their battle against the evil sorcerer
who has taken over their kingdom.
Paul R. Fisher was still a teenager himself
when he began the Ash Staff series.
If you are looking for something to read after Tolkien
or Lloyd Alexander — try Mole and his friends.*

—— 03115-3 — $2.25

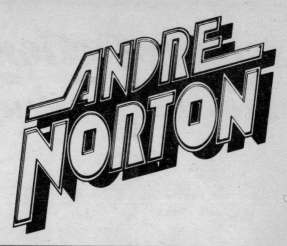